D0961007

ALSO BY IAN FRAZIER

THE
CURSING
MOMMY'S
BOOK OF
DAYS

THE CURSING MOMMY'S BOOK OF DAYS

IAN FRAZIER

FARRAR, STRAUS AND GIROUX   NEW YORK

Farrar, Straus and Giroux
18 West 18th Street, New York 10011

Distributed in Canada by D&M Publishers, Inc.
Printed in the United States of America
First edition, 2012

Portions of this book originally appeared, in somewhat
different form, in *The New Yorker.*

Library of Congress Cataloging-in-Publication Data
Frazier, Ian.
      The cursing mommy's book of days / Ian Frazier. — 1st ed.
         p.   cm.
      ISBN 978-0-374-13318-4 (alk. paper)
      1. Mothers—Fiction.   2. Family life—Fiction.   3. Stress
(Psychology)—Fiction.   4. Domestic fiction.   I. Title.

   PS3556.R363 C77 2012
   813'.54—dc23

                                                2012018505

Designed by Jonathan D. Lippincott

www.fsgbooks.com

10   9   8   7   6   5   4   3   2   1

TO JAY

THE
CURSING
MOMMY'S
BOOK OF
DAYS

To all of you, a cheerful and warm "Good Morning!" I am no-body special, particularly in the eyes of other drivers and some of the clients of my husband, Larry—I am just the Cursing Mommy, your neighbor and friend. Sitting with my morning coffee here at the kitchen table after children and husband have been safely dispatched to school and the work he complains so bitterly about, I take a quiet moment for myself, and you. Wrap your hands around your coffee cup, close your eyes, and share this moment with me.

The goddamn fucking kitchen ceiling needs to be repaired. Excuse me, I did not mean to curse right then, but that is what I get for disregarding my own advice for as much as a second and opening my eyes. Accidentally I glanced up at the mess the kitchen ceiling has become, plaster sagging in two places and a couple of pieces even breaking off and falling down, and I let out some curse words inadvertently. Well, that happens sometimes! Also, I won't think about that horrible night when the toilet in the bath-room above the kitchen overflowed, leading to the problem with the plaster. Apparently Larry had never heard of such a thing as a shutoff valve.

Now my eyes are closed again, my fingers laced comfortably around the cup, and the Cursing Mommy is with you in her mind. The wonderful philosopher Pierre Teilhard de Chardin—in French his last name sounds something like "of the garden," isn't that lovely?—once wrote, "My son is probably trying not to faint at school right now, I should have kept him home, and that awful assistant principal will probably be a jerk to me about it again."

I am sorry—no. Pierre Teilhard de Chardin did not write anything of the kind. Rather, he wrote, "We are not human beings having a spiritual experience. We are spiritual beings having a human experience."

SPIRITUAL beings having a HUMAN experience—doesn't that sound so perfectly right? As spirit, we are at once infinitely more and infinitely less than the steam rising off our coffee cups. Spirits on a human journey, we tread our common path through time. Isn't it glorious, when you think about it, that we're all on this human journey together? Each morning like this forms another stepping-stone along our way.

Today, at this exact quiet moment at the kitchen table, the Cursing Mommy begins the journey of another year. To all my fellow spirits out there, who have followed the Cursing Mommy through her columns and other products, I extend a friendly invitation to come along. Please join the Cursing Mommy on my year's journey, day by day, as our spirits grow.

JANUARY

And so, we set out. Ideally, this daybook would have started on Saturday morning, January 1, but Larry and I had to be in Encino. A client of Larry's invites the whole office out there to stay over in his gigantic house for New Year's Eve and New Year's Day every year. This client brings in a huge amount of business and Larry says we might be sleeping in the car if it weren't for him, so of course we have to go. And I do mean *we*, because the client is a big believer in wives attending, though they don't have much to do. Husbands, on the other hand, the client isn't so crazy about. That's another story.

As a result, we weren't here for New Year's Day. We flew back on the second, and on the third I drove to the assisted living to see my fucking father.

I feel that I must start this day, month, and year over again. Just thinking about that weekend and then the trip to the goddamn horrible assisted living makes me want to put that nonsense far, far behind. I will clear my head, get a refill on my coffee, and go back to the kitchen table where I began.

We must always remember to be grateful for what we have. On this winter morning, with the temperature in the twenties and snow covering the ground outside, I am grateful just to be sitting here sheltered and indoors. My eight-year-old, Kyle, breaks out in hives and faints if you look at him cross-eyed, and he's probably doing exactly that right now in gym class, and any minute the phone will ring and it will be the snotty assistant principal, and I will have to go out and hope the car will start so I can pick up my swooning son. But that hasn't happened yet. Who was it who called worry "negative prayer"? I will keep my hopes and prayers positive on this first day (fourth, technically, as I already explained) of our journey year.

The children had such fun in the snow yesterday. I was at the fucking assisted living, Larry was down in the basement doing something or other with his boxes of capacitors, and the kids had an absolute ball outside, he said. God knows he probably wasn't paying much attention. From where I sit in my favorite kitchen chair I can see the snowman they made. I am grateful for my children's happiness and the small monument to it remaining on our front lawn.

Actually, as I look more closely at it, it's not so small. Moving to the front window I wonder how they ever built a snowman that high! In fact, it doesn't really resemble a snowman . . .

The reason it does not resemble a snowman, I now see, is that it is not a snowman, it is a snow penis. A giant snow penis on my front lawn. How could I not have noticed it before? I got back from the fucking assisted living after dark, that's why. They did quite an inventive job of it, with large snow testicles, as well. This must have been Trevor's idea. He is going on twelve, going on whatever age you can be sent to prison. He got poor Kyle to go along.

Those of you who keep up with my regular Cursing Mommy columns know that at some point in almost every one of them—okay, every one of them—the Cursing Mommy regrettably becomes frustrated with some aspect of daily life, and she flips out, screams curses, breaks things, gives people the finger, etc. Today, on the first or fourth day of our journey year, the Cursing Mommy is not going to do any of that. Serenity is the new watchword. I am now simply going to pull on Larry's boots, put my coat on over my bathrobe, go out in the front yard, and knock the revolting snow penis down.

Now I am in the yard and I smack the snow penis—why did I forget my mittens?—and *ouch!* Shit! The thing is solid ice! It has frozen solid overnight, I see. So I am giving the snow penis a good swift kick and GODDAMN FUCKING STUPID SNOW PENIS! FUCKING GODDAMN THING IS LIKE—*OUCH!!*—FUCKING CEMENT! I'LL KICK YOU DOWN IF IT'S THE FUCKING LAST THING . . . AHHH! SHIT! I SLIPPED ON THIS FUCKING SLIPPERY ICE AND I'VE FALLEN IN THE SNOW!! LYING IN MY FUCKING FRONT YARD IN MY FUCKING BATHROBE! FUCKING GODDAMN LARRY! FUCK GEORGE BUSH! FUCKING GODDAMN JOHN BOEHNER, THAT FUCKING ASSHOLE!! . . .

[*pause*]

In just a minute I will get up and go inside. Let fucking Larry knock the fucking thing down when he gets home. It will melt eventually anyway.

Oh, what a fucking horrible day this is going to be.

WEDNESDAY, JANUARY 5
"Open thou my lips, oh Lord, that my mouth may show forth thy praise."

Do we always remember to praise? I'm not talking about praising our spouse or our kids or our coworkers, the "self-esteem routine," though of course that's important, too. I mean praising the power or powers that placed us and everything around us upon this spinning cinder we call our earth—yes, I mean exalting generally the simple beauty of the world. We should devote ourselves to this every instant from the moment we awake. First thing when we open our eyes in the morning we must say, "Open thou our lips, that our mouths may show forth thy praise!"

I wish I could always be conscientious about that, but sometimes, unfortunately, I am not. For example, this morning Larry was up, sitting on the edge of the bed and putting salve on his toe fungus, and I woke and looked at the ceiling and sighed, and I forgot to praise. Instead, I said, "Shit."

Of course, I am the Cursing Mommy.

THURSDAY, JANUARY 6

Hello again, my friends, on another dark winter's morning. My, it is cozy here in the kitchen—and out on the patio, and even in the yard, for that matter, where according to our outdoor thermometer the temperature is a shirtsleeve sixty-eight degrees. Thank goodness the "snow sculpture" is no more. Yesterday's torrential rains that also filled part of the basement washed most of it away. Often all we must do in life is wait, and our wishes will be fulfilled.

This morning I am counting my blessings. That goddamn snow penis is gone. Water got in some of the boxes of Larry's capacitors down in the basement, apparently. I suppose that's not a blessing, technically, but what the hell.

Do you sometimes have your first cocktail at 8:15 a.m.?

SATURDAY, JANUARY 8

I meant to write an entry for yesterday, but Kyle stayed home from school. All of Christmas vacation the kid is a picture of health, and then when classes start again, suddenly he feels poorly. The awful assistant principal did, in fact, call. I couldn't find my cell phone, which I spend my life looking for, and all at once there's this muffled ring and the cat goes shooting about five feet in the air. He'd been sleeping on it. Molkowski, assistant principal, on the line.

Kyle was in a swoon again in gym, no surprise. Molkowski gave me the usual blah-blah-blah and I went and got him. I kept him indoors all of yesterday, but I made him go back this morning. His school now has some goddamn mandatory fucking Clean the Boiler Room Day every Saturday, because they repealed the school levy. Parents are supposed to help, too. I went along and took some rags, and Kyle and I made a morning of it. He managed not to faint from the horror of it all, poor guy.

MONDAY, JANUARY 10

One old tradition I absolutely adore is that of devoting every Monday to the family's weekly baking. Bright and early every Monday, my gramma Pat used to get up, pack a lunch for Grampa Hub, give him his bicarb, and shoo him out the door. Then she would light a Chesterfield and start to bake.

And I do mean *bake*! Gracious, what that woman couldn't do. Gramma Pat is long dead of emphysema, but I can still smell the delicious and enticing aroma of her kitchen, mixed with secondhand smoke, as I used to hang on her apron strings and watch her every gesture. Pies, cakes, fruit crumbles, strudels, lebkuchen dusted with powdered sugar and the odd bit of cigarette ash—all appeared effortlessly, as if by magic. She never used a lighter. While she rolled dough with her left hand, she could fold a match from a matchbook and light it with her right! She also did all the family's bread baking—white and brown bread, both—and would never think of buying store-bought.

Can you excuse me for a second? It's the goddamn phone.

TUESDAY, JANUARY 11

Sabrina from the fucking goddamn assisted living cheerfully ruined yesterday by calling just to let me know that "Dad" had assaulted another patient. I had to drop everything and go over there, natch. Enough said. Let us return to:

"The Cursing Mommy's Baking Day (continued)"

God, I hate my fucking father.

I'm sorry, that was what the shrinks call an "intrusive thought," and it has no place in the making of this pie. Excuse me.

Today, just because I thought it would be a hoot, I am following a tasty-sounding recipe for chocolate pie that I found printed on a pie pan I bought yesterday at Food Superior. I get a lot of my best recipes from just such unexpected places. I have already melted the semisweet chocolate in the microwave, as instructed, and added a cup of strong coffee, and then combined these with the instant chocolate pie filling, for an extra chocolaty flavor. I then crushed the gingersnaps for the crust, and they are on this wax paper here.

I now spread the crushed gingersnaps evenly in the pie pan. After this step, I carefully pour in the filling mixture. Do I now add the extra cookie pieces to the top, or do I do that after baking? And to what temperature do I preheat the oven? And how long do I bake the pie? I will consult the recipe.

And now I see there is a problem. The recipe is on the bottom of the pie pan. Which I have just covered with gingersnap crust and a two-inch-deep layer of chocolate filling.

Oh, fuck everything.

I fucking give up. Why did I not see that the FUCKING MORONS PUT THE DIRECTIONS ON THE FUCKING INSIDE BOTTOM OF THE FUCKING PAN? All right, I'll just scrape a little bit aside—oh, no! I tipped the pan over! AHHH! The fucking gorpy filling is spilling out! Trying to catch it—AHHH!—I slip and fall on the kitchen floor! WHAT A FUCKING MESS!! I'M ON MY BACK ON THE KITCHEN FLOOR IN A PUDDLE OF FUCKING CHOCOLATE GORP!! FUCKING STUPID PIE-PAN COMPANY! FUCK-

ING MITCH MCCONNELL, THAT FUCKING ASSHOLE!
HELP! HEL-L-L-L-P!!!

[pause]

Actually, it's not so bad lying here, except for the overpowering chocolate smell. I swear I'll never eat chocolate again. Why
did I ever try this? I detest baking. In just a minute I'm going to
get up.

Oh, what a fucking horrible day this is turning out to be.

WEDNESDAY, JANUARY 12

This morning I want to tell you about a little game that I sometimes play with myself. It has brightened many a day for me, and
perhaps it can do the same for you. This is a secret I have never
told anybody, but if you like it, and if you find it works for you, I
won't mind at all if you pass it on.

Sometimes, when I am feeling challenged by life, as, for
example, right now, when I look out the back window and see
that the Honda has a flat tire again, and I'm going to have to
call the recently released criminal tow truck driver who runs
the AAA account around here, and I'm wondering what kind
of cheap party balloons Steve's Sunoco has been selling Larry
in the guise of car tires—Jesus, Larry, why didn't you fucking
deal with this before you left for work, or at least give me a
heads-up?

As I was saying, at moments like this, I play the Elsewhere
Game. In my mind I simply go elsewhere, to a distant place that's
marvelous and far away and steeped in leisure, the kind of place
where people like the client of Larry's in Encino that I was telling you about who insist on the presence of certain wives on company business weekends spend all their time. To myself, I say
sentences I would be saying in that lovely, faraway place:

"Think I'll take the boat out this morning! Haven't been to Lower Matecumbe Key in a while! Maybe there are some new shells washed up on the Gulf side! First let me make sure all the wire transfers are going through! Which sandals would I rather, the flats or the slingbacks? Should I walk down to the dock, or ride my bicycle?"

Oh, God, it's not working. Perhaps with a pitcher of sangria . . .

THURSDAY, JANUARY 13

Trevor, our older son, is a wonderful boy. His mind goes faster than his words can keep up with, one of his teachers has told me, and as a result he lashes out and sometimes exposes himself in class. We are working on this. He does not always tell the truth. "The truth is not in him," as Grampa Hub used to say about the serial killer, I forget his name—not that Trevor is in such company! Ted Bundy. That was the name. Grampa Hub and Gramma Pat were fascinated with that case.

My husband, Larry, does not take enough time with Trevor, I think because he (Larry) is often at work on the weekends, and when he's home he's very involved with whatever he does in the basement with his boxes of capacitors, and that occupies a lot of the attention he might give his son.

Do you ever get panic attacks? I think I'm having one right now, thinking about Trevor and how in God's name he will ever get through life. He is just a horrible, wretched child. I know it's wrong to say that about my own son but he should be under police supervision all the time and I absolutely do not know what we're going to do with him. That is wrong to think, yes, I am aware of that, but what should I do? You tell me.

Trevor, honey, if you ever read this, please use words to express your reaction, not hitting or knives.

FRIDAY, JANUARY 14

Still sort of panicked about Trevor, so I thought I would try a simple yoga exercise. I'm going to put on my yoga slippers—which are made out of stitched-together pieces of real yoga mats!—and then I stand, centered and quiet and mindful, in the vicinity of the liquor cabinet. I let my mind drift freely, accepting whatever comes into it, and to my surprise, I'm thinking, "Walnut liqueur."

SATURDAY, JANUARY 15

God, that stuff was awful. I am still gagging, and the horrible moldy walnut taste will not leave my mouth. Sabrina called again. This is not the way I want my mouth to feel as I drive in mysteriously heavy Saturday morning traffic to the goddamn fucking assisted living.

SUNDAY, JANUARY 16

Although I consider myself a deeply spiritual person, I am impatient with the creeds and dogmas of organized religion. (Actually, it's the creeds I am impatient with, while the dogmas I don't so much mind.) The one therapist who would accept Trevor agreed to see him only at seven o'clock on Sunday mornings, so every Sunday I get him up and dressed and drag him off, not to his great liking, obviously. Then I wait in the car in the parking lot while he has his appointment, and after it I drive him to McDonald's and then home. This is our usual Sunday. I am not a regular churchgoer, in other words.

This morning as I waited in the car in the therapist's parking lot, I was fooling with the radio and one of those radio preachers came on. The guy had a quavery, ancient voice that sounded like he was practically in the grave. His topic was the story of Mary and Martha, in the book of somebody or other, when the Lord comes to visit at their house. The Lord is sitting there in the house preaching, and one of the two women, Mary or Martha, I forget which, "busies herself with much serving," while the other sits at Jesus's feet.

The one who is serving—let's say it's Martha, I have a fifty-fifty chance of being right—says to the Lord something like, "Hey, Lord, tell Mary to help me, because I'm doing all the work and she is just sitting there." And he replies (I'm paraphrasing), "Martha, you are too busy with small things, you should be like Mary, who knows that it's better to sit and listen to me"—i.e., you, Martha, are just wasting your time.

The near-death radio preacher's message was that we are too much concerned with worldly cares when really we should yadda yadda yadda. Okay—got it. The more I thought about it, though, the stupider it seemed. These ladies have Jesus over to their house, he brings an entourage, the apostles or whoever are standing or sitting everywhere in the living room, they've all been out in the hot Holy Land sun, and they want something to eat. Martha is running around preparing it and setting up tables and chairs and so on, and the Lord tells her she should be more like her sister, who has not lifted one finger to help. I began to wonder how in hell—excuse me—the good Lord managed to get away with that. Seems to me, the minute he said that to Martha, both he and the do-nothing sister would have been looking at a flying platter of baby goat with lentil sauce heading straight their way. How the good Lord kept that woman from chucking something right at his ha-loed head has to be ranked as one of the true miracles of the Bible, up there with the loaves and fishes and the parting of the sea.

Or am I missing a deeper meaning here? Could be. The Cursing Mommy might not be the best person to go to for Bible commentary on this Sunday morning.

MONDAY, JANUARY 17
Today is Martin Luther King Day, and then Tuesday, Wednesday, and Thursday are Unpaid Teacher Appreciation Days, when

we appreciate the teachers by repaving the school playground and they give up their salaries for those days. Trevor and Kyle and I have a certain quota of asphalt we are expected to bring. Last year I was one of the organizers—never again, I vowed, when it was done. But I am organizing Kyle's class's parents again this year.

Why in the goddamn hell did I agree to this? Did I suffer some temporary insanity? Now not only do I have to deal with the kids being home all week except Friday, but I must also spend today calling the fucking other parents to set this thing up before going to Spong's Supply and buying nine fifty-pound sacks of fucking asphalt and driving them to the school over potholes in our car with its party-balloon tires. Sometimes I despise my fucking life.

TUESDAY, JANUARY 18
[See above.]

WEDNESDAY, JANUARY 19
[That goes double for Wednesday.]

THURSDAY, JANUARY 20
[Never, *never* do this again!]

FRIDAY, JANUARY 21
Back in my favorite kitchen chair again with my coffee cup and you, my friends—and oh, so happy to be! How are you? It's been a while! Let's just be silent for a moment together, as real friends can be with one another, and take in the pleasant, peaceful rhythms of an ordinary morning.

The refrigerator motor is loose in its housing, I think. That's the reason it makes that *ka-bump* sound when it turns off, as it did just now. I will remind Larry to tighten the bolts, or the belt, or whatever has to be done, not that he will do it. Let's consider the refrigerator's *ka-bump* merely an upbeat punctuation note to our morning, like a double tap on a calypso steel drum on that sunny Elsewhere Island we go to sometimes. *Ka-bump.* Now it's turning on again. Larry will do nothing, and I will have to call the repairman.

Sitting quietly and just listening, in the unseen, sustaining presence of our friends. Thank God there was at least one day of school this week, and the house is calm this morning, relatively. How did you sleep last night? It's awful to toss and turn, isn't it? I did not sleep very well, myself. When I came downstairs this morning, I had a newspaper headline running through my brain:

> It Will Be Easy, Easy, Easy:
> The Shag Helicopter Is No More

Now, did I only dream that, or am I remembering a real headline I saw recently? And if that is a real headline, where did I see it, and what could the story have been about? "Shag Helicopter"? What in the world could that mean?

SATURDAY, JANUARY 22

The headline cannot be found anywhere online, so I probably dreamed it. That is no help with my current indisposition, however, which is that I now have the fucking headline permanently stuck in my head.

It Will Be Easy, Easy, Easy: The Shag Helicopter Is No More.
It Will Be Easy, Easy, Easy: The Shag Helicopter Is No More.
It Will Be Easy, Easy, Easy: The Shag Helicopter Is No More.
Please, brain, stop saying that over and over. I already have

enough to deal with. I need some kind of shock to jolt the insane sentence out of me, the way you scare somebody to cure them of the hiccups. I am sure I will not have long to wait for a curative distraction. I must be patient. Something will come along.

It Will Be Easy, Easy, Easy . . .

SUNDAY, JANUARY 23

Begging my brain to shut up already about the fucking Shag Helicopter as I sit in the therapist's parking lot and wait for Trevor at seven fifty.

MONDAY, JANUARY 24

> *Be careful what you wish for.* —Anonymous

And thus we see the truth of this old unhelpful saying, because today I am no longer thinking about that goddamn headline, which I won't mention for fear of recurrence. No, now I am thinking and tearing my hair out about a phone call I just got from Larry. He had his annual performance review first thing when he arrived at work today. His hourly rate is being reduced.

Oh, God, what're we going to do? The review was a one-on-one with the client who has the house in Encino, who turns out also to run a private equity company that holds a controlling share in Larry's firm, which means the client from Encino is actually the client of himself, it seems. Larry's numbers for last year were down. In the previous few months he didn't bill enough. There were complaints about his bringing some of his boxes of capacitors into the office.

Oh God oh God oh God. Why doesn't he just stop with the fucking goddamn capacitors?—but they're so important to him. Why didn't he bill more hours? Basically what this means, Larry says, is he will be working more to bring home less. He is about ready to shoot himself.

TUESDAY, JANUARY 25

I will say one thing, though—no problem is big enough to affect how ol' Larry sleeps at night. Last night he's lying there snoring away, sawing logs, and I'm next to him with my useless goddamn annoying earplugs, wide awake and staring at the ceiling. After a while it starts to stare back, and it says to me, "Hello, I'm your ceiling. I've watched you many a night as you lie there asleep and unaware, and only now do you notice me?" Then it goes into this self-congratulatory ceiling monologue about how it was there before me and will be there after me, and some other woman will lie where I'm lying and stare up at it, and so on. I didn't mind, actually. It passed the time.

Let me tell you a little bit about the client with the house in Encino. The man is a multigazillionaire, whatever that means, but you would never know it to look at him. He appears just like an ordinary guy, or even less than ordinary. He is not aloof at all but acts like anybody. You wouldn't pick him out as one of the richest people on the planet, which I guess he is. The only thing that you could call different is that he loves heavy metal, which he has piped through the whole house and even in the pool, where if you swim underwater it practically crushes your eardrums. Also, at the start of his New Year's weekend, he does a strip on the diving board, beginning with his cell phone and his BlackBerry, which he takes out of his pockets and throws into the water without a thought! Of course losing them is nothing to him, he can easily have them replaced.

Late in the evening if he catches you alone he can be a hazard. Kicking him in the shins, however, was probably not the best idea.

WEDNESDAY, JANUARY 26

When I'm feeling low and blue, nothing perks me up like a little shopping. In fact, sometimes I can be almost a shopaholic! How about you? Do you like to "shop 'til you drop"?

Well, we shouldn't give in to that, in these economic times. I know *I* certainly shouldn't, with the smaller income our family is likely to be looking at due to Larry's terrible performance review—so I have developed a strategy. I shop, but I use my head, and I get all the fun of shopping without breaking the family piggybank. I call it my "splurge smart" technique, and today I'm going to share it with you.

Splurge Smart: A Cursing Mommy Wised-up Shopping Spree

Normally I would drive to a store to do this, but today the goddamn car is being repaired. No problem—I'll simply shop online! I have my credit card handy, and I begin by going to Merchants' Markdown's website, where they have some wonderful things. I am looking for a new raincoat . . . no, I do not want any Viagra, thank you . . . and Jesus Christ, no, I do not want to know my credit score rating . . . don't care if Rennie Lister's dress at the Peabody Awards went too far . . . Here we are! Merchants' Markdown! And I simply click on "women's raincoats," give my credit card number (with expiration date and security code and zip code), and away I go!

Goodness, they all look lovely, don't they? Too bad I can't buy them all. But do you know what? I *can*, or I can pretend I can. I go along from raincoat to raincoat—here's a tan belted number with a hood that might be perfect for me—and I put each one in my shopping cart. At the end, of course, I will cancel every purchase except the one I like the absolute best. I get all the fun of splurging without the high cost—I splurge smart! And now, with my shopping cart brimming full of raincoats, I click on "cancel," because in truth I don't think any of these would be really right. I hit "cancel" . . . I hit "cancel" . . . I hit fucking "cancel"! Cancel! Cancel! Cancel! Jesus Christ, why won't it fucking cancel?

"Thank you for your purchase"? I didn't make any fucking purchase! *"Cancel cancel cancel cancel!"* Nothing fucking happens!

"Your order will ship within three hours"? But I haven't fucking ordered anything! Why can't I fucking cancel this! FUCKING GODDAMN STUPID MERCHANTS' MARKDOWN! FUCKING BUNCH OF THIEVES! FUCKING STUPID COMPUTER! Okay, I'll just unplug the fucking thing. I'm on the floor crawling behind the fucking goddamn computer, WHY ARE FUCKING COMPUTERS SO FUCKING EXPENSIVE THAT YOU CAN'T JUST SMASH THEM—OUCH!! Pulling the plug out, I accidentally yank the pole lamp down on top of me! FUCK GODDAMN EVERYTHING!! FUCKING GODDAMN BUSH ADMINISTRATION!! FUCKING RUMSFELD, YOU FUCKING ASSHOLE!! HELP! HEL-L-L-L-P!!!!

[*pause*]

Actually, it's kind of restful back here, among the wires. I should clean out some of these dust bunnies, I suppose, but who fucking cares. Now I have about six dozen pointless goddamn raincoats arriving soon by UPS. I'll merely fucking ship them back. In just a minute I'm going to get up.

Oh, what a fucking horrible day this is going to be.

THURSDAY, JANUARY 27

> *I often think thoughts*
> *That need not*
> *Have been*
> *Thought.*
> —M. Foler Tuohy

Are you aware of the work of M. Foler Tuohy? He is my very, very favorite poet / philosopher / life coach / armchair guru, and if you don't know about him, he is somebody you simply HAVE to read. I press copies of his books on all my friends. Universally, they agree with me. M. Foler Tuohy has devoted himself to leading an intentional life. He always tries to see through the surface appearances of things, and above all he is about removing clutter, such as the clutter many of us carry around in our minds.

I love the way M. Foler Tuohy is also a storyteller. Like the Bible, he illustrates many of the most important truths with stories, because, as he emphasizes, telling stories is what we human beings have done since caveman days. Stories are how we connect to one another as people, as well as by hollering, as I sometimes do myself. M. Foler Tuohy also describes himself as "a great lover of language," and that is also very true. Much of his writing uses wonderful, ravishing vocabulary.

FRIDAY, JANUARY 28

In daily life we can see many examples of the mental clutter M. Foler Tuohy is warning us against. This morning my mind is filled with clutter about how fucking Larry showered and left for work and did not clean up the cat mess on the goddamn bathroom floor. Instead he left it for me. Obviously Larry saw the cat mess and SIMPLY STEPPED AROUND IT! This is Larry's new thing. His terrible performance review and his new reduced billing rate have made him so oppressed and preoccupied that whereas he was doing almost nothing around the house before, now he is doing totally and completely absolutely goddamn nothing, not even cleaning up a cat mess right under his nose. He must not be bothered—that seems to be Larry's new policy. Therefore *everything* around the house will now be up to me, even on days like, for example, today, when I have a Cursing Mommy column to do.

My friends, can I confide in you? I think of you, the Cursing Mommy's silent and sustaining companions invisibly surrounding her, and I know you're the only ones I can tell this to. The client with the house in Encino who is making Larry's life miserable gave me his phone number when we were there over New Year's. He put it in my travel bag somehow and I didn't find it until I unpacked. The piece of paper just says "Call me" and a number, with no signature, but I recognize the insane handwriting because it's the same as on his insane New Year's card. It's written in black graffiti-size laundry marking pen. I don't know if he put this in my bag before or after I kicked his shins.

Okay, I did not throw the number away. I mean, it seemed too valuable—how many people have this guy's private number, after all? And now I am wondering if maybe I could call it and get him to go easy on Larry. At least I could apologize for kicking him.

Talk about mental clutter! Do you see what I mean?

SATURDAY, JANUARY 29

Today at Food Superior I ran into Margaret from book group and she pointed out that the bottles of Perrier and Pellegrino sparkling water are now found in the aisle for sodas, while the bottles of vitamin water and skinny water are now in the aisle for bottled water. This is an odd change. Margaret and I tried to figure out the logic. Perrier and Pellegrino are bottled natural water, and so you would think they would be with the other bottled waters, while the various colored and flavored vitamin waters are man-made drinks and thus would seem to belong in the soda aisle. At first the switch makes no sense, but you have to put on your thinking cap. The Perrier and the Pellegrino are now with the sodas because, like them, they are carbonated (though naturally so), while the various vitamin waters are with the plain bottled water—your Poland Spring and Deer Park waters and the rest—because they are not.

Hmmm . . . interesting . . .

SUNDAY, JANUARY 30

At Trevor's therapist this morning, I sat in the parking lot and didn't even listen to the radio because I could hardly hear it over the rain. I would not have been surprised if I had been washed away, car and parking lot and everything. When I ran the windshield wipers I could see the chain-link fence around the lot with a couple of sawed-off tree branches still stuck in it where they had grown through. It must have been too much trouble for the workmen to remove them entirely, so the branches were sawed off on either side, and the chunks with fence wire in them just left there in the fence. I try always to park in the same space next to the tree pieces, for a sense of security, I guess. Isn't that funny of me?

Last night I was trying to make the rain stop by thinking against it and saying "fucking goddamn rain," and so on. Then I started hearing a strange watery sound inside the house, and it turned out to be water running down the inside of the basement walls! The rain had filled the window wells and water was pouring in around the casements. What a headache! At 3:00 a.m. Larry and I were vacuuming the water on the basement floor with the Shop-Vac and dumping it into the sink in the laundry room. I don't even want to know what happened to Larry's boxes of capacitors. I didn't ask.

MONDAY, JANUARY 31

Still raining, but not to worry. I've heard it is very good for the reservoirs!

FEBRUARY

People don't like this month, but I think that is unfair. I always try to be very positive about February and look for what is good about it. This morning, for example, it is not raining so much as I sit here in the kitchen with my coffee. The sandbag emplacements we made with plastic trash bags filled with sand from the children's sandbox (which they haven't used in years) seem to be keeping some of the water out of the window wells. Kyle seems to have entered a phase in which he breaks out in hives less, and he has made it through two whole weeks without having to come home once. The Eutopophane that Trevor's therapist insisted he take appears to be working, though it does make him rather groggy and his urine is blue. He has been somewhat less disruptive in class, his teachers say.

Today I have come to a big decision: I am going to call that number. I want you, my unseen cohort of wonderful, supportive friends, to sit in with me while I do. I'll simply ring up the client with the house in Encino whom I've described to you, and I will tell him that I regret having kicked him in the shins though he more than deserved it, and I'll ask him to please increase Larry's billing rates because he's being too hard on Larry and Larry will get his numbers up this year. How hard can this be? Wish me luck. Here goes:

Beep. Beep-beep-beep. Beep-beep-beep, beep beep, beep beep.

It's ringing . . . God, I am nervous about this . . . "Hello?
Hello?" . . . Why am I getting a recording? I thought this was
his private number . . . "Yes, I am calling from a touch-tone
phone" . . . Why is that important, for heaven's sake? . . . "Yes, I
will stay on the line" . . . Jesus, what in hell is this all about? . . .
"No, I do not wish to participate in a survey at the end of this
call!" . . . *A survey?* How many people does this asshole give his
number to? . . . "Yes, I will hold until my call can be answered" . . .
"Yes, I will continue to hold" . . . "Yes, I will continue to hold" . . .
Holy Christ, come on, already! . . . "Yes, I will continue to
hold" . . . What a popular guy! . . . "Yes, I will continue to
hold" . . . "Yes, I will continue to hold" . . . We're going on fifteen
minutes here! . . . "What? WHAT? *'No one can take your call
right now'*??? After all this fucking time you made me wait? Yes,
I most certainly would like to leave a message after the tone!
Listen here, you fucking rich asshole prick, this is Larry's wife,
who kicked you in the shins on New Year's Eve, and I only
WISH I'D FUCKING KICKED YOU HARDER, YOU STU-
PID FUCK! FUCKING RICH GEORGE BUSH–LIKE ASS-
HOLE, PAY YOUR FUCKING TAXES, YOU FUCK, AND
STOP PICKING ON HARDWORKING PEOPLE LIKE
LARRY, YOU HEAVY-METAL-LOVING DICK CHENEY–
RESEMBLING SHITHEAD, HOGGING ALL THE FUCK-
ING MONEY SO THERE'S NONE LEFT FOR ANYBODY,
YOU CAN GO FUCK YOURSELF, YOU STUPID FUCK,
AND IT'S ME, LARRY'S WIFE, THE CURSING MOMMY,
WHO TOLD YOU SO, *AND DON'T YOU FUCKING FOR-
GET IT!*"

. . . My God, what have I done? What came over me? I have
ruined us. What should I do now? I'll stay on the line . . . maybe
a human being will come on that I can explain myself to. I'll say
I was rehearsing for a play . . . Now there's an announcement
coming on . . . *Thank you for calling A Touch of India Carpet*

Cleaners? . . . Oh, thank God. I dialed the wrong number. Oh, thank God.

Would anyone besides me like a cocktail?

WEDNESDAY, FEBRUARY 2

It is very important to breathe. Since the phone call yesterday I have been trying to get my heart rate back to normal, and we know from yoga that proper breathing technique is how this is done. In fact, since yesterday all I've really been able to do is breathe. In, out. In, out. If I am perfectly honest with myself, I will admit that I am still not calm. When Larry came home last night I was sitting here just breathing—and working through a slight hangover—so I let him get his own dinner. If he knew something was wrong, he did not inquire, and of course I'm not volunteering anything.

All our experiences, good and bad, should be regarded as opportunities to learn. On the last day of his life, Auguste Renoir, the great Impressionist painter, finished painting a vase of flowers, and as he put his brushes away, he said, "I learned something today." And then he died! Isn't that a beautiful story? Of course it does not make me as calm as it might, because he dies at the end. Actually, I think it's making me less calm. Forget I said anything.

Now there is someone at our front door. As I answer it, I will remember to breathe.

THURSDAY, FEBRUARY 3

The person at the front door was Chris, the UPS lady, delivering the thirteen dozen raincoats I did not order from Merchants' Markdown. According to the enclosed invoice, or invoices, by ordering in bulk I received a 6 percent discount, so my credit card was charged only $13,456.98. The boxes filled the living room to a height of three feet. By working feverishly all day I was able to open all the boxes, repackage the raincoats in the return mailers, and make four trips to the UPS place to ship them back. Thankfully the shipping was free. Now I just pray the damn things get there in time for the charge to be taken off our card before the bill goes out.

Just another day's work for the Cursing Mommy!

FRIDAY, FEBRUARY 4

May we remember everywhere and always to value the basic dignity of every human being.   —Mission Statement, the Ecumenical Council

Sometimes I must try very hard to keep this fine goal of the Ecumenical Council in mind. Today when I checked the liquor cabinet I discovered that I was out of scotch, sort of an emergency situation, so I went immediately to Lariat Liquors in the plaza, picked up a big bottle of Dewar's, and handed my credit card to Richard, the person behind the counter. Richard is someone who makes it a challenge to put the Ecumenical Council's statement into practice in daily life because he has the kind of face you want to punch. Do you know the kind of person I mean? Just, you know—*ka-pow!* Right in the nose! Of course I would never do that, and I don't even think about it usually, I hope.

Richard took my card and swiped it through the machine. He was looking at the machine's display, which I couldn't see, and suddenly his eyes got a small glint in them. He swiped the card again, waited, and the glint in his eyes grew brighter. With quiet pleasure he lifted his eyes to me and said a single word: "Declined." Then he handed back my card, took the bottle of Dewar's from the counter, and replaced it on the shelf.

Fortunately I had another card. I silently prayed it would

work, and by some miracle it did, and we got things sorted out. Valuing Richard's basic dignity as a human being by not punching his goddamn fucking purple veiny nose when he said "Declined" has been the great humanitarian achievement of my week so far.

"Declined." *Ka-pow!* Then Larry could make a special trip home from work to bail me out of jail.

Later I called the credit card company. Because of the raincoats, I am $8,973.63 over my limit. Fucking Merchants' Markdown.

SATURDAY, FEBRUARY 5

Poor Kyle had to leave his Saturday morning cartoons this morning so we could attend Repoint the Bricks Day at his school. All third through sixth graders and their parents had to erect scaffolding and repoint the bricks on the school's northern and western exterior walls, which took quite a beating in the recent rains. One of the teachers, Mr. Elledge, who has some experience in construction because of his second job, was in charge. Sometimes I wish they had never repealed the school levy but that was the voters' decision. Kyle did start to faint, but only twice. We were lucky that the temperature stayed in the seventies, making the grouting mix more pliable.

SUNDAY, FEBRUARY 6

Trevor had a good session with his therapist and I think we can see some real progress. The therapist put him on two additional medications along with the Eutopophane—Simulose and Ridiculin. These are lobotomy derivatives of the nightshade family, if I'm remembering that right. They are more effective than Eutopophane alone and they give Trevor a very level mood. In combination they can cause you to grow a second row of teeth, and we will have to watch for that. Trevor was a terrible biter when he was small.

MONDAY, FEBRUARY 7

Another call from Sabrina, and another trip to the fucking goddamn assisted living. When I say I wish my fucking father would just fucking die, sometimes it gives people an impression that is negative and wrong. What I mean is that my father has been a blight on the world all his life and it would simply be *better* if he died. I mean, here's this person who abandons his wife and family when I was twelve and my sister was ten and my brother was four, and he disappears to become an opera singer, which he fails at, then he becomes a real estate agent and makes millions that his ex-wife and kids never see a penny of, then he blows his money on a woman twenty-five years younger than he is, then she dumps him, then he becomes more or less a street bum, then he gets money from his own father's estate (not a penny of which do his ex-wife or his kids ever see), then he starts to become weirder, possibly because of dementia that consists of him being even more obnoxious than he was already, then he ends up at the goddamn assisted living, and then we—make that I—am expected to oversee his goddamn care and deal with his goddamn insurance company and visit him every goddamn day. That I'm even still speaking to this man is a huge concession. So for him to just fucking die would be really okay! Except maybe for himself. And I definitely mean all this in the most positive sense possible!

TUESDAY, FEBRUARY 8

Today at Food Superior I went to get some vitamin water and it had been moved back with the carbonated beverages. I checked, and sure enough, the Perrier and Pellegrino were once again with the bottled water. I do not know what is going on, but I think it is a sign that Food Superior is having management problems and will soon go out of business. That would be a shame. It's the most convenient store to where I live.

WEDNESDAY, FEBRUARY 9

Friends, here's a useful hint that I wonder if most people know. When you are wearing your best silk blouse and you're on your way to a fun brunch with your friend Gail from book group, and you stop at the kitchen sink to rinse some mascara from your thumb, and you turn the faucet on all the way, and the water rushes out and hits a cereal bowl from breakfast that's in the sink, and there is a spoon directly below the faucet in the cereal bowl, and the curvature of the spoon causes the rushing water to leap up out of the sink, and a bunch of dirty milky leftover goddamn cereal water splashes all over your blouse, ruining it, remember to take a deep breath and count to ten, and not do as I did, which was to grab a hammer from the tool drawer next to the sink and SMASH EVERY FUCKING DISH IN THE SINK TO TINY PIECES! FUCKING GODDAMN SPOON IN THE FUCKING CEREAL BOWL! WHY DON'T PEOPLE PUT THEIR FUCKING GODDAMN DIRTY DISHES IN THE FUCKING DISHWASHER, FOR CHRIST'S SAKE?!!

By following this hint you will save on blouses, dishes, and hammer marks on the sink that can never be washed out—not to mention wear on the nerves.

THURSDAY, FEBRUARY 10

Gail and I had a fabulous time talking about the book we're reading for book group, *Why the Bush Administration REALLY Sucks*, by Abner McShane and Walter Steinmann. Gail had suggested the group read it, and I had seconded the suggestion, despite some of the other book group members saying that the subject is somewhat out of date. Gail replied that we've read other books with the same basic theme and always enjoyed them, but there were so many that we never had time to get to this particular book. What we liked about this one was that it concentrates on members of the Bush administration whom we had not hated before, not having known of them—real assholes nobody ever heard of in Bush's Environmental Protection Agency, for example. In book group we believe it is the responsibility of each and every citizen to keep herself informed.

FRIDAY, FEBRUARY 11

Today's news from Sabrina is that "Dad" is doing so well in the Jazzercise program that he's thinking of taking part in tomorrow's three-kilometer Seniors' Run.

Hooray.

SATURDAY, FEBRUARY 12

Kyle had to bring a floor-polishing machine to his school today, because his class was chosen as Janitors of the Month. Of course, he didn't tell me this until nine o'clock the night before. Where the hell was I supposed to come up with a floor-polishing machine at nine on a Friday night? I went online and found an industrial-equipment rental place forty miles away that opened at eight this morning, and Kyle and I were there at eight, and they had floor-polishing machines, luckily. I must admit I was not very nice to poor Kyle about leaving this to the last minute. He always does that.

SUNDAY, FEBRUARY 13

I'm sitting in the therapist's parking lot by the sawed-off branches again. Today I must run the car heater because of last night's ice storm. It made the roads a skidding nightmare and we were late this morning. Friends, I know you're out there. The sun is glinting on the icy bushes and trees and telephone wires, and when I walked Trevor into the building—he sometimes dozes off and needs help to get going, it's the medications—a wind blew, and the ice-covered twigs were clicking like millions of tiny castanets. I don't know why, but the sound reminded me of you, the Cursing Mommy's unseen wonderful companions, who are always all around, and who understand what she is talking about. If you weren't there, the Cursing Mommy does not know what she would do.

MONDAY, FEBRUARY 14

A tree in our backyard broke because of the ice and fell on the garage. Larry, to his credit, at least told me about this before he took off this morning at five thirty. I don't know why we didn't hear it—it had to've happened last night. Calling the insurance people and arranging for a damage estimate is what I get to do today. So, FUCKING GODDAMN FUCKING SHIT, STUPID GODDAMN FUCKING TREE!! FUCKING GODDAMN LARRY WHO ISN'T HERE TO HELP EVEN THOUGH IT'S NOT HIS FAULT! FUCKING GODDAMN SHILL FOR RICH PEOPLE CONGRESSMAN FUCKING WHAT'S HIS NAME RYAN, though I have to admit his connection to the ice storm is indirect, so what, FUCK WHAT'S HIS NAME RYAN ANYWAY! *FUCKING GODDAMN ICE STORM!!*

Now I feel slightly better and can turn to the day's tasks.

TUESDAY, FEBRUARY 15

In the middle of dealing with the goddamn garage yesterday I got a text message on my cell phone, and it was from Larry's boss. I realize he's not technically Larry's boss, he's the client with the house in Encino who happens to own a company that owns Larry's firm, and Larry is not really the guy's employee, being technically a so-called independent contractor, which basically means that we have no pension plan and buy our own health insurance—

Anyway, be all that as it may, I got a text message from Larry's boss, the guy with the house in Encino, and as near as I can determine, he asked me out on a date. How did he get my cell phone number?

What to do? I don't even know what to think. Obviously I can't trust myself to respond to the guy in any way, after the debacle of my phone call to A Touch of India Carpet Cleaners. I loathe and detest and want to murder the guy. But God help me, I am both horribly weirded-out and not unflattered. And much as Larry drives me up a fucking wall, I hate not telling him things, but I'm not going to tell him about this.

WEDNESDAY, FEBRUARY 16

Latest from Sabrina: "Dad" has been working out in the weight room. He no longer always recognizes me, he can't feed himself reliably, and he is bench-pressing 150 pounds. The doctor says he will last another twenty-five years.

Yippee.

THURSDAY, FEBRUARY 17

Today is Cursing Mommy Crafts Day, in which the Cursing Mommy picks out a lovely red wine and pours a big glass and settles down to the comfortable task of arranging treasured family photos in this handy accordion book she has made. So let's start with:

The Cursing Mommy's Crafts Day, Part I:
How to Make Your Own Accordion Book

Take sheets of the heaviest-weight poster board your art store has in stock and cut them into rectangles of equal size. Their dimensions are up to you, but remember that you will want to store your accordion book on a shelf where you can take it out and look at it whenever you want. I made my accordion book fifteen inches by ten inches—big enough to hold a lot of photos, but not so big that I'll have to store it in the attic where it's seldom seen. Cover the first and last panels with colorful fabric as I've done, and connect all the panels with loops of ribbon so the book can be opened out, accordion style. You'll need to punch holes in the panels, as shown, to put the ribbon through.

Finishing all that takes at least a bottle and a half, you can see. Ideally you want to do this in somewhat less, which I believe should be my limit on a day like today. Maybe open only one more bottle, just in case.

Now you stick on these little photo-holding doohickeys, I don't know what they're called. They're to hold the photos, obviously. Now, here's a photo I haven't looked at in a while. It's Larry and me on our wedding day. My God, was I ever that thin? You'll have to excuse me, this kind of chokes me up . . . *oh, boo hoo hoo* . . . I'm sorry, some thoughts just came over me . . . And here's us on a sailboat that same day, what a nightmare . . . My fucking father, uninvited, who came to the ceremony anyway . . . Gramma Pat, with her oxygen tank . . . Forgive me, I need to blow my nose . . .

God, I can't bear to look at these fucking things . . . *boo hoo hoo* . . . What the fuck was I thinking to wear that dress? . . . What a goddamn horrible wedding . . . The stupid minister, a total fucking bozo . . . There's my brother, standing on his hands and doing a donkey kick in his tuxedo . . . *boo hoo hoo WAHH-HHH!! Oh, I'm feeling overcome. Oh, how did I ever end up like*

this? WAHHHHHHH! Sob! Sob! . . . Excuse me, I'm going to—
sniff!—take a break and stretch out on the carpet here for just a
bit, with this cushion from the sofa over my head for protection
against what I'm thinking about . . . We'll get back to the accordion book in just a moment . . . yes . . .

[*long pause*]

Okay, I'm up and walking around again. I see in the mirror
that the floor has made one side of my face kind of flat, with
the pattern of the carpet pile imprinted on it. It'll probably be
normal again by the time the kids get home. So now let us
move on to Part II of the Cursing Mommy's Crafts Day, which
consists of:

Dumping All This Shit in a Huge Box

Yes, sweep it all off the table with a large gesture of your arm as
you observe me doing here, accordion book and loose photos and
all, and then put the box in the goddamn attic where you never
have to look at any of this shit again as long as you fucking live.

Oh, what a typical fucking horrible day this has been.

FRIDAY, FEBRUARY 18

> *God respects me when I work, but She loves me when I sing.*
> *—popular saying, quoted by M. Foler Tuohy*

The chain saws started at seven thirty this morning because
they're removing the tree that crushed the roof of the garage. It
is inspiring to see the workmen in their blue coveralls and bright
yellow hard hats bustling about their jobs on this gray winter day.
They have attached ropes to parts of the tree and they are lifting
the bigger pieces, once they are cut free, by means of a bucket-
extension-type thing that goes up and down on top of their tree-
service truck. The garage roof is quite flattened, and there is

still some question about exactly what our rather uncooperative insurance company will pay.

I think the important point Tuohy is making in the above quotation is that we must turn with pleasure to the tasks we have been given, knowing we are respected for them on high, while at the same time always striving to sing "the miracle that is to be found in everything," in Tuohy's beautiful phrase. I am helping myself to accomplish all of that this morning by drinking a cup of special wake-up blend coffee with 38 percent more caffeine.

SATURDAY, FEBRUARY 19

Such a busy Saturday morning for the Cursing Mommy household, with me yelling and cursing, Larry rushing out the door to put in weekend work time as part of his ongoing attempt to impress the heartless fucks who pay his salary, Kyle donning his janitor clothes for today's mandatory stint at the school, and Trevor simply trying not to nod off. Today Trevor and I have a great opportunity to reduce the family's health insurance payments by participating in Sphagnum Health's Rate-Payer Volunteer Service Program (RPVSP), which allows us to deduct a small amount from our payment each month in return for responding to requests for voluntary service when called upon. Don't know what today's assignment will be, but we got the call from Sphagnum at five this morning and we are to meet the company bus in the plaza in twenty minutes.

Wish us luck!

SUNDAY, FEBRUARY 20

Well, it sounded like a wonderful idea, but it turned out to be a bit more complicated. At eight thirty Saturday morning, Trevor and I boarded the Sphagnum bus with about three dozen fellow insurees, including some other parents and kids. I recognized none of the parents, but a few of the kids knew Trevor. We went about twenty minutes to an absolutely enormous mansion in McKinley Springs Gated Community, where we were given rakes and set to raking the gravel in an immense Japanese garden they had out back—all these little white stones, perfectly round. We were told each stone had been chosen by hand, and our job was to rake all of them into exactly straight lines. Trevor was not good at this and I let him rest on a bench.

The work was rather tedious and a Sphagnum associate kept encouraging us in a friendly way you couldn't help but kind of hate. At noon we broke for lunch and ate the sandwiches we had brought. I was talking to a man named Franks who said this mansion belonged to the CEO of Sphagnum, Mr. Sandor A. Stattsman. This guy Franks was excited, as I was, at the prospect of keeping our health insurance payments to under thirty thousand a year. A little gravel raking seemed a small price to pay.

After raking, we picked up twigs, of which there were millions, probably left over from the last ice storm. Then about five o'clock the Sphagnum associates gathered us in a circle on the driveway turnaround and had us give our names and policy numbers and say what we liked about the day. I asked why Sphagnum wasn't covering Trevor's therapist visits (he is at the therapist's right now, by the way), and this caused Trevor to stomp on my toe to show I was embarrassing him. The associates said today was not the appropriate time for coverage questions and gave me a number to call.

MONDAY, FEBRUARY 21

I have to continue with the Sphagnum Health volunteer day because I have not yet told you the most incredible thing. After we were standing in the turnaround, we started back down the long drive to where the bus was parked by the security booth. A white limousine was coming up the drive and we moved over to one side to let it go by. The whole limo was throbbing with the reverberations of the music playing inside, and as it came up beside us suddenly it stopped and a dark-tinted window went down and the music came blasting out. Trevor later said the song was by Cannibal something or other, a song about intestines and power tools. Anyway, the window opened and someone stuck his head out and yelled my name—it was the client with the house in Encino! I turned and saw him and was so surprised I almost forgot to give him the finger.

Then I kept walking down the drive with the rest of the volunteers. He shouted after me that I should answer his text messages, but I just continued to give him the finger over my shoulder without looking back. Trevor asked me who that was and I said it was nobody. I guess he must have been there to visit Sandor A. Stattsman, head of Sphagnum Health. Who knows, maybe the fuckhead owns him, too. I could not get over this coincidence and I kept thinking about it on the bus going home.

What do you think about that, all my friends out there?

TUESDAY, FEBRUARY 22

Today I am doing nothing. Do you ever have those kinds of days? I contributed my bit this weekend, helped slightly reduce the health insurance payment, took Trevor to the therapist, made dinner for everybody. Today I will devote myself to doing nothing at all.

WEDNESDAY, FEBRUARY 23

The kids are out of school because of teacher conferences. Theoretically I have to go in and meet with Kyle's and Trevor's teachers, but I forgot to sign up, so instead I will lie in bed. I refer the family to my well-known column "Get Your Own Goddamn

Lunch: A Cursing Mommy Guide to Quick-'n'-Easy Mealtimes,"
available online or someplace.

THURSDAY, FEBRUARY 24
Today's big piece of news is that M. Foler Tuohy will be coming
to our local library speaker's program in April! Our whole book
group is going. I can't wait!

FRIDAY, FEBRUARY 25
Started out to have an ambitious day, take old DVDs to book
sale, get car washed, go to Food Superior, etc. When I stepped
out the back door the wind blew extra hard and I didn't like the
color of the sky. I went back inside, took off my coat, went upstairs, got undressed, climbed back into bed.

SATURDAY, FEBRUARY 26
Still in bed, I'm afraid. I let poor Kyle go to Scrape-and-Paint
Day by himself.

SUNDAY, FEBRUARY 27
Yoga teaches us that we can meditate anywhere—while doing
laundry, bathing, eating, making a shopping list, or sitting in a
parking lot outside a therapist's office where our son is getting
counseling early on a Sunday morning. Here by the sawed-off
tree branches with the chain-link fence wire still in them is my
own private ashram, if I can only persuade my mind to settle
down, which, as it happens, I can't, because I am just starting to
become aware that I gave Larry's boss the finger. At last it's beginning to sink in.

How could I have done such a stupid thing? *How could I have done such a stupid thing?* The guy has since sent me a few text messages I erased without reading. There's still a possibility he thinks I did not recognize him. I can only hope that is the case. It is not the case.

Screaming in the car can be a good release, as I have learned from experience. There is a four-story apartment house on the other side of the fence, but I don't think the people in it can hear me, although once a man came out on a balcony as I was screaming at the top of my lungs and I had my mouth open wide and my eyes squeezed shut, and suddenly I opened them and saw the guy. I suppose at that distance my screaming was a rather faint sound, but my facial expression with the wide-open mouth probably struck him as unusual. Yoga does not teach us much about screaming at the top of our lungs, but perhaps it should, because I, for one, do quite a bit of it, and I find yoga helpful as well. Perhaps a combination of yoga and screaming would be a good idea. I am sure someone has already thought of that. To help my screaming I usually vocalize it into a curse word, such as *"Sh-i-i-i-i-i-i-i-i-i-i-i-i-i-i-t!"* or *"F-u-u-u-u-u-u-u-u-u-u-u-u-u-u-u-u-u-u-ck!"* Screaming in the car for the full fifty minutes of Trevor's therapist appointment clears out psychic cobwebs, though it does also kind of make me want to scream some more, and I can't really do that while I'm driving Trevor on his post-therapist trip to McDonald's. So there is a downside.

MONDAY, FEBRUARY 28

I have never understood about leap years, have you? This is not a leap year, so today is not a what—a leap day? It is just an ordinary day, with no extra leaping. That is fine with me, although it makes February the most expensive month of the year on a per-day basis, from the point of view of people who pay for things by the month. You get fewer days for your money in February. This may be why people have a bad view of February, as I stated at the beginning of the month.

Another thing I have never understood is bowling scores, with all those X's and the little boxes in the corner of the squares on the scorecard. I have been asked to leave a bowling alley because I was cursing about the goddamn complicated fucking incomprehensible scorecard several years ago. I no longer bowl, though Kyle requested a bowling birthday party last year. I agreed on the condition that Larry keep score. Kid birthday parties have been some of the absolute worst experiences of my life and that bowling party was one of them even without my having to deal with keeping score. I also do not really understand how when it is fall up here it is spring down in South America, although I am willing to take the experts' word for it, as we must do with so many things.

We just have to proceed on faith, don't we? But faith in *what*? That is a tough one! Another February is almost past, and it did not even do a good job of keeping up with the pitiless flow of time, and so must leave a day's worth of debt to be paid by a future February, just as Kyle and Trevor will probably be stuck with the big pile of debt that Larry and I are getting into. To be fair, we would probably never have accumulated such debts if we'd never had kids in the first place, so the debts are partly the kids' doing. But then the kids did not ask to be born either, they might reply—kids are excellent arguers. All kids are F. Lee Bailey, as my friend Gail says.

But spring is coming soon! Let us take joy in that, my friends. Its annual renewal will bring flowers like the crocuses (unless they were killed off by blooming when the temperature went into the seventies a few weeks ago before the ice storms). We will wear garlands in our hair and dance the ancient dance around the maypole, and the sap will rise.

MONDAY, FEBRUARY 28, 11:44 P.M.

This fucking month just will not quit. God, I *so* despise it. I am awake at this hour with Larry snoring beside me and the goddamn smart-ass ceiling staring down and leering at me again. I have been trying to get to sleep by imagining I am in the middle of summer on some plush country estate with twenty million dollars in the bank and our fucking garage roof repaired and Trevor no longer a crazed demon child and Kyle no longer fainting and Larry retired from his god-awful job and happy in the basement with his goddamn beloved capacitors . . . And the ceiling keeps its relentless gaze on me. How to get through this fucking life? There's really nothing so terribly wrong, except fucking goddamn everything. How to get through? How to finally fall asleep? Maybe I'll try drinking some warm milk with a bit of vanilla, or maybe a triple dose of Nyquil. "I am watching," says the ceiling. "You won't sleep tonight. Do not even bother trying. Find something pointless to think about. It is still February. Even when it's March it will still be February. It will always be February. There will always be a ceiling watching as you try unsuccessfully to sleep. In several lifetimes the red numbers on the digital clock on your nightstand will not move beyond 11:44:04 p.m. I am watching you constantly. Just give up and lie there."

MONDAY, FEBRUARY 28, 11:47 P.M.

It is still fucking February. On the plus side, three more minutes of it do seem to have gone by.

MARCH

TUESDAY, MARCH 1

February was perfectly awful, to be honest, so we can thank God it's finally gone and look ahead to a "do-over" in March. Countless great possibilities shimmer on our horizon and wait unseen in March's yet-to-be-filled-in blank calendar pages—I find that rather thrilling, don't you? We are not yet what we shall become. Let us proceed into the new month with this uplifting thought: "Something WONDERFUL will happen to us today!"

WEDNESDAY, MARCH 2

In the "who would've guessed it?" department, I recently learned a fascinating fact: People who are trying to lose weight sometimes employ the assistance of specially trained dogs. Now, I had not known that! These "weight-reduction dogs," as they are called, help the dieter to stay on his or her plan by encouraging good eating habits, countering bad ones, and providing positive reinforcement through companionship and discipline. What a super idea! With the help of weight-reduction dogs, many participants in the program have dropped twice the pounds in half the time, according to the website. (The accompanying before-and-after photos are impressive indeed.)

As most of you know, one important consumer aid the Cursing Mommy provides is the testing of household products and services. So, in the interest of that, the Cursing Mommy has

rented a weight-reduction dog for the day! Yes, I picked up this
cute beagle-Samoyed–pit bull mix, Boris, at a weight-reduction
dog rental center just this morning. (Apparently, mixed breeds
are preferred for this kind of work.) Before bringing Boris into
the house, I shut the cats in the basement, and I laid out a typical
diet menu, plus some yucky, yummy nondiet foods, to see how the
pooch performs. Hello, Boris, are you ready? He responds with a
cheerful wag of his tail, so I guess we can begin.

The Cursing Mommy Weight-Reduction Dog Test, Part I:
Breakfast

At this end of the dining room table I have set a healthy breakfast of one half cup of oatmeal with three ounces of no-fat milk,
an eight-ounce glass of tomato juice, and one-third of a banana.
As I start to eat the oatmeal, my goodness! Look at the dog's tail
wag! Boris is practically cheering as I force down the healthy but
rather unpalatable (to be candid) meal. He rubs his head against
my knee and seems to grin with approval. Amazing!

At the other end of the table, for contrast, I have laid out a
nonhealthy breakfast consisting of a large, heavily frosted cinnamon roll from a fast-food place and a twelve-ounce cappuccino
with whipped cream and three teaspoons of sugar. I sit down, I
put my napkin in my lap—the ever-watchful dog starts to growl—
and I reach for the cinnamon roll. As I lift it to my mouth—
HEY!—the dog leaps up and snatches it with his jaws right out
of my hand! Holy Christ! Incredible. Boris is now gobbling the
roll on the floor, making quite a mess and growling and snapping
his jaws. Okay, very impressive. Now I think I'll have a sip of the
cappuccino and WOW! That was fast! Boris hopped up, knocked
the cup away with his paws, and is now slurping up the spilled
liquid on the floor along with crumbs of the roll. Okay, he's done
his job, and I begin to understand why the dog himself is actually pretty fat.

All right, I will put some of the leftovers back in the refrigerator. WHOA! The dog leaps in front of me! He won't let me near the refrigerator, he's baring his quite vicious-looking teeth and snarling. Listen, Boris, I'm not trying to get something more to eat, I just want to put this stuff away YIKES! He nipped my foot! Listen, you crazy dog, get back! I just want to put this stuff—hey, wait!—he bumped the refrigerator door open with his head and is eating the chicken casserole from last night! Hey, I made that casserole with low-fat sour cream, you stupid—get out of there! Now he's scarfing down some bacon, package and all! GET OUT OF THERE, YOU GODDAMN MUTT!! Okay, that does it. I'm taking you back . . . I get my car keys from the holder on the wall and WHAT IN TH— The dog grabs the keys with his teeth right out of my hand! I hate to curse at a dumb animal, but COME BACK HERE YOU FUCKING GOD-DAMN BEAST, I'LL FUCKING STRANGLE YOU WHEN I CATCH YOU!! GIMME BACK MY FUCKING CAR KEYS!! Oh, no! The cats have somehow gotten loose! Chasing after them with my keys still in his mouth the rotten creature leaps on the bookshelf and knocks over a vase and . . . AHHH!! Now I've tripped on the coffee table! I'm skidding facedown on the god-damn floor straight into a box of Larry's goddamn capacitors! FUCKING GODDAMN WEIGHT-REDUCTION DOG!! STUPID FUCKING CAPACITORS!! FUCKING CATS!! GOD-DAMN STUPID FUCKING BUSH ADMINISTRATION!! *GODDAMN FUCKING STUPID FUCKING EVERYTHING!!!*

[*pause*]

I think the goddamn dog has gone to sleep on top of the bookshelf. I just heard a snore. He *should* sleep, after the amount he ate. In just a minute I'm going to get up and call the rental place to come and get him. "Weight-reduction dog"—ha, what a joke. Let him keep the car keys, for all I care. I am not going near that animal again.

Oh, what a fucking goddamn horrible day this has been.

THURSDAY, MARCH 3

> *The nose that smells the flower*
> *Is not the flower.*
> *The ear that hears the song*
> *Is not the song.*
>
>   —*M. Foler Tuohy*

Sometimes M. Foler Tuohy says things that are so obvious we would never have thought of them, but then when we consider them a little bit longer, they become more obvious still. "Of course," we say to ourselves, "the nose is not the flower, they are two different things, and nobody ever suggested otherwise."

But then with deeper reflection, Tuohy's thought opens out like an onion revealing its many layers, and sometimes, also onionlike, making us cry. I believe the truth Tuohy is trying to convey here has to do with personal humility. Take my own experience of yesterday. There I was running around chasing after that horrible dog. Why? I had mistaken myself for the thing I was experiencing, i.e., a deranged animal tearing up my house. What I should have done instead is separate the two, self and dog, in my mind. Then with humility for my own weakness in contending with a faster and stronger creature, I should've found Grampa Hub's old hunting rifle in the closet upstairs and shot the fucking dog right in the fucking head. I will know what to do next time.

FRIDAY, MARCH 4

Tonight is book group, when we finally get to discuss *Why the Bush Administration REALLY Sucks*, by McShane and Steinmann. I have many points I want to bring up and several key parts I want to read aloud, but I bet almost everybody else does, too. The book is very rich in detail, with areas of the Bush administration that other books we've read did not touch upon. A few members of book group—Angie, for one—will probably go back to the old objection that the Bush administration has been out of office for a while. That is definitely a minority opinion, though, because the rest of us still are very interested in the subject. I am making my crabmeat-and-cream-cheese dip for an appetizer.

SATURDAY, MARCH 5

A lively book group last night, with a lot of soul-searching. Margaret, Gail, Holly, Sandra, and I brought up a difficult point—we kind of don't hate Condoleezza Rice. Eventually everybody agreed that book group will just have to fall short in this area, because the world is a complicated place. Some of us then also admitted that we don't completely despise Laura Bush, either. I said I like that she is said to be a heavy smoker. Anne then admitted she had felt sorry for Nancy Reagan when Reagan was sick, and that opened a whole other can of worms. We want to be consistent about our feelings but sometimes we can't. We must take ourselves as we are. At the end of the session we returned to the old dependables, Rumsfeld and Cheney.

While Kyle and I and the rest of his class and their parents work this morning to reglue the linoleum tiles on the school cafeteria floor, that is what I am wondering about—who to despise slightly more, Cheney or Rumsfeld, Rumsfeld or Cheney?

SUNDAY, MARCH 6

Early Sunday morning finds me parked as usual in my same spot by the sawed-off logs in Trevor's therapist's parking lot. Trevor has not been taking all his medications, apparently, because yesterday afternoon he set our local commuter rail station on fire. He has an explanation for why he did this, but I, for one, find it unpersuasive. Had he been keeping up with all his meds he probably would have been too impaired to get the fire burning so briskly, especially considering the day, which was damp. The fire department was able to contain the blaze and the police released Trevor to us, his parents, due to his age. We must go back and see a youth services judge next month for further monitoring. Thank God Trevor got this out of the way before his twelfth birthday, otherwise they would have shipped him off somewhere. The damages are yet to be assessed and we, his parents, will of course be stuck with the tab.

I have reminded Trevor again and again about not committing arson, and Larry has, too. I guess this rule has not yet taken hold in his still-developing mind. He enjoys fires and is a very strong-willed child. He may need more effective medications and I told the therapist as much when I brought him in this morning.

MONDAY, MARCH 7

Don't you just hate Mondays sometimes? I imagine all of you, my wonderful unseen friends, on this ordinary Monday sitting down at your desks or your kitchen tables just as I am sitting here. Maybe you look out your back windows, like I do, and see goddamn blue tarps on the roofs of your garages where they were crushed by trees. And maybe your heavily medicated kids have just zombie-walked onto the school bus, or have had a last swooning session on the couch (as my Kyle did) while begging not to be sent to school because the substitute teacher will make him sort rivets for the stairwell repairs. Maybe your own spouses left for work this morning quietly weeping at 5:00 a.m.

We are all more or less in the same boat, aren't we? Well, let's find comfort in sailing it together! Join hands with me, your friend the Cursing Mommy, on this ordinary awful Monday, and resolve to overcome the goddamn fucking miserable gray awfulness of the horrible goddamn day, week, month, and lifetime of however long that stretches before us like a desert of endlessly repeated bleak fucking Monday morning hells like today. (That previous sentence is how we DON'T want to think, obviously.)

On this particular Monday morning we are going to consider instead exactly what we'll do when we all win the lottery. Note I did not say IF we win the lottery, but WHEN. I am borrowing a bit from Tuohy here when I remind us all that it is, in fact, only a question of WHEN we win it, because in a spiritual sense, each of us has won already. All we must do is recognize what we've won and take ownership of our inner selves and of the internal riches present in our own lives. With this hopeful and forward-looking attitude we can defy Monday morning and charge cheerily on into our day, which, in my case, involves dealing with my fucking father's stupid goddamn doctor's phone messages about possible treatments for "Dad's" anal warts.

TUESDAY, MARCH 8

Food Superior has gone insane. I am really concerned about that store. Shopping there this afternoon I noticed that the advertisements they now have on the floor, ceiling, and hanging from the light fixtures are all for couples' websites or walk-in clinics. Also, the whole business about the bottled water and the vitamin water has gotten even more confusing. Top-of-the-line gourmet cat food is now in the middle of the bottled water aisle—yes, for real!—while the sparkling waters have been moved to Ethnic Foods, I guess because some of them are French. On top of that, a photographer now roams the aisles offering to make freestanding life-size photo cutouts of shoppers to be propped up next to their favorite products. You receive a free coupon for participating. What has gotten into that store?

WEDNESDAY, MARCH 9

More goddamn text messages from Larry's goddamn client / boss / whatever he is. Finally I got curious and—I know I shouldn't have—opened one of them. The message was lines from some

German metal band, something about love being a cistern or something. I erased it immediately. Larry's paychecks are 15 percent smaller now, and I am just aching to tell this fuckhead how unfair he is. On the other hand, I'm afraid of making things worse. Friends, you know the Cursing Mommy. What should she do?

THURSDAY, MARCH 10
Squirrels in the fucking goddamn chimney, running up and down. We have these glass folding-door things that close off the fireplace, and inside them is like a chain-mail curtain to keep sparks from flying out when the glass things are open. The squirrels scamper down the chimney and then climb around on the wire mesh curtain and look in at us. If the glass doors were open, they could just scoot around the curtain into the living room. I hear this scrabbling of claws on wire and I look over and see a squirrel's beady little eyes. I hate that stupidly observant expression they have.

FRIDAY, MARCH 11
Gramma Pat was a marvelous seamstress. A blouse that had lost a button or socks that needed darning or trousers with holes in them went into the big wicker bin in her sewing closet off the back hallway, and then on Fridays, before the weekend's church events, Gramma Pat would take out all the garments in need of repair and spread them on the dining room table. As a little girl, I used to stand at her side, enthralled. Next to the table she would park her old foot-pedal Singer machine on its wheeled stand, with the dark green wooden base worn through to the bare wood where countless yards of cloth had passed over it and where little black lines showed the many cigarettes Gramma Pat had left burning there.

  Whirrr! Whirrr! I can still hear the cheerful, busy sound of that trusty old machine as Gramma Pat worked away, a fresh pack of Chesterfields at her elbow. How her fingers flew in the haze of smoke so thick you almost couldn't see her sometimes! She could keep one of those extralongs between her lips until the ash seemed to defy gravity, when with a deft tap she would add it to the ashtray.

I no longer work on a foot-pedal Singer, of course, though I still have Gramma Pat's someplace out in the garage where it probably got crushed by the tree. Today I am using my modern five-speed electric (also a Singer), which can easily handle most domestic sewing tasks. So, let us now begin with:

The Cursing Mommy's Sewing Basket, Part I: Mending a Torn Pair of Denim Jeans

Unlike my gramma, I do not smoke except when I drink a lot at parties, so today I will simply place this glass of spiced vodka on ice here where I can reach it to relax my nerves. (I love these new flavored vodkas, don't you?) Here is my pair of absolute favorite all-time-best-fitting jeans that unfortunately have a small tear across the right knee. I plan to mend the tear first from the inside using cross stitching on a patch I will cut from an unworn place on this old pair of jeans of Larry's that he was about to throw away.

First, with my seam ripper, I slice up the inseam on the old jeans, laying open the pant leg to make a single piece of fabric from which a patch can be cut more easily. Another little soupçon of vodka in the glass will help this go better, I believe. Mmmm, tasty! I trace the outline of the patch on the lighter side of the denim like so, and then carefully cut it out with my shears. Then I cut four more patches, just to have some extras handy.

Now, turning to the jeans to be repaired, I pull the pant leg inside out so I can pin the patch in place on that side before I begin to sew . . . Wait a minute . . . what jeans are these? Why are these jeans so large? . . . What the—? Oh, no. It can't be.

I see now, as I examine the pair of jeans I am patching, and the pair I just ripped to pieces in order to cut out five patches, that I have fucking mistakenly CUT THE PATCHES FROM THE GOOD PAIR OF JEANS! WHAT THE FUCK WAS I FUCKING THINKING? I HAVE RUINED MY BEST JEANS! JESUS FUCKING CHRIST, WHAT A FUCKING GODDAMN IDIOT I AM!! FUCKING GODDAMN LARRY'S FUCKING INDISTINGUISHABLE FUCKING JEANS!! I'LL SHOW YOU, YOU FUCKING JEANS, I'LL CUT BOTH PAIRS OF YOU TO FUCKING RIBBONS, YOU FUCKING GODDAMN THINGS!!! I'M SHREDDING YOU WITH SCISSORS!! NOW I'VE FALLEN FROM THE CHAIR IN A HEAP OF DENIM FRAGMENTS!! OH, FUCK WHAT'S HIS NAME BROWN, THAT FUCKING HURRICANE KATRINA MORON FROM FEMA WHO DESTROYED NEW ORLEANS!! FUCK GOD-DAMN RONALD REAGAN, I DON'T FUCKING CARE IF HE FUCKING DIED ALREADY!! *FUCK GODDAMN EVERYTHING!!!*

[*pause*]

In just a minute I'm going to get up. I'll throw all these denim shreds into my rag box. I can always use more rags. Soon the kids will be coming home and I'll get started on dinner. Well, there goes my best pair of jeans.

Oh, what a fucking horrible day this has been.

SATURDAY, MARCH 12

Today was one of those glorious spring mornings that make the heart glad. I wish all of you could have been with me as I stepped out the back door this morning and inhaled the intoxicating scent of the freshly crushed grass and other plants battered by last night's hail, with heaps of hailstones scattered all about and melting refreshingly in the sun. Seventy-five degrees, practically

Caribbean weather, and perfect for sunbathing—but no time for that on this busy day! Larry was loading the car with his boxes of capacitors on his way to the annual Capacitors' Convention, while Trevor and Kyle and I would put in another maintenance day at school.

Larry dropped us there as he was heading off. We were all in happy moods, even Trevor, as near as I could tell. Our workday went smoothly, though I broke two fingernails chiseling paint, Trevor slept, and Kyle broke out in hives temporarily. At the end of the work session, my friend Gail from book group (Gail's son, Matt, is in Kyle's class) kindly gave us a ride home.

As we were approaching our house, a strange thing occurred. From a distance I noticed a vehicle parked by our driveway, and as we came closer I saw it was a white limousine! Even from inside Gail's car I could hear the throb of heavy metal. I quickly scrunched down in my seat and told Gail to drive on. She had no idea what I was talking about but she is a faithful friend and kept going. "Drop us off on Christopher Street," I told her. Mystified, she did. I said I would explain later. The kids and I got out at the Skenazys' house and cut through their yard and went into our house by the back door. We slipped down into the basement and sat there in the dark for half an hour not answering the doorbell—which rang several times—until the limo went away.

When I finally came upstairs, I found a huge bunch of pink and white roses on the front steps but no card. I sealed them up in a leaf bag and set it out by the trash barrels so I won't have to explain to Larry when he gets home tomorrow.

SUNDAY, MARCH 13
This morning I asked Trevor's therapist if he had any extraheavy sedatives he could prescribe for me. He only gave me a puzzled look and said I should ask my own doctor about that. What the hell—I figured it was worth a try.

MONDAY, MARCH 14

Larry had an absolute ball at the Capacitors' Convention and it seems to have restored his confidence. He did not do his usual quiet weeping as he got ready for work this morning. He said he had met some true kindred spirits at the convention and was thinking of making a business of his capacitors full-time. Apparently he has some of the most prized capacitors in the world in his collection, and to insure them he must install a sophisticated security system in our house. I said that would be a great idea. (Where the money for it would come from is something else again.) Putting in a security system appeals to me right now, although I didn't say why.

TUESDAY, MARCH 15

Beware the ides of March!   —*William Shakespeare,* Julius Caesar

As we go through life, we are constantly being told to beware. Like the toothless old seer who warned the emperor Caesar that he would meet his downfall on March 15, self-appointed doomsayers pop up in our path. We must do this or that, we are told, or we will plummet into disaster! And we listen, and we step frightenedly through our lives from one day to the next, expecting the worst, never sure we aren't doing the very thing that will lead directly to our wrack and ruin.

Well, if all of you will pardon my French: the hell with that applesauce! As the Cursing Mommy, I hereby give you permission to jump off the waiting "cliff." You will find it's only about six inches high! And if you don't believe me, believe M. Foler Tuohy, who writes (in his latest book, *Ouch! That Smarts!*), "More mischief has been done in the world through excessive caution than through all deliberate wickedness combined. Never listen to those who will tell you that the hill is too steep, the way too long, the goal too high. Forge onward, always, and never fear!"

May I get metaphysical, or philosophical, or maybe even a bit corny here for a moment? The way I look at it, friends, is this: If I were a soul existing in some mystical prebirth nowhere zone, and God or whoever came to me and said I could go to Planet Earth and take my chances with living in human shape, and told me I'd be here for a while in good or bad or wonderful or terrible circumstances, or maybe in all those circumstances mixed together, and after a while I would die, and leave the planet, and return to the nowhere zone where I began—would I say yes, let's give it a try? OF COURSE I WOULD! Wouldn't you? It might be fun! Why not? I'm sure I would jump at the chance. So, knowing we would have chosen to be here anyway, we should embrace with open arms whatever the hell we happen to encounter in this life, and trample and stomp on obstacles, and not hesitate to curse once in a while when things go wrong, as (let's face it) they generally do.

The Cursing Mommy replies to the toothless old seer, "Let the fucking ides of March beware of ME!"

WEDNESDAY, MARCH 16

My father's minor surgery (those horrid warts) was today. I had to drive to the goddamn assisted living and ride with the old jerk to the outpatient center for the "procedure," hold his hand before and after, ride back with him to the goddamn assisted living, consult with his doctors and caregivers, see that he was made comfortable, and yadda yadda. Is it okay if I not go into further details?

And meanwhile some of the staff are giving me the eyeball like I'm a bad daughter because I didn't visit last week. I just want to knee them in the fucking groin, truthfully. That's how I really feel. In fact, I say nothing, and smile, and am nice. The fuckheads. Experts say that old people with daughters taking care of them live longer than ditto with sons. Just my luck.

THURSDAY, MARCH 17

Oh, I just can't stand it! I feel like I want to "murtilize" some-body, as Gramma Pat used to say. I opened the morning mail and found a notice from Sphagnum Health saying they were adding a 7 percent "fuel increase surcharge" to our bill! The amount more than wipes out the little rebate we received for raking all that gravel. How does the price of fuel figure into health insur-ance costs, anyway? I am really furious about this. I feel like call-ing Mr. Sandor A. Stattsman himself. Or going to his house and messing up his fucking gravel.

FRIDAY, MARCH 18

I completely forgot St. Patrick's Day this year. Yesterday I was so livid about that Sphagnum Health bill, I was calling their ridicu-lous goddamn customer service number and bouncing around a phone tree, and—of course—getting absolutely nowhere. As a result I neglected to lift a glass to St. Paddy, so therefore I am correcting the oversight this morning.

SATURDAY, MARCH 19

Kyle got the day off from maintenance because the commercial he wrote for Platt's Fruit Leather, one of the school's corporate sponsors, has been chosen for the spring program. We are very proud of him. He broke out in hives at the news—he has an es-pecially hard time with "good stress" of this kind. As a reward I took him to the mall. It only allows children accompanied by parents who spend at least thirty-five dollars on mall purchases, so I used the opportunity to shop for odds and ends. Meanwhile Kyle, armed with the validated sales slips, went to the food court and met some other children who were making paper airplanes from food wrappers and having races with them. He had a wonderful time. On the way back to the car he held my hand and thanked me and said he would remember today forever. He told me that he much preferred it to hanging Sheetrock.

SUNDAY, MARCH 20

Trevor's therapist has gone to Bonaire, so for once we were able to sleep in. I can't remember the last time I did that on a Sunday. Larry hopped out of bed before dawn and disappeared down in the basement, and I had the luxury of just lying there with the whole bed to myself and thinking about people I despised. Sandor A. Stattsman, for one. The fucking client with the house in Encino, naturally. A guy whose name I don't remember from freshman orientation at college—what an asshole. The fuckhead who invented trickle-down economics, whatever his name might have been. And what's his face who used to work at the bank—God, I detested that guy. Plus that fuckhead at the gas station who accused me of lying about the spilled gas in order to—Jesus, I don't even remember what stupid con he thought I was trying to run on him. What a complete fucking jerk! I can't recall his name.

Then I got up and made my special cinnamon pancakes for everyone, with big cups of 38-percent-more-caffeine coffee for me. Larry prefers the decaf version of that, which is like very strong regular coffee.

MONDAY, MARCH 21

School canceled due to sandstorm.

TUESDAY, MARCH 22

Sandstorm worse. Larry just phoned to tell me he almost couldn't get to work.

WEDNESDAY, MARCH 23
Sandstorm letting up. Sand everywhere. What a job of digging out awaits us!

THURSDAY, MARCH 24
[no time to write in this]

FRIDAY, MARCH 25
[ditto]

SATURDAY, MARCH 26
Well, if that wasn't the wildest thing! A sandstorm completely buried our area in fine brown sand to the depth of four feet in places. Scientists said this rarely happens. In fact, there has not been a sandstorm of this size here since possibly the Precambrian era, as near as anyone knows. We took away some valuable lessons from the storm, which we can apply in the future. One is to buy sand guards for windows, doors, and pet entries. The other is to protect plants, such as our daffodils and grape hyacinths, which were just starting to come up when the influx of scorching sand withered them. In the yard this morning I was pleased to see that a few of them have survived and are starting to poke their hopeful little heads through the sand drifts that remain after the removal process. Everyone pitched in on the cleanup and I think we came together in the work and learned a lot about one another.

SUNDAY, MARCH 27
Community is so important in our lives. Gail picked me up early this morning because we were having a book group "sandathon"

where we would go to each member's house, one after the next, and clean from floor to ceiling. There is sand *inside* the threads on the tops of the toothpaste tubes, if you can believe it—that's how fine some of these sand grains are. We started at Margaret's and went through like a squad of cleaning fiends! Oh, we were a jolly crew, and enjoyed the lunch Holly and Susan provided, and by dinnertime we had finished with each member's house, including mine. Of course, some sand still remains, and probably always will be there as a reminder of this once-in-a-planet happening.

MONDAY, MARCH 28

With relief I return to familiar routines on this Monday morning, the sounds of Larry's quiet sobbing and Trevor's groggy cries as I try to get him to move. Then the two of them and Kyle are out the door, and quiet once again reigns, and I can return to my kitchen table, my coffee cup, and you, my encouraging and wonderful unseen friends. When the Cursing Mommy fears she is losing her way in life, she sits down for a good talk with you and feels better every time.

Today I want to discuss exfoliating. That's right—basic skin care, a subject few of us have enough time for in our busy lives. I was reading a supermodel's beauty tips in the paper last week where she said her secret for a fresh complexion was drinking fourteen twelve-ounce glasses of water every day. I am sorry, but with that amount of water, the young lady must be spending her entire life in the loo! Yes, staying well hydrated does provide a fresh and blooming look to the skin, but, I mean, come on. Try drinking a few twelve-ounce glasses of water and then sitting for two hours in a traffic jam with a carful of third graders on their way to the Ice Capades. Your skin may look dewy fresh, but what good is that when your features are contorted in agony?

The horrible sand everywhere had me feeling so dry that I

decided to exfoliate using a mild facial astringent to cleanse the pores and remove dead skin cells before remoisturizing. We have all been through that drill, and frankly, it is not what it is supposed to be! Your skin can become addicted to the process. I am not kidding. On this jar of extremely expensive moisturizer whose brand name I will not reveal (the Cursing Mommy does not endorse individual brands), the consumer is told, "The skin actually eats [the product] as a food!" Creepers! Do you want a product your skin *eats*? Do you want to walk around with hungry skin, on top of everything? That is just too science-fictiony.

TUESDAY, MARCH 29

Anyway, to go back to skin care, yesterday I finally broke down and used the skin-eats-it-as-a-food moisturizer just to see what would happen, and by about nine o'clock at night my face was *starving*. It wanted more moisturizer and it wanted it *now*. I had just showered with a new "volumizing" shampoo and it had volumized my hair to about three times the size of my head. In desperation I slapped on a marvelous facial moisturizing mask I make in the blender using avocado, aloe vera, and a lovely fragrant Indian root called vetiver, with a smell that is wonderfully restorative and divine.

Well, I covered my face with that soothing mixture and put cucumber slices on my eyelids to hydrate them as well, and as I was feeling my way back into the bedroom I happened to knock over a night table, and that woke Larry. He sat up and looked at me and let out such a scream. I guess with the mask and hair I did look different, and startled him. I told him to please be quiet for Jesus Christ's sake or he'd wake the children—but too late. Kyle burst into the room and saw me, and he screamed, too, and then Trevor followed, took one look, and began to bellow sluggishly. I ran to the shower and jumped in before the situation could get out of hand. Proper skin care has many risks, obviously. Please don't ever let me try this again.

WEDNESDAY, MARCH 30
As we know, owning pets teaches kids responsibility, brings the family together for fun sharing, and even provides health benefits such as stress reduction for older members of the family. In the light of all that, I can only regret I don't feel very positive about our own goddamn fucking cats. In fact, I detest and loathe them—they rip up our furniture, and make messes I alone clean up, and shed, and fight, and snarl, and strew kitty litter all over, and jump up on the kitchen counter with their filthy feet, and hiss at me, and make my life a general hell. In fact, I would toss the fucking goddamn cats out in the street if the rest of the family (Kyle and Larry, mainly) would agree. "Let's get kittens! Oh, please, Mommy, can't we get kittens?" the children cried, way back when, in a younger and simpler day. Moronically, I gave in. And who takes care of the cats nowadays, you ask? The children? Larry? *Au contraire!*

Now our wretched goddamn cats have developed some damn thing that's wrong with them. They are listless, they sneeze, they get this gross filmy stuff around their eyes, they rub their eyes with the backs of their paws. We are all worried, but exactly who is going to do anything about the problem? The kids? Larry? The fucking adorable cats themselves?

THURSDAY, MARCH 31
So I chased the cats around the house—they weren't so listless they couldn't run—and I finally caught them and I put them in their cat carriers (which they hate) and I drove them to the vet and I waited for about three hours in the waiting room and brought

them in to him, finally, and he examined them and he did some tests—and guess what? Our cats have allergies, the vet says. More specifically, they are allergic to us! Yes, our poor sad cats are allergic to human beings, mostly to Larry, who of course at his age is losing some hair, and the cats have developed "adult-onset feline allergic reaction" to his hair. Now all I have to do is give the cats a dose of not-cheap anti-allergy medicine with an eyedropper twice a day from now on, permanently. One more goddamn thing I have to deal with.

Oh well, it could be worse, I guess. Onward, friends!

APRIL

Good morning and hooray for this lovely new month, April, the month of hopeful fresh beginnings. Spring takes off in April, as if we didn't know, and what a blossoming, brimming, blessed time this will be! We are all familiar with spring cleaning, and spring planting, and those sexy spring makeovers we devote so much of our time and resources to. But what about a spring rejuvenation of the soul? Have we been careful to set aside some of our happy springtime energy for that good purpose?

Yes, if we put our minds to it, our souls can "green up" in the springtime just like the flowers and trees. But unlike in nature, this rebirth won't happen automatically. We must be cultivators of our spirits, gardeners of our good thoughts, fertilizers of our very own wild and irreplaceable dreams. We must irrigate our aspirations and pull out the noxious mental weeds, such as complacency, and habit, and all the ordinary old ways of doing things. Imagine if we could take our hearts out of our chests and polish them up and put them back in again, humming and shiny and new, better able to love and feel—wouldn't that be wonderful? Well, that is what our springtime rejuvenation of the soul should be.

I never was much for New Year's resolutions (and of course I hardly had a moment to think about them this year, with the god-awful New Year's we had), but springtime resolutions is a concept I can get behind. Let us resolve this April to blossom inside ourselves and become all-new individuals in our souls. I believe that is a project of which M. Foler Tuohy (coming to our local library later this month!) would definitely approve.

SATURDAY, APRIL 2

Goddamn Sphagnum Health to eternal hell, those goddamn, fucking, asshole, THIEVES. I just paid their monthly bill after subtracting the deduction we earned for raking that CEO's goddamn gravel, and they just now e-mailed me to say they had received the check and it was insufficient because my deduction for Rate-Payer Volunteer Service had been disallowed. There followed a fucking raft of fine print that seemed to say I was not entitled to the deduction because I had not filed for it in a "timely" way, which, as near as I can determine, would have been two fucking months before the aforesaid goddamn volunteer service occurred.

Well, friends, the Cursing Mommy did not take this lying down. I sent an e-mail back to Sphagnum Health saying that I was disallowing their disallowing of my deduction, and how did they like that? They e-mailed back that I could not disallow things, because only they were allowed to disallow things. I then e-mailed back saying "Says who? I disallow your disallowing of MY disallowing! So there!"

They then replied that our coverage would be canceled if they did not receive payment of the outstanding balance within seventy-two hours.

God, how I despise them.

SUNDAY, APRIL 3

Yesterday's work day at Kyle's school was quite arduous. Some of the electrical rewiring the fourth graders did in the gymnasium last week was not up to code, apparently. The principal shamed the fourth graders by having the third graders (and their moms and dads and caregivers) do it over. What a crock of cranberries *that* was!

On top of that, Trevor's therapist has delayed his return from Bonaire. This makes me nervous because some of Trevor's prescriptions have run out or are about to. I'd hate to see that child go unmedicated.

MONDAY, APRIL 4

Our fifteenth wedding anniversary. I made Larry his favorite dinner (pork and sauerkraut with applesauce; no, I did not make the applesauce myself, it came out of a jar, and the sauerkraut came from a plastic pouch). He said we would go out to dinner next year when we can afford it. For an anniversary present he gave me a heat gun. It is used to soften old paint for removal. A heat gun is not what I had always wanted, but I am sure it will be useful in some way. He included a very sweet card.

TUESDAY, APRIL 5

Sent the check to Sphagnum Health via overnight mail. Goddamn them to eternal, fucking, deepest, HELL.

WEDNESDAY, APRIL 6

Oh, friends, I know I shouldn't complain, but my soul is not growing new shoots this morning. No, it is lifeless and parched and cracked. I feel I am swimming in wet concrete. It's like I'm wearing an overcoat with many pockets, and every pocket contains a big bar of lead, and the weighted coat is weighing on my shoulders, pulling me down . . .

Friends, I know that is far from the proper attitude. I don't want to think like that. Here by myself again at my kitchen table

I will take comfort from your invisible companionship, and pick myself up, and remember instead all that's good . . .

Have you ever seen one of those monkey islands at the zoo? You know, those big displays made out of rock with some old tree stumps and tire swings and so forth for the monkeys to climb on? And the monkeys swarm all over and run up and down and scamper and make chittering sounds and bump into one another and bare their gums? Well, that is what the problems swarming on me resemble, on this low-down April day.

However, I must not think like that, as I have pointed out already.

THURSDAY, APRIL 7

Oh good God, the garage caught fire! We looked out the window last night at dinner and flames were leaping from it. The fire department came and ran over the flowers I'd just rescued from the sandstorm and the firemen hosed down the whole structure and saved most of it—but the construction guys had just put up a new roof frame! Which is now totally gone! Larry is lying in bed in a fetal position. I hate to think Trevor left something smoldering out there, but I admit the possibility does exist. I couldn't refill his prescription for Dystopial, which contains an anti-arsonic, and that may have led to the problem. When and if the therapist returns I must get the drug renewed so this won't recur. I think we'll probably now tear the whole garage down and just leave our car and stuff under pieces of plyboard. It will look rather informal but it will be just for a little while. Hopefully.

FRIDAY, APRIL 8

Never set out to clean your house unless you are angry and in a throwing-away mood. This is a rule of Gramma Pat's that I always adhere to. Gramma Pat used to fire up a Chesterfield and stick another behind her ear so she could get to it quickly, and then she would plug in the old Hoover and start her vacuuming. After that it was "Katie, bar the door!" until Gramma wore herself out or went to buy more Chesterfields. Oh, she could make the dust fly! One time I'll never forget she threw her cigarette down without putting it all the way out and it got in the vacuum bag and started a fire there. Nothing (except severe emphysema) ever stopped Gramma Pat. I'm in an exactly similar mood this morning for:

The Cursing Mommy's Vacuuming Day; or, Dust Bunnies, Begone!

Today I am using a SukMore Ultra-Inhaling Rug and Carpet Beater-Cleaner I was sent on trial to see if I like it, and so far I do. I plan to really go to town with this machine as I attack (first) the living room carpet, where there is still some sand and horrid fluff and cat hair and Larry's hair and whatnot despite the going-over my book group gave it just last week. As Gramma Pat used to say, 99 percent of all household dust is actually human skin cells from the people who live there. Pretty unappetizing, right? Well, now I am vacuuming like gangbusters, pushing this machine all over (and it is making quite a roar!) to vacuum that awful accumulated stuff right out of here.

And yes indeedy I am mad this morning (*roarrrr*) about the garage burning down (*roarrrr*) and Larry's reduced pay (*roarrrr*) and the thieves at Sphagnum Health (*roarrrr*) and our horrible street that has orange traffic cones all around the potholes (*roarrrr*) so we're going to have to buy a huge goddamn SUV with steel tires just to drive on our own goddamn road (*roarrrr*), and the therapist who is still in Bonaire (*roarrrr*), and the goddamn cat allergist I now have to take the cats to because Larry refuses to wear a hair net around the house (*roarrrr*), and LARRY'S GODDAMN AWFUL CLIENT/BOSS/OWNER, that fucking too-cool limo-riding shit, who underpays Larry and keeps sending me text messages that I know are creepy even though I never open them (*roarrrr*)! Vacuum all that nonsense right out of here (*roarrrr*)! Yes! And at least you don't have to dress your best to vacuum—the Cursing Mommy is doing her cleaning today in a comfortable old floor-length housecoat that used to be Gramma Pat's, and I swoop the SukMore right at my feet and GAHHH! NOOOOO! The goddamn machine inhaled the hem of my housecoat! Let go, you goddamn thing! Where the hell is the Off switch? Goddamn machine has inhaled the housecoat up to my knee! I'm yanking and ripping at the fabric! GODDAMN FUCK-ING PIECE OF SHIT DANGEROUS GODDAMN VACUUM CLEANER! FUCK THE GODDAMN INCOMPETENTS OF THE CONSUMER SAFETY BUREAU UNDER THE FUCK-ING BUSH ADMINISTRATION, WHOEVER THEY WERE, THAT LET THIS—OUCH!!—DANGEROUS PIECE OF SHIT BE SOLD!!! FUCK GODDAMN ARI FLEISCHER, THAT VACUUM-CLEANER-DEREGULATING ASSHOLE!! NOW I'M WRESTLING WITH THE GODDAMN VACUUM ON THE FUCKING FLOOR!!! *OH, GODDAMN FUCK FUCKING GODDAMN EVERYTHING!!!!* (*rrriiippp, tearrrr, putt putt. Click.*)

[*pause*]

Finally I got the wretched thing turned off. I see the bag has spilled some of its contents during the struggle. In just a min-ute I'll sweep it up with a good old-fashioned broom. So long, housecoat. From now on the dust can smother us all to death for all I care.

Oh, what a fucking horrible day this has been.

SATURDAY, APRIL 9
What next? On top of having a tree fall on it, and catching on fire, the garage has now collapsed completely. Larry, in between

moans, says it might've been termites—but how would that be possible? I don't believe we have termites in the garage. I hate to think that Trevor might somehow be responsible for this. The collapse left quite a mess and scattered the remaining things that were in the garage far and wide. Fortunately we had moved most of our belongings out and now park our car in the driveway.

God, what will we do? Larry is finishing the taxes along with everything else and that also upsets him. More of his hair is falling out from stress, which further sickens the cats. We are really sort of overwhelmed right now. Plus, this is the start of Easter vacation, so both kids will be rattling around the house all week.

I have to suspect that Trevor is behind both the fire and (somehow) the collapse. He has never liked the garage. When he was little he said a monster he called Mr. Libby lived there.

SUNDAY, APRIL 10

This morning finds me back in Trevor's therapist's parking lot by the sawed-off tree branches in the chain-link fence. The therapist has finally returned from Bonaire. It is a nice warm spring day, eighty-three degrees at 7:30 a.m., and going to get warmer, the weather lady says. I have the windows rolled down. I am forgoing my usual restorative fifty-minute screaming session as I wait in the car today, because to do it and not disturb neighbors I would have to roll the windows up and run the car engine and have the air conditioner going, and that seems silly and not very relaxing at all. So I am trying to enjoy this warm spring morning without screaming.

Last night Gail, that angel, brought us over a complete turkey dinner. She knew I would be too busy after everything with the garage to plan and cook a good meal. Gail included stuffing and cranberry sauce and mashed potatoes and gravy—the works! It was like having Thanksgiving in April. She is a simply wonderful friend and she has no idea how much she lifted our mood, God bless her heart.

MONDAY, APRIL 11
Took the kids to buy new shoes. They both needed them. Kyle wanted fancy new sneakers and made a fuss when I said that wasn't what we were shopping for. He loves sneakers and spends hours designing special ones. I suppose I should've just given in and let the kid have them. He gets so little pleasure out of life.

TUESDAY, APRIL 12
The awful client or whatever of Larry's sent me a huge box of fancy cheeses yesterday and they arrived just as we were sitting down to dinner. When Larry looked at the delivery slip and saw who the package was from he became pathetically happy and began to say his star must be on the rise again at work, our troubles would soon be over, and so on. It kind of broke my heart. I had slipped the card into my pocket by then and naturally I never showed it to him. Later when I read it, it was as creepy as I expected it would be. If the damn package had arrived during the day when only I was home, I would have just sent it back. But Larry insisted we open it and have some Amish bleu or whatever, right goddamn then! I declined. He went ahead anyway. God, I wanted to run upstairs and hide under the covers and not come out. Friends, tell me what I should do! Now Larry will go to work tomorrow and gratefully thank the guy. I hate to imagine.

WEDNESDAY, APRIL 13
Yes, lying in a steaming tub with a bottle of Kahlua and ignoring the children's knocks on the bathroom door all afternoon is not

the most mature coping strategy. So stipulated, your honor! The Cursing Mommy pleads no contest.

But Jesus Christ, what the hell am I supposed to do? "*Watch TV, kids! That's what it's for! Watch anything you want! Play video games! Haven't you ever heard of video games? The kind where you shoot people? Just leave me the hell alone right now, okay?*" I shout.

My friends, I repeat: What am I supposed to do?

THURSDAY, APRIL 14

Everything important happens at parties. —*a very wise person*

So after thinking and agonizing and rethinking and racking my brain, and arguing under my breath with the goddamn snide, defeatist, no-help ceiling all night while Larry snored beside me, I finally came up with a solution: I will throw a party! This guy, Larry's horrid Client/Boss, is obviously living in a cloud-cuckoo-land fantasy of which, creepily, he has made me a part. So I'll invite him over with a whole bunch of other people and give him a dose of reality. Let the bozo see me with my husband and my kids—no sending the kids away for this party! I want them here, and Larry, too, at my side. I'll be as nice as pie and refer to "my husband" and say "Larry and I" did this or that all evening, without being too obvious about it, of course. Let the creep see what is actually going on, and who I actually am, and that I'm already FUCKING GODDAMN MARRIED SO HE SHOULD LEAVE ME THE HELL ALONE, FOR CHRIST'S FUCKING SAKE!! But nicely, of course. I'll puncture his fantasy dirigible that way.

I'll invite everybody in Larry's office. Now, normally they might not come to a party given by someone as far down the totem pole as Larry. But when they hear the Boss/Client is coming—and he will come—the others will fall in line. And I'll invite my whole book group, too! I've told nobody in book group about this goddamn problem with the creepy Client/Boss, although by now Gail certainly suspects something. But our book group is so great! We love parties! And it will be great to have book group there with me because it is armed against people like this Client/Boss asshole because of all the reading we've done.

Will this work? I don't know. But I always feel better when I come up with a plan—don't you?

FRIDAY, APRIL 15

Told Larry we're going to throw a party in two weeks. He was so stressed about the taxes he barely heard me at first. Then he finally focused and said nobody from his office would want to come to a party at our house. I assured him they most certainly would. He asked why, and I said because nobody throws parties in April and people are really in the mood for one after paying taxes because they're so down, they need some fun. Larry bought this explanation, incredibly. For all I know it may be true.

SATURDAY, APRIL 16

Sent out the e-mail invitations this morning, and the first—*the very first*—person to respond was Mr. Client/Boss with the Huge House etc. himself. Did I call it, or what? He said he would be a party of two: "Myself + Security." How festive! But how sensible! By all means, bring the bodyguard. More the merrier!

SUNDAY, APRIL 17

You'd suppose that Trevor's therapist might want to take Easter morning off, but no. That's okay with me, I don't mind. I'm kind of attached to sitting in this parking lot on Sundays. It's such a nothing place, it's kind of soothing. Today I got up earlier than usual and did the kids' Easter baskets and hid them, and then I roused Trevor, who was particularly slow this morning. I told him that he and Kyle could hunt for their baskets when we got back. That is about as much Easter as we are going to do.

I searched for my old pal, the preacher from the crypt who I've listened to before, but all I could find on the radio today was Easter hymns. They got me thinking about when we went down to Florida one Easter when I was about ten, and there was a huge old Spanish church there, with this same kind of music, plus a lot of weird stuff like wooden saints with photographs of people's broken legs and other things the saints were supposed to cure safety-pinned to the saints' robes. Our mother hid our Easter baskets in the motel courtyard, full of spiky plants and lizards running around, and when I found my basket there was a lizard with a forked red tongue sitting on it. I'll never forget that.

Afterward we went out in a glass-bottom boat. Have you ever been in one of those? Oh, it was dreamy—we could see way down into the clear water, all the coral and sea fans and little striped fish, and an old anchor and a pirate skeleton that they had put there previously, of course. That boat makes me think of you, the Cursing Mommy's precious unseen friends out there. I am going to have this party, and tell you all about it, and you will be able to see deep into it just as if you were looking down from a glass-bottom boat. And I will try to watch it from your perspective, too, and that will make me calm and serene.

MONDAY, APRIL 18

Woke up in a flurry of excitement about this party, so I hustled the children off to school and took out my yellow pad and a fresh Sharpie and started to make a list. Gramma Pat always used to say, before starting any major task, "The very first thing I do is, I sit down and make a list!" Actually that wasn't the *very* first thing because of course then right away she lit up a Chesterfield. She meant, the very first thing after *that*.

Now, I need my calendar, too. I have to know *what* to do *when*, because this is going to be a busy couple of weeks and I want the scheduling to be exact. My fucking father has several "postprocedural" appointments I must take him to, and book group is reading M. Foler Tuohy's latest writings so we'll be prepared for his visit to our local library (the night before our party!—crowded days, but that can't be helped), and I must figure out the food and when I'm going to shop for the various things. I want a varied menu. With so many people the supper will be buffet style, of course.

All right—so where is my calendar? I can't proceed without my calendar. Normally I keep it right here on the shelf in the kitchen with my address book and the list of frequently called numbers and the emergency list of local hospitals and the number of the Poison Control Board and so on, which thank God I've never called, and all the recipes I've saved from newspapers and WHERE IS MY FUCKING CALENDAR? All right, take a deep breath. I have to locate this calendar. I can't start making my list without my fucking goddamn stupid calendar that should be right here on this shelf where it usually is. I'm sure it's here. I'm probably looking right at it right now!

The fucking thing isn't here. WHERE THE FUCK IS THE GODDAMN CALENDAR? Fucking Larry took it. He hid it. He hates the goddamn calendar, and whenever I approach him with it to make arrangements of any kind he backs away like I'm carrying a dripping syringe. If I have lost the fucking calendar I am totally fucked because our entire schedule for the year is on it. Now I'm throwing stuff from the shelf all over the fucking KITCHEN goddamn it. WHERE THE *FUCK* IS THE FUCK-ING GODDAMN STUPID FUCKING CALENDAR?

Not here. It is definitely NOT HERE, I am definitely NOT LOOKING AT IT, but it's someplace close by. Goddamn scientists invent all this goddamn useless shit, why don't they invent fucking goddamn locator chips you can put in important frequently lost objects like fucking goddamn calendars and then you'd just hit a button on your phone or something and a light would blink on a locator panel or something showing where the fucking goddamn calendar was. But no, they have to invent a new kind of solid-titanium catheter or some damn thing so Sphagnum Health can rip you off even worse WHERE THE FUCK IS THE GODDAMN CALENDAR?!!

Okay, it must be behind the refrigerator. It must've slipped behind there somehow. I'll simply move the refrigerator out enough so I can see back there—Jesus this's heavy!—and I'll just look and GODDAMN STUFF IS FALLING OFF THE TOP OF THE REFRIGERATOR!! GODDAMN SALAD BOWL WE NEVER USE JUST BOUNCED—*OWWW!*—OFF THE TOP OF MY HEAD!!! Now I stepped on the salad tongs and WHOAHHHH! fell flat on the kitchen floor!! The other stuff on top of the refrigerator now is sliding off, following the salad bowl, which was propping it all up there, and that other stuff is also . . . *falling on me*!!! WHAT THE FUCK WAS I THINKING, MOVING THAT FUCKING REFRIGERATOR???!!! GODDAMN FUCKING BUSH-ADMINISTRATION-ENABLING HERITAGE FOUNDATION, COULDN'T EVEN INVENT A FUCKING CALENDAR-LOCATING CHIP, THE FUCKING ASSHOLES!!! HELP!!! HEL-L-L-L-L-L-L-LP!!

[*pause*]

Actually, it's not so bad here on the kitchen floor, with my head propped on the upside-down salad bowl, listening to the stupid refrigerator turn off. In just a minute I'm going to get up. I'll go to the store and buy a new fucking calendar, I guess. What choice do I have?

Oh, what a horrible disastrous fucking goddamn week this is going to be.

TUESDAY, APRIL 19

It's only three days since the e-mail invitations went out, and already we have forty-seven people who say they're going to attend! Every single person I invited from Larry's office has said he (or she) will be here. Word must've got out that the main man is coming, and that did the trick. Just as I predicted! All of book group and their husbands will be coming, too, with the possible exception of Angie and Russ. Angie called in a terrible state and said she didn't know yet if they could come, because Russ had been having some problems. I'm not sure exactly what is going on. She said he apparently suffered a mental breakdown while trying to roll up a garden hose.

WEDNESDAY, APRIL 20

Can you believe it? People I don't even know are e-mailing me asking if they can come to our party! Some couples we met at Jerk's house in Encino over New Year's are going to be in town and he e-mailed me saying they would e-mail me because they're going to be in town etc., and can they come? In my reply I pretended to be an events planner who is working for me. Ms. Events Planner (Saskia J. Jones is her "name") wrote back and said that I said it would be all right, and we will add them to the guest list.

THURSDAY, APRIL 21

I am continuing with the party planning in the best of upbeat and positive moods, thanks to the spring season, and the nice weather, and a wonderful springtime anticipation on the breeze, and this new margarita mix. And also thanks to you, the Cursing Mommy's invisible, wonderful comrades-in-arms and friends! Splendid vistas await us, don't you agree?

And I must say it is a joy to be rereading the work of M. Foler Tuohy during whatever free moments I happen to find in my day.

Just this morning I underlined this sentence: "When it comes to the details, great and small, of our own lives, each and every one of us is the leading expert in the world." In the margin I wrote, "How true!"

FRIDAY, APRIL 22
Richard, that veiny-nosed killjoy at Lariat Liquors, did not believe my one still-working credit card actually still works when I stopped by this afternoon to place my order for the party. While he was making a special call to the credit card company, I reached over and took my card from his hand and simply walked out. Oh, my, that was satisfying! Suddenly I remembered Omar's Discount Alcohol Warehouse out on Route 11—a bit of a drive, but worth it, definitely.

SATURDAY, APRIL 23
This morning Kyle and I were making newel posts for his school's back staircase on a metal lathe in the school basement when he stopped for a moment, pulled up his safety glasses, and asked me, "Mom, did you know that the kiwi is the only bird with nostrils?"

Now where do you think he came up with that?

SUNDAY, APRIL 24
As you can imagine, my head is so full of thoughts and plans and worries and concerns and so on, it's just a swirl. Our party is only five days away! I have been thinking frantically about what to do with our garage. Or, I should say, with the awful wreckage of our garage. If our guests happen to look out the back windows or go out in our driveway they will wonder why we have this heap of awful wreckage in our yard.

Just now, in the parking lot of Trevor's therapist, I came up with a solution: I will get a huge tarp. Not one of those little blue ones like we had on the garage roof, but a huge camouflage one like they use in the military. Larry and I will put the camo tarp over the garage wreckage and stake it to the ground, and because of the camo it will blend in, and our guests won't even notice it's there.

Fabulous!

MONDAY, APRIL 25

The trouble with goddamn Larry is he doesn't THINK. I found the perfect tarp at an army surplus store, I laid the tarp out over the garage wreckage, and I crawled under it with a flashlight to move some of the junk around so the tarp would look more natural, like a small hill. Meanwhile Larry goes around the outside with camo tent pegs nailing them through the grommets to hold the tarp firmly to the ground, and then he HEARS THE FUCKING PHONE RING AND GOES INSIDE THE HOUSE TO ANSWER IT! LEAVING ME THERE UNDER THE FUCKING TARP!!!

What a fucking idiot. What a complete fucking total idiot Larry can be sometimes. There I am struggling and hollering and bumping around under the tarp, and eventually Trevor comes wandering by and he hears me, and he says, very slowly, "Is that you, Mom?"

The call was from one of Larry's fellow capacitor collectors and he got so caught up in it he completely forgot about me, the tarp, and everything. He'd've left me there all night, I have no doubt.

But the tarp does look pretty good, I must say. It's a Jungle Fern camo pattern and it blends right in with our yard, which we need to prune back a bit. (When and if we ever get around to *that*!)

TUESDAY, APRIL 26

Another trip to the fucking assisted living to bring my father to the doctor. He now thinks I am the ex-wife who took all his money, and he sometimes calls me Marjorie (that was her name). I don't even bother to correct him. The old heller got exactly what he deserved with Marjorie, and when I'm with him I really don't mind being her.

WEDNESDAY, APRIL 27

The day of our big party approaches! So much to arrange, from the decorations to the hors d'oeuvres to the buffet supper to the desserts. I am praying—*praying*—that our single working credit card is up to the job. Today I thought it might be fun as well as instructive for you, my friends, to see how the Cursing Mommy plans and prepares a party. We want it to be entertaining for the guests and effortless (or effortless seeming—that's the real trick!) for the hostess. How do I do it? Just watch!

The Cursing Mommy's No-Fuss Party Planner: Rule #1:
Make Sure There Will Be Enough to Drink!

The greatest single thing I have ever discovered in my entire life is that Omar's Discount Alcohol Warehouse out on Route 11 DE-LIVERS! Yes, with orders of over a certain amount, Omar's drives right to your door anywhere within a seventeen-mile radius, and according to MapQuest we are exactly sixteen-point-three miles from Omar's parking lot!

I cannot believe this place delivers. It is absolutely WON-DERFUL!! I just sit here, make a call, give my credit card number, and forty minutes later a truckload of alcohol is unloading in my driveway. Before the guy leaves, I sample some of the Prosecco sparkling wine to make sure it's what I ordered and it's DELICIOUS! I simply cannot believe that I just ask and these marvelous things appear at my home. The next bottle could be bad, however, but as I take a sampling of it—it, too, is very good!

Well, great! The main task I had scheduled for today is done, so I will devote the rest of the afternoon to resting up for all the work I will have tomorrow. It also might be prudent to tap these kegs and make sure the beer is fresh.

THURSDAY, APRIL 28

Up this morning bright and early at about 3:00 a.m. with an absolutely raging thirst and a headache and so on, but now the delivery from the liquor store has been spot-tested and is ready for the party. Larry came down and asked what I was doing at that hour banging around in the kitchen. Making a huge vat of potato salad, of course! Everybody loves potato salad! Got that done, baked the ham, unwrapped the cheeses from the gift box to let them air and ripen—yes, I'll be serving the Client/Boss's gift right back to him—boiled and cleaned six pounds of shrimp and put them on ice to chill, peeled and diced the crudités (raw vegetables—a must!), and made four kinds of dipping sauce.

This new coffee with 38 percent more caffeine is terrific! In fact, it is ABSOLUTELY FUCKING GREAT!!!

FRIDAY, APRIL 29

Well, where to begin? Today is the day of our party, and already so much has happened I hardly have time to tell all of it to you, my wonderful unseen friends out there. In just a few minutes Gail is coming over to help with the preparations, so I'll make it quick and try to summarize.

Last night was M. Foler Tuohy's long-awaited appearance at the local library. Our book group arrived forty-five minutes early and almost didn't get seats! Well, there was so much excitement, we were all looking forward to it, we had our copies of his books for him to sign and—can I tell you this?

He was kind of awful!

I am sure he must be under a lot of strain, traveling the country and meeting devoted fans. But for heaven's sake, he is this little round man with a bright red face—not at all like in the book jacket photos—and he came out and started to read from his new unpublished book, and—I don't know, I may not be a judge of literature—I think it was pornography. It seemed to be about a famous author who meets a local wife and mother while he is on a book tour and . . . well, you get the drift.

But that was not the worst part. This guy is reading along, having a wonderful time with all his descriptions—and, friends, here's a word of warning: When an author tells you he is "a great lover of language," LOOK OUT! M. Foler Tuohy is chuckling to himself over his brilliance and rolling these anatomical terms off his tongue, and suddenly there's a ringing, and he stops reading, fumbles in his pocket, pulls out his cell phone—

AND HE TAKES THE FUCKING CALL!!! FOUR FUCK-ING MINUTES (from when I started timing it) THIS GUY TALKS ON HIS CELL PHONE!!! WHILE STANDING AT THE FUCKING PODIUM!!! WHILE THE AUDIENCE FUCKING SITS THERE AND *WAITS*!!!

It was just amazing. After the reading he signed books, and our book group lined up with everybody else, and when Angie got to the head of the line she talked to him and talked to him, until the organizers practically had to drag her away. It seems Angie's husband, Russ, who was feeling kind of fragile after the recent incident with the garden hose, had an episode two days ago where he was trying to get a window shade to go up and he kept pulling it down and pulling it down until it reached all the way to the floor and it still would not go up, and he lost his mind. Now he is at Fresh Springs Research Hospital for observation, and

Angie is naturally distraught. She said M. Foler Tuohy was very caring when she told him about this. And guess what? Angie ended up inviting him to come with her to our party tonight, since Russ is in the hospital! And M. Foler Tuohy said he would!

Gail's car is turning into our driveway—I have to run. Tomorrow I'll let you know how it all turns out. Wish me luck.

FRIDAY, APRIL 29

The party is going on right now. I am down in the basement all alone with Larry's capacitors, taking a breather. My God, this is crazy. I hear talking, music, cocktail glasses clinking—just now something smashed on the floor, somebody probably dropped a wineglass. I'm hiding out down here for a moment because I know I said I would let you, my friends out there, see into the party as if you're in a glass-bottom boat—but now someone's calling for me. I'll ignore them and maybe they'll stop. There are many people I don't even know here. They're still calling for me. I am not above it all, I'm not floating and serene, I am right in it—now they're shouting—gotta go.

SATURDAY, APRIL 30

[blank]

MAY

Somehow I got Trevor to his therapist appointment this morning. Don't ask me how. I am sitting in the parking lot again. It's a nice day.

NO NO NO NO NO NO NO!!! I DO NOT WANT TO THINK ABOUT THAT!!!

Sorry, a memory of the party just popped into my head.

It was a good party. A successful party. I think it was a good party. People said they had a good time. I got e-mails from people saying they had a good time. As they were leaving they told me they had a good time. It's hard to tell about your own party, but I think it was a good party.

GAHHHHH!!! I DON'T WANT TO REMEMBER THAT!!!

After everybody was gone, and the kids were long in bed, and Larry had fallen asleep on his couch in the basement, and I was by myself, I put on Ella Fitzgerald comfortingly low, and I cleaned. Oh, friends, I cleaned 'til the sun came up, filling big black trash bags with plastic cups and paper plates and putting away the leftover food—there wasn't that much of it!—and stacking the chairs to go back to the party-rental and putting the house back the way it was. I wanted it to look like no party had ever happened. Then I went to bed and slept most of Saturday.

This morning as I was dragging Trevor out the back door I glanced down, and there behind the door was a plastic cup with some leftover drink in it and about forty cigarettes of all different kinds stubbed out and crammed in the cup, and the liquid in the cup, whatever it was, had turned this nicotine reddish brown, and there was also an old lime wedge with a red plastic sword toothpick through it. During the party some people went into the backyard to smoke and I guess that was how the cup ended up there. When I looked at it I almost got sick, I honestly did. I just left it there. I'll get Larry to do something about it later. (I smoked a few cigarettes at the party myself, to tell the truth.)

That was one of the things I was thinking about before, when I said I didn't want to think about that AHHHHH! I JUST THOUGHT ABOUT SOMETHING ELSE I DON'T WANT TO THINK ABOUT!! NO NO NO NO NO NO NO NO NO NO NO NO NO NO!!!

MONDAY, MAY 2

I am back at the kitchen table—my life raft—with my cup of ordinary (not 38 percent more caffeine!) coffee, and I sense the supportive presence of you, my unseen wonderful friends, and thank God I am feeling almost normal again, and I am now ready to try to tell you about the party.

So: the party.

I had everything ready by six forty-five (it was supposed to start at seven). I was dressed and had done my hair and makeup, and I was giving the kids their supper in the kitchen, and at seven o'clock ON THE DOT the doorbell rings. (I kind of hate people who arrive at parties right on time—don't you?) Of course it's the Client/Boss from Encino. The white limo is out front, and there off to the side is the bodyguard, a bald Brazilian guy, and we're standing at the door, and Larry is crazily saying something or other, and ANOTHER white limo rolls up. The Boss/Client says he hopes we don't mind, he's invited his friend who lives nearby, Mr. Sandor A. Stattsman!

So I'm hanging on Larry, trying to remember my objective.

I'm telling Client/Boss, "Larry and I bought the house because blah blah blah, Larry and I love it here, Larry and I this, Larry and I that," et cetera, et cetera, and meanwhile I'm thinking that Sandor A. Stattsman, CEO of Sphagnum Health, which I despise beyond almost anything on earth, is about to come into my house.

My mind is speeding because now I have another objective. Not only am I going to show the Boss/Client he should leave me alone, and maybe simultaneously persuade him to give Larry a break—but now I am also trying to figure out how to get Sandor A. Stattsman to . . . what? Stop robbing us? What do I say to this awful criminal?

Well, then everybody started to show up. Sometimes with a party you get lucky because it's not so much anything you do as hostess, it's just that people are in the mood for a party. There's something in the atmosphere. People were coming through the door and I was so busy with all the guests and everything I hardly had time to get another drink. Mr. Sandor A. Stattsman walks up to me, and . . . he's a toad! Almost literally! He's in a wrinkled white shirt, a little guy with a huge watch on his skinny, white, toadlike arm, and for just a second I give the Client/Boss a look, like, "*This* is your friend?" And I may be wrong, but I think he was embarrassed. God bless book group, they showed up with their husbands and they had all brought a dessert or an appetizer— I must remember to return those bowls and plates—except for Angie, who was with M. Foler Tuohy, whose face had become even redder than ever.

AHHHHH!!! NO NO NO NO NO!!! I DO NOT WANT TO THINK ABOUT THAT!!! SHUT UP SHUT UP SHUT UP SHUT UP, BRAIN!!!

TUESDAY, MAY 3

Sometimes when we are having a lot of thoughts that we do not wish to have (as has been the case with me, regarding our recent party), it can be helpful to try to organize the thoughts into categories in our minds. This leads to greater confidence, restores a sense of being in control, and actually promotes endorphins, scientists say.

So, friends, please follow along now as the Cursing Mommy organizes her thoughts, misgivings, fears, regrets, bitter self-reproaches, rare happy recollections, etc., about this party into three simple categories: Positives, Negatives, and Completely Horrible Fucking Disasters She Can't Believe She Was Stupid Enough to Fucking Let Herself Become Involved In.

Category I: Positives

- The party is over.
- The house is still standing.
- Larry is still employed, as of this morning.
- The limousine Trevor drove off in was recovered a few blocks away.
- Damage to the other vehicles was minor.
- Many people have called or e-mailed to say the party was great and they had a wonderful time.
- Angie was probably going to do something like this anyway.
- The Client/Boss may have been too drunk to remember everything I said.
- Mr. Sandor A. Stattsman deserved it, anyway.
- There must be one or two other positive things I'm not thinking of right now but will remember later.

Category II: Negatives

- The slap fight.
- Calling the Boss/Client "a disgusting creepy stalker."
- Telling him he is a moron and Larry is ten times smarter than he is.
- Saying he is such a revolting pig he should be ashamed of himself.

- Not making sure, before saying these things, that we were someplace where fifteen other people couldn't hear.
- Throwing the glass of cabernet.
- Using that tile-and-tub cleaner to remove the stain. (Note to self: Ask Stattsman to return Larry's trousers that he borrowed; no, on second thought, forget it. Those trousers are gone.)
- Getting into that horrible conversation with M. Foler Tuohy where he kept saying, "The best of me is in my writing!" and "You have the best of me in my books!" and "I am merely my art's disreputable poor relation!" and "Before I met Angela, I was completely dead inside!"
- Angie telling me, "Before I met Skip [M. Foler Tuohy's stupid nickname], I was completely dead inside!"
- Me hollering at Angie, "I don't care how fucking dead you are inside, you have two small children to look after and a husband in a mental institution!! NOBODY FUCKING CARES IF YOU'RE DEAD INSIDE!!!"
- My horrible sense of guilt that I ever introduced Angie, and book group in general, to this louse M. Foler Tuohy.

Category III: Completely Horrible Fucking Disasters, etc.

- Can we skip this category? I can't face it. I'm feeling overwhelmed.
- Although I will say—AHHHHH! THIS IS ONE OF THOSE THOUGHTS I FUCKING DON'T WANT TO HAVE!—that the way some of the people from Larry's office looked at me when I was talking to Boss/Client Whozits gave me the TOTAL FUCKING CREEPS!! Like I was *privileged* to be talking to this fuck! Meanwhile he didn't even notice them, his own employees, at all. He's just looking at me with his intent I-always-get-what-I-want stare. EEEEEEHHHHHCH!! Makes me shudder!! I mean, I'm not the suck-up here. *He* was privileged to be talking to *me*, because I AM THE CURSING

MOMMY!! AS BECAME APPARENT WHEN I STARTED TELLING HIM EXACTLY WHAT I THOUGHT OF HIM!! AHHHH!!! WHAT A HORRIBLE MEMORY!!! AHHHH!!! OWWW!!!

[pause]

I'm sorry, friends. Again, I got carried away. You see why the Cursing Mommy doesn't want to talk about, or even think about, certain things.

WEDNESDAY, MAY 4

> *The slower you travel the faster you go.*
> —*Carole Hegedus and Dean Beeman*

Today I am going to slow things down. I have been rushing, rushing, rushing through my life, and this morning I need to simply stop and heed the above advice of Carole Hegedus and Dean Beeman, from their thoughtful book, *Do Exactly as We Say*. To be perfectly honest, I never used to like Carole Hegedus and Dean Beeman that much, because I found them bossy and thought their book was a rip-off because it had only about four words on each page and cost $29.95. Usually when I wanted to reconnect with my spirituality, I would turn to M. Foler Tuohy, but the memory of him enrages me now and sets me to cursing. So I have revisited the writings of Hegedus and Beeman and discovered much I had overlooked before (although I still think a few more words per page, a shorter book, and a more reasonable price tag might have been in order).

I slow down my movement by putting on my yoga slippers (made from pieces of real yoga mats!) and sitting quietly in the middle of the living room floor. I slow down my breathing by holding each indrawn breath for twenty-two seconds before I exhale. I slow down my heart rate by . . . well, I'm not sure how to do that. It's still going pretty fast. And I slow down my thoughts by concentrating on a mental image of a white orb, as Hegedus and Beeman recommend.

Breathe in . . . count to twenty-two . . . breathe out. I think this is working, possibly. Everything is slowing down. The white orb hovers (mentally) before me. I do not know what an orb is, maybe I should have looked it up in a dictionary. I am trying to picture hibernating animals, continents moving a few millimeters every year, deserted railroad stations . . .

Yes, it's working. Now I think I am actually *too* slowed down, frankly. So I'll picture the orb jittering around a bit, and the hibernating animals hopping up in their burrows, and the continents hurrying slightly more, and . . .

Now I'm going too fast again. I will never fucking get this right.

THURSDAY, MAY 5

As if we didn't have enough to worry about, Angie has run off with M. Foler Tuohy! Although that is awful, it's not the worst part. She also sent out a group e-mail to everybody in book group asking if we would take care of her kids until Russ is released from Fresh Springs Research Hospital. Of course she does not know just when that might be, and as the news of her departure will probably not be very helpful to his recovery, I imagine it could take a while. Gail, that sweetie, drove right over and picked the kids up. They were with their babysitter, who had stayed the night.

The kids, Destiny and Antony, are both five. They're not twins—Russ and Angie adopted them, I think they are Cambodian or Vietnamese. I don't know much about them but Gail says they are quiet and well behaved.

FRIDAY, MAY 6

At an emergency meeting of book group last night we discussed the situation. Holly pointed out, quite reasonably, I thought, that dealing with this type of problem is not what book group is supposed to be for. Alice put in that Angie was the one who wanted to read books not about the Bush administration, and look where that had got us. (I felt terrible then, though no one was tactless enough to mention the fact that reading M. Foler Tuohy had been my suggestion.) Susan, who had brought an absolutely scrumptious lemon velvet cake, said we should take turns having the kids at our houses, maybe a week at a time, so as not to upset them by moving them around so much. Gail said she couldn't keep them after tomorrow because she is going out of town for work. I jumped right in and volunteered to have them at my house for a week after that.

Now, why did I volunteer so quickly? I'm already worrying about Trevor, and about Kyle's fainting and hives, and about our wretched goddamn allergic cats, and our garage disaster, and Larry's job, and the stalker Client/Boss (who continues to send me texts that I continue to ignore—nothing I said at my party affected him at all), and of course there's always my fucking father.

I will tell you exactly why I volunteered: GUILT. Guilt is what will get you, every time.

SATURDAY, MAY 7

Why did no one inform me that these kids came with their own prairie dog colony? It is in a terrarium four feet long and it must weigh a hundred pounds and the kids have to keep it with them because the prairie dogs need constant watching and feeding and so forth. Larry, Trevor, Holly, Fred (Holly's husband), and I had to wrestle the thing out of Angie's basement and into ours this morning. We were nice about it, but—*sheesh*! I guess the prairie dogs are kind of cute, and Destiny and Antony are very serious and sweet about caring for them. But honestly, this was not something I had bargained on.

SUNDAY, MAY 8

Back in Trevor's therapist's parking lot on this snowy May morning, with wet snow piling up on the yellow blossoms of the forsythia, giving them a strange corn-and-mashed-potatoes look. Fortunately the snow is not sticking to the ground and the roads are clear. This morning I am too tired to scream. I have no desire to listen to the radio. I am just slumped over the steering wheel like a Mafia hit victim—all I need is some fake blood splashed on the inside of the windshield and a couple of those bullet-hole window decals. That would be a good joke on Trevor when he opens the car door.

Dealing with Angie's kids on top of everything else has worn me down. They were awake all night. I moved Kyle in with Trevor, put extra mattresses on the floor, tried to make it fun, like a campout (have we ever had fun on a campout?), but Destiny and Antony wouldn't sleep. They didn't fuss or cry, they just kept consulting quietly about the prairie dogs. In between Larry's snores, the ceiling and I could hear them whispering at one in the morning. Then I heard them going downstairs. Turns out, I bought the wrong kind of food at the pet store yesterday. Now, if you had asked me what prairie dogs eat, I would've guessed it was other prairie dogs that have been run over on the road. That's all I've ever seen them eating.

But, no—they eat seeds, like you put in bird feeders. So I got a couple sacks of those. But, it turns out, the kind I bought have hot chili pepper seeds mixed in, so that squirrels (who hate hot food, apparently) won't raid the bird feeder. Problem is, prairie dogs won't eat a mix with hot pepper seeds, either. Somehow the kids had figured all this out. So there I am in my bathrobe at 1:30 a.m. with two five-year-olds and a bunch of seeds spread before us on the Ping-Pong table, picking out the hot pepper seeds. They were little bitty things and it took forever. The kids were better at it than I was. And meanwhile I'm thinking, obviously, "What the fuck am I doing with my life?"

Once again peace returns, if ever so briefly, with my kids at school, Destiny and Antony in the all-day (thank God!) private kindergarten they go to, and Larry departed hours ago for his office. Today the Cursing Mommy is going to sit and commune with you, her real-but-unseen wonderful friends out there, and try to get back into a good daily rhythm.

This morning in the paper there's an interview with an international peace activist who says she wants to "increase the possibilities for tenderness in the world." Friends, isn't that a beautiful goal? I adore the promise in that word, "possibilities"—because how can tenderness ever exist at all if we haven't already created the possibilities for it? Now, how do you suppose each of us can do that?

Well, I see in the mail today another little uptick in our rates from Sphagnum Health, for "submarine-watching fees," whatever in the world those might be. So, in my opinion, a good first step for increasing the possibilities for tenderness in the world would be to blow up fucking Sphagnum Health. Also, destroy all leftovers from the fucking Bush administration and make jerks like Larry's overbearing crummy Client/Boss pay some actual fucking taxes for a change so maybe he will have less time for bothering me, and then get the fucking goddamn county to pave our fucking street, and my fucking father should then—

I am missing the point about tenderness, I know. Thank you, friends, for correcting me. I will set those wrong thoughts aside for now, knowing, unfortunately but realistically, that they probably will return.

TUESDAY, MAY 10

You know who I fucking hate? That guy from Lithuania who's on TV—do you know who I'm talking about? That guy who's such a fucking asshole. Oh, you know—I can't think of his name.

WEDNESDAY, MAY 11

The flowers are up and blooming, if they survived the recent snow, and the forsythia's spring yellow smiles in the hedges, while the beautiful big saucer magnolias and the cheery red and pink and bridal-white azaleas burst forth like neon lights. And in the grasses the little wildflowers, the violets and the pinks, modestly show their hidden glories—and it's bouquet season! Today I want to revive a column topic from a previous year and share with all of you:

Creating the Perfect Bouquet, Part II: A Cursing Mommy
Guide to No-Fuss Flower Arrangement

This morning I have gathered together a wide selection of in-season flowers and greenery, as you see here—some from my own yard and some from our local florist and garden shops. I have them in this plastic tub with a little lukewarm (never cold!) water and a solution of plant food to keep them in the best condition until they go into the vase.

Do you remember May baskets? Those little paper baskets of flowers that girls used to make for their sweethearts? Gramma Pat often told me about them, and about the "language of flowers," as she called it, in which different flowers in the basket meant different things. Once, she told me, she sent Grampa Hub (then just a young man) a May basket that not only informed him she was "sweet" on him but also let him know, by means of flowers, the exact day and hour when her family expected him to call, and the brand of cigarettes (Chesterfields) he should bring.

Excuse me, but there is a man walking around in my backyard

with a clipboard. I must hurry and see what that is about. Don't
go away—I'll be right back.

THURSDAY, MAY 12

Well, that was interesting. The man with the clipboard was from
the municipal zoning board, and guess what? It is a violation of
the zoning laws to have a wrecked garage in your yard, even if
you cover it neatly with a Jungle Fern camouflage tarp. We have
sixty days to get the whole business carted away and then apply
for a permit to build a new garage (assuming, of course, that we
can afford that!). Or else they will fine us!

That was a nice how do you do! I was on the phone to Larry
and the town commissioner, but there was nothing to be done
about it. I did not have time to return to my flower arranging,
and now I have to pick Angie's kids up at their kindergarten,
which only goes for a half day today because of gift-shop inventory (don't ask).

Anyway, I'll freshen the water these flowers are in and return to the flower arranging tomorrow.

FRIDAY, MAY 13

Well, wouldn't you know, today would be the day a minor sink-
hole opened in our street. Nobody can get in or out, so all four
kids are home all day. Yeeeks! Again I have to put off the flower
arranging.

SATURDAY, MAY 14

Can't do the flowers today because Kyle and Trevor's school has
Tote 'n' Carry Day, when we bring up sandbags full of masonry
rubble from the collapsed foundation. This will occupy all of
Saturday with a brief break for lunch.

SUNDAY, MAY 15

In Trevor's therapist's parking lot I had planned exactly how I would arrange these flowers, and what thrilling, hidden message their colors and shapes and positions would convey. Oh, I had an entire floral poem all mapped out! But when we got back, Destiny and Antony, the poor kids, somehow had BOTH developed toothaches, and I had to hunt around for a dentist who could see them on a Sunday. What a nightmare! Finally Dr. Mejia, whom I reached at home, agreed to see them, and he pulled one tooth from Destiny and two—count 'em, *two*—from Antony. We saved the teeth to put under their pillows for the tooth fairy. During the whole thing the kids were really brave and hardly cried, though you could tell they hurt. But as a result I had no time for flower arranging.

MONDAY, MAY 16

Today after everybody was out of the house and I finally had a minute to myself, I went to check on the flowers and they were looking rather peaked. The water had evaporated, and some blossoms had withered. But, nothing daunted, I proceeded to make my arrangement anyway, and the hidden message in the bouquet was "FUCK THIS GODDAMN LIFE WHERE I CAN'T EVEN FIND TEN GODDAMN MINUTES TO ARRANGE SOME GODDAMN FLOWERS!!" The pretty yellow daffodils, ducking their heads so shyly, seemed to say "GODDAMN FUCKING GARAGE, WHAT A FUCKING PAIN IN THE ASS!!!" while the fragrant sprigs of pale lavender lilacs whispered, "OUR TIME IS BUT BRIEF, AND IT IS BEING STOLEN BY BULLSHIT!!!" The hydrangeas, pink as cotton candy, declared, "FUCK THE FUCKING BUSH ADMINISTRATION, THOSE GREEDY BOUGHT-AND-PAID-FOR CORPORATE TOADY FUCKS!!!" and the pristine white azaleas replied, "AND FUCK GODDAMN SPHAGNUM HEALTH AND THAT FUCKING REPTILIAN

ASSHOLE SANDOR A. STATTSMAN, THOSE FUCKING
VAMPIRE ASSHOLE THIEVES!!!"

Now I will set the vase with my new (albeit already rather
wilted) arrangement on the mantelpiece and wait for the goddamn stupid cats to knock it over while I lie quietly facedown on
the floor.

[*pause*]

In just a minute I'm going to get up. Soon I have to call
Fresh Springs Research Hospital and find out if they are ever
going to release poor crazy Russ. Why is my life like this all the
time? Why?

Oh, what a fucking horrible day I predict this is going to be.

TUESDAY, MAY 17

> *Where we put a period, God puts a comma.*
> —*sign in front of the local Methodist church*

I do not know exactly what this saying means, but I find it encouraging anyway—don't you? Now, I can be rather un-optimistic
from time to time, as I was as recently as yesterday, in fact, but
I must remember that my sometimes downbeat conclusions are
never the final word. At the end of our gloomiest thoughts, always
let us put a comma, and never a period (or exclamation point),
because much that is good, and that we don't expect, is sure to
follow.

The unexpected good news for this week is Larry's better
mood because of improvements at his job. People there loved
our party and thanked him for having it and noticed him for
the first time. Then yesterday he learned he has been chosen to
handle a prestigious overseas travel assignment in Lagos, Nigeria!
He is very excited about this. (Although when I asked him if that
meant they were restoring his 15 percent pay cut, so maybe we

could do something about the huge credit card bills from the party, he got testy with me.)

WEDNESDAY, MAY 18

Food Superior has been closed for a month for a design make-over. This morning it reopened and—my God! A big new sign on top of it says STUFF, ETC . . . The place is now a truck terminal, basically. You go in, there is a bare concrete floor, bare girders up above, and hundreds of truck bays around this central area covered with plastic-wrapped piles of crates on pallets. You wheel your shopping cart up metal ramps into the bays and hunt for what you want in the trucks themselves. Checkout is self-service. The prices are low—I will say that.

While I was shopping I ran into Margaret from book group. She had been looking for sparkling water for over an hour. She said she thought our book group should open our own supermarket, like the old Safeway. I said I was afraid book group was getting farther and farther away from books.

THURSDAY, MAY 19

> *"Stop, drop, and roll" won't work in hell.*
> *—sign in front of the local Baptist church*

On this wretched goddamn day I am sorry to report that my mood is more Baptist than Methodist. Oh, friends! I have to tell you what just happened.

This morning, after everyone had left, I received an overnight-mail delivery. Why did I even open it, when I saw it was from Larry's office? I wasn't thinking. I opened it, and inside was a yucky romantic note from the horrid Client/Boss, folded around a first-class plane ticket to Aruba. I don't even want to describe—

I hate even to talk about it. That he would even think he

could send me this . . . My objective in having that party failed completely. Looking more closely I saw that the date of the ticket is the day after Larry is supposed to go to Nigeria.

Excuse me, I'm going to go lie facedown on the living room floor again for a moment. I'll try to think, "Comma, not period. Comma, not period."

Or perhaps, on the other hand, fuck that.

FRIDAY, MAY 20

Sent the ticket back to Jerk by overnight mail. On his note I just scrawled, "Give me a break!" We'll see what good that does.

Today is Trevor's twelfth birthday. Twelve years ago I became the Cursing Mommy. The video Larry made of the birth starts with him walking down the hospital corridor and then in the distance you hear a baby crying, and me saying, "WHERE THE FUCK IS MY FUCKING HUSBAND?" Well, that was twelve long years ago, and the reward was our dear (if rather heavily medicated) son Trevor, whom we love. Tonight in his honor we are having his favorite dinner: chopped-ham-loaf-on-white-bread sandwiches with lots of mayonnaise, and fudge cake with fudge icing, whipped cream, and hot fudge.

SATURDAY, MAY 21

After a half day of caulking at Kyle and Trevor's school, I took Trevor and two friends, Matt Z. and Matt R., to an indoor paintball arena for Trevor's birthday. Because they are underage I had to accompany them inside and put on the hard hat and safety glasses and smock and the whole bit. I brought along a book to read but that was not to be. I got hit with paintballs four times— three reds and a green. (The red gun was Trevor's.) Goddamn Larry can do this particular fun duty next year. The kids loved every second of it.

SUNDAY, MAY 22

Back in Trevor's therapist's parking lot by the sawed-off tree branches, and time for my weekly recap. But first, some screaming.

SH-I-I-I-I-I-I-I-I-I-I-I-I-I-I-I-I-I-I-I-I-I-I-I-I-T!!!

F-U-U-U-U-U-U-U-U-U-U-U-U-U-U-U-U-U-U-U-U-U-U-U-U-CK!!!

That feels somewhat better.

For complicated reasons we ended up having Angie's kids at the house for two weeks rather than one. Alice and her husband are coming by to pick up Destiny and Antony and the prairie dog colony later today. Angie sent a mass e-mail to everybody in book group saying that she and M. Foler Tuohy ("Skip") are having a wonderful time in Hawaii at his endive ranch. I'm reading this, and meanwhile I'm taking care of this woman's children, and Larry's asshole Boss/Client is sending me that fucking disgusting plane ticket to Aruba, which I've decided not even to be insulted by because he's too much of a worm to be capable of insulting anybody—

And, I mean, come on! This asshole dispatches Larry to Nigeria apparently to get him out of the way and then sends me a ticket so I can run off with him the day *after*? Yes? And who is supposed to take care of *my* kids, pray tell? Not that I would ever do such a thing in a million years, but the fact that the guy is so fucking clueless on top of everything else somehow really infuriates me. And here I'm pawing through seeds to feed the prairie dogs while Angie is in the south of France—

Not the south of France, excuse me—Hawaii. On the ol' endive ranchero.

MONDAY, MAY 23

Larry has never been happier. He just learned that the Lagos city dump is supposed to have the largest concentration of a certain kind of 1950s-era capacitor in the world.

TUESDAY, MAY 24

Went to the goddamn assisted living today to look in on "Dad" and make sure all the "Do Not Resuscitate" papers are on file, in the remote chance they are ever needed. The old reprobate is completely recovered from his anal wart surgery and will be performing a gymnastics routine in the Seniors' Talent Contest next week, to the song "Some Enchanted Evening."

WEDNESDAY, MAY 25

Did you ever have one of those days where everything goes wrong? Well, today was "one of those days" for me! I went into the city this morning to look for a portable hair dryer for our vacation, and wouldn't you know, I got caught in the most awful rainstorm I have ever SEEN! Truly! I was walking down the street and the skies just opened up, and I had my umbrella in one hand and my shopping bags in the other, and I went to jump over this absolute *river* of rainwater rushing along the gutter, and I was wearing my low-heel sandals that don't really have any backs, and as I jumped my right sandal fell off, and it landed in the rainwater river and started floating away!

Well, there I am hopping along the sidewalk on my one remaining sandal in pursuit of my other sandal, and the river runs along the curb and turns the corner and suddenly disappears down a storm drain! And my sandal goes with it! These were my best sandals, my Clive Kimberlies, which Larry bought me four years ago for my birthday. Gone for good. I simply could not get over it.

Unfortunately, in certain circumstances I really do curse quite a lot, and I am afraid this was one of them. As I stood there hopping on one foot in the rain and cursing, a woman who was walking past stopped, turned around, and asked, "Excuse me, are you the Cursing Mommy?" I said I was, and she said, "Oh, it's such a pleasure to meet you! I just *love* your fucking column!"

Friends, we must never forget that there are angels out there.

This wonderful woman—her name was Felicia—happened to be on her way back to her office from the gym, and she had her running shoes with her, and when I told her about losing my sandal she made me take them. Can you believe that! She insisted that she had another pair at home. I asked for her card, so I'll send the shoes back to her right away. What a sweetie pie!

THURSDAY, MAY 26

Yes, there *are* angels out there. This important, wonderful fact bears repeating, as we go on with our lives that sometimes seem like unmitigated hell crushing us into nothing for all eternity. Angels like Felicia, and like you, my unseen friends, walk among us every day.

Last night as Kyle and Trevor were getting ready for bed, I told them the story of losing my sandal. I made them take their earbuds out and *listen* for a change. So they did, and paid attention with apparently thoughtful expressions on their faces. I finished my story, and they looked at me, and then Trevor asked, "What do you think was the loudest-decibel burp ever?"

Why do I even bother? Why do I go on?

FRIDAY, MAY 27

Larry leaves for Lagos, Nigeria, this evening, and although in most situations I tell him to pack his own goddamn suitcase, today I am going to pack his own goddamn suitcase for him, just this one time, so as to be able to demonstrate for you:

How to Pack Your Spouse's or Partner's Own Goddamn
Suitcase: A Cursing Mommy Helpful Pretravel Primer

Today the suitcase I will be using is a convenient new model featuring a little handle that pulls up like so, and wheels at the bottom enabling the suitcase to be easily wheeled behind you in airports and on sidewalks and in other places where otherwise it would have to be carried. I believe the technical name for this type of suitcase in the airline industry is a "roll-aboard." It is a very handy type of suitcase and has revolutionized travel with its ease of movability.

So the first thing we do is unzip this thing here—what is this weird zipper? Oh, okay, it doesn't do anything. I love zippers like that, don't you? Let's try this other zipper. Hmm, well, that seems only to zip the first zipper back up.

Okay, here is the main zipper that actually unzips the suitcase—or does it? No, this seems to just make this outer compartment more expandable. Useless goddamn fucking zipper. Okay, now I get it. This other zipper with the lock on it is the one I want. It's not locked, but . . . the goddamn thing is stuck, apparently. Yes, a piece of totally unnecessary inner lining has become entangled in the zipper's teeth. All right, I'll use this pair of pliers to YANK the fucking goddamn zipper THE FUCK OPEN!! Goddamn thing, I'm yanking on it and JESUS FUCKING CHRIST—I've snapped the zipper tag thing in two!!! Now the pliers have nothing to hold on to. So I will simply take this pair of metal shears from the tool drawer and GODDAMN FUCKING OVERDESIGNED POINTLESS FUCKING SUITCASE!!! cut the fucking suitcase open. I'LL SHOW YOU, YOU GODDAMN THING!!! NOW I'M FUCKING SLICING THE FUCKING THING OPEN, TRY TO JAM ON ME, WILL YOU, YOU FUCKING GODDAMN THING!!! Now I've got it down on the floor GODDAMN FUCKING STUPID SUITCASE THAT WE BOUGHT DURING THE FUCKING BUSH ADMINISTRA-TION, WHEN SUITCASES IN THIS COUNTRY STARTED GOING TO SHIT!!! FUCKING GODDAMN DICK CHENEY, PRIVATIZING "ROLL-ABOARD"-TYPE ASSHOLE SELF-ISH FUCK!!! GODDAMN ZIPPER!! FUCKING SUITCASE!! HELP! HE-L-L-L-LP!!"

[*pause*]

Actually, it's not so bad lying here on the floor with my right arm and part of my right shoulder inside this sliced-open suitcase that I have just destroyed. What the hell, I'll throw a bunch of Larry's stuff in there anyway and tape the whole thing up with duct tape, what's the fucking difference? If Larry doesn't like it he can fucking well pack some other suitcase himself. In just a minute I'm going to get up.

Oh, what a fucking wretched goddamn horrible day this has been.

SATURDAY, MAY 28

Out and about on a beautiful spring morning, with no reconstruction work on the kids' school scheduled for today, due to Memorial Day Weekend. What to do on a lovely day that opens before us like a sunny, beckoning path? Larry is in Lagos, Nigeria, by now, and the kids and I are home by ourselves with nothing pressing on the schedule. I know what we'll do—finally, maybe, I can get them to write their Christmas thank-you notes.

SUNDAY, MAY 29

Well, what a chore *that* was! I had to argue and cajole and threaten before they would turn off the video games and get to it. Then they just wrote a line: "Dear Aunt May, Thank you for the sweater. Trevor." Not even, "Love, Trevor." Then they printed them out on the computer. I kept making them redo them until they sounded more like they were written by living human beings.

Eventually, thank God, we got through that batch. Today we'll start on the ones from last Christmas. After that we'll do the last three birthdays and be up to date.

MONDAY, MAY 30

Followed the Memorial Day Parade out to the cemetery. God bless Grampa Hub and Buddy Wilcox and everybody else who was in the wars! Kyle and Trevor ran ahead because they wanted to get the bullet shells from the ten-gun salute. Alice from book group and I walked together. She had Angie's kids with her, so that meant we couldn't talk about Angie, which was too bad. Destiny and Antony are very smart for five-year-olds. Apparently they have been negotiating on their own with Fresh Springs Research Hospital for their dad's release.

TUESDAY, MAY 31

Larry called last night from Lagos, Nigeria, so ecstatic he could barely get his breath. I haven't heard him sound like that in years. Then we got cut off.

My husband, Larry—ecstatic? What could that be about, I wonder?

JUNE

> *Love is the furniture of the soul.*
> —Bhagavad-Gita *(Brooke Hogan, translator)*

This morning for a meditation aid I turned at random to a page in the calfskin notebook where I write down all my favorite quotations, and this one just jumped out at me. It is such a charming, homely, homey thought, written in distant India all those centuries ago, yet equally applicable to our own day. Also, like many great sayings of philosophy, it makes us smile.

Then as I was smiling and thinking about this saying I happened to catch a glimpse of my face reflected in our living room mirror, and—I don't know, maybe I should have been meditating harder—anyway, I sort of looked like an idiot. I mean, here I was smiling and grinning about a saying that actually was, I don't know . . . stupid? "Love is the furniture of the soul"? Does that make any sense? Is it possible that I copied it down incorrectly?

Now I was in a horrible pickle of doubt and my meditative frame of mind was on hold. What if I have been sitting here meditating and contemplating based on a saying that is totally dumb? Does that make the meditating less valid? I thought I should go and look up the saying somewhere and get to the bottom of this. Then I became tired and poured myself a great big scotch.

THURSDAY, JUNE 2

Finally had a long phone conversation with Larry in Nigeria and found out what's going on. I suspected it had something to do with capacitors, and I was right. He went to one of the Lagos dumps (there are a whole bunch of them) where old capacitors are brought to be sorted through. To hear him tell it, he found a gold mine. He says that just by refluxing some of the old capacitors he can make them better than new and import them to the U.S. and resell them (he says) for a fortune. All the Nigerian capacitors are 000-series and date from the period of British rule, so in addition they have that Oxford-Cambridge style, he says. Nobody there is aware of their value. His contact who will sell him the capacitors in bulk (not knowing their value) is a high-ranking bishop of the Nigerian Apostolic Church, Archbishop Kwesi Adjoa Mfune. Larry had me write down his name and phone number.

FRIDAY, JUNE 3

Last night I brought Trevor and Kyle to the goddamn assisted living so we could watch their grandfather perform his gymnastics routine to "Some Enchanted Evening." The old snake in the weeds wasn't bad, although with his operatic "training" he started to sing along to the Ezio Pinza recording, which was a distraction. Evidently he is not very popular at the goddamn assisted living because the other seniors booed him throughout and threw rolls at him. Of course, in the past he has beaten some of them with his fists.

SATURDAY, JUNE 4

Summer has arrived early, with unseasonable temperatures of a hundred degrees. I am a warm-weather person so I do not mind the heat as much, but it was a challenge for some of the first and second graders today during Mandatory Tech Day, when parents, caregivers, and students set up an outdoor stage for next week's spring show. (The regular auditorium is off-limits, having been condemned.) Some of the teachers were furloughed one month before the end of the school year as a savings measure, so we came up a bit shorthanded. But as I kept reminding the kids, staying hydrated is the main thing. A major soft-drink company provided sodas and bottled water.

SUNDAY, JUNE 5
Today was even more unseasonable than yesterday, with a high temperature of a hundred and three. At seven fifteen in the morning in the parking lot at Trevor's therapist's office, I was simply *roasting* in the car, even with all the windows down. I didn't want to turn on the AC so I walked a little way up the block and sat at the very edge of a sprinkler on the lawn of an orthodontist's office. As the cooling drops hit me, such a delicious feeling! Trevor didn't even notice I was wet from head to toe when he came back to the car.

MONDAY, JUNE 6
Talk about unseasonable! The high temperature today was even more unseasonable—a hundred and seven. Now, *that* is unseasonable.

No word from Larry since last week. I'm sure he's fine. Probably he's just wandering around checking out new capacitor troves.

TUESDAY, JUNE 7
A bit cooler today, although, at a hundred and one, still unseasonable. Went with Kyle to the equipment rental as soon as school was out and rented three industrial-size fans for this evening's

show. Couldn't fit them in the car without keeping the back open while I drove the forty miles home. People kept honking at me and pointing, as if I didn't know the back was open.

WEDNESDAY, JUNE 8

Well, the school's spring show is over, the fans have been returned, and I am ready to collapse in a heap. Kyle hyperventilated so much he had to carry a bag around with him almost the entire time (except when he was onstage, of course). But he did just fine in his first-place commercial for Platt's Fruit Leather, which was in the form of a game show about fruit leather. I was so proud of him. The evening's entire program was really clever, based on a combination of a talk show and a game show, with commercials just like actual commercials for the school's corporate sponsors. Each grade and each class in each grade also did a commercial for itself that was loosely based on real commercials—you could tell which ones they were. Oh, it was fun! The evening had a few technical glitches, mainly because of the june bugs, which crashed into the lights and sometimes fell on the performers, who screamed. Many of the parents were recording the show and the cameras were pointing all different directions, depending on the kid being filmed, and a few squabbles broke out over tripod placement. At the curtain call, the parents rushed the stage with bouquets of flowers for their kids, and Kyle and Trevor were a bit put out that I had forgotten to get roses for them—the first time in their lives either one of them ever cared about flowers! What can I tell you? I forgot. So I'm a bad mom. Shoot me.

THURSDAY, JUNE 9

It's been a week, and still no word from Larry. He must be really getting into those Nigerian capacitors!

FRIDAY, JUNE 10

Friends, would you like to hear about a wild day? Let me tell you about a wild day.

I am wrung out like a dishrag. I almost never had so much stress. It started peacefully—I was getting ready to do my yoga. Then I happened to look out the front window, and there it was—the white limo, pulling up to the curb. The Client/Boss gets out, comes to the front door. I open it, ask what he wants. His face is grim. He asks if he can come inside, he has something to tell me.

It must be serious, because for once his limo isn't throbbing with music. I don't want to let him in, but I have no choice. I sit on the couch, he sits on a chair. He says he has bad news. Larry has been kidnapped, he says.

It's like I was hit with a hammer. I just sit there, stammer questions. He says they had reports, something happened, Larry has disappeared, kidnapping is suspected, no ransom requests as yet. He gets up from the chair, comes over to me, puts his arm around me. I jump up and say I'll be right back. On my way through the dining room I grab my cell phone. I go into the bathroom, lock the door. I call Gail, get her voice mail. I tell her to please come over right away. Then I call Margaret. She picks up. She is out at Stuff, Etc . . . , searching for various groceries. I ask her to come over immediately. I say it's an emergency, Larry has been kidnapped in Nigeria.

I stay in the bathroom as long as I can. Finally I come out, I go back in the living room, the guy is on his phone. He gets off immediately. The doorbell rings—Margaret is here! God bless her, she must have driven like crazy. Boss/Client doesn't look pleased to see her, he seems surprised and barely says hello.

Meanwhile outside it's been getting blacker and blacker because a thunderstorm is building. After the heat we've had, this is going to be a doozie, and sure enough—suddenly it's pouring like fifty fire trucks are above the house with their hoses pointing straight down. Lightning is cracking and the thunder is coming in explosions. I run around turning on the lights, but one minute later the power goes out and we're in the dark. In the middle of all this I'm trying to think of what to do, Margaret is in the kitchen heating up water for tea on the stove (which is still working because it's gas), Boss/Client is saying they've been unable to get in touch with their contacts in Lagos, and suddenly it occurs to me—I have the phone number of the guy Larry was going to buy the capacitors from. It's on a notepad by the phone.

So I go to the phone, which is also still working, and I dial the number, after the long distance code and the code for Lagos, Nigeria (234-1), and there are these weird foreign-sounding rings, like buzzes, and then a voice answers, "This is Archbishop Kwesi Adjoa Mfune speaking, whom am I speaking to?" He has a deep, deep voice, like he's talking out of a barrel, but also jolly, too. Trying not to babble, I explain who I am, I say we haven't heard from Larry, we're afraid something has happened to him. And this man says, "Lawrence is doing quite splendidly, you know. I put him on a plane for U.S.A. this morning!"

"He says Larry's fine! He's on a plane coming home!" I tell Client/Boss. For a moment his face goes white with relief, and he says, "That's impossible!" unable to believe the good news. Meanwhile Archbishop Mfune is reminding me to remind Larry to wire him the down payment for the capacitors first thing tomorrow. I assure him I will, and I thank him profusely and ring off. Well, I collapse with Margaret on the couch in the living room with our tea—Client/Boss didn't want any, he went in the next room and muttered into his phone. Suddenly the power comes back on, all the digital things are blinking "12:00, 12:00, 12:00." My cell phone beeps. It's a text message from Larry asking if I can pick him up at the airport!

So I call him just to make sure it's really him, and it is. He's not "doing quite splendidly." He's in a whiny mood, he's been sitting on the runway waiting for a gate for over an hour because of the storm. Briefly I explain about how he was supposed to have been kidnapped, and then I get off.

Well, the Client/Boss says some things about what a relief etc., but Larry should've kept in better touch with the office blah blah blah. I'm thinking, "Fucking fire him, then, asshole. See if I care," but for once I keep my mouth shut. Just then there's a scrabbling sound on the fireplace screen—the squirrels are running around on it again. Their nests must've been drenched by the rain. They stop for a moment and sort of strike a pose, and they're looking up at Boss/Client with their observant-idiot expressions, and he turns around and sees them, and he goes, "Gahhh!" and jumps. Margaret and I had to laugh.

For a wild day, friends, can you beat that one?

SATURDAY, JUNE 11

And then, wouldn't you know, no vehicles could get into or out of the airport because of downed power lines, and Larry had to spend the night there, twenty miles from home! He slept in the baggage claim and was looking pretty rumpled when I picked him up this morning. I was very glad to see him anyway. He said he had missed his last three appointments in Lagos, just completely forgot them, because he went with Archbishop Mfune into the countryside to check out some Soviet-made capacitors. Now he had got himself all in a fret that he was going to be fired. Somehow I do not think he will be fired.

I skipped whatever work project they've cooked up for today at the kids' school. Trevor and Kyle and I have been there almost every Saturday and I know plenty of families that missed more than we did. What did I do today instead, you ask? I drank martinis. In bed. All day. While watching old movies on our DVD player. Had a marvelous time, and for dinner we ordered Chinese.

SUNDAY, JUNE 12

Trevor's therapist says that as of next week he is going on summer hiatus. He says he needs some time away from his patients—he did not add, "especially Trevor," but I could hear him thinking it—and he will give us prescriptions to last Trevor until September, when he returns. I don't know about my son, but I think I will miss sitting in the therapist's parking lot. I may drive over and sit there for an hour every Sunday just for the hell of it.

MONDAY, JUNE 13

Last night we had book group, but we hardly spent any time at all on the fascinating book we had chosen, *Lesser-Known Criminals of the Bush Administration*, by Susan Goldfein-Prester and Lyle Gunning. Everybody in book group wanted to know first about Larry's kidnapping false alarm. So Margaret and I started regaling them with that story, and then we all began talking about the Client/Boss, and the party at my house, and Angie, and that louse M. Foler Tuohy—and as a result, our original topic barely was touched upon. But later we agreed that tonight's had been one of the best book groups ever.

Anne did notice one detail that I thought was interesting. When I told the part about promising Archbishop Mfune that Larry would wire him the down payment for the capacitors, Anne said she had heard that wire transfers to Nigeria can be problematic sometimes. She said she wasn't sure, and she didn't want to be unfair to an emerging third-world country with lifeways different from our own, but she had heard some rumors, possibly untrue. In any case, she suggested it might be a good idea to go slow on that wire transfer.

When I told Larry this at five this morning as he was getting ready for work, he became indignant and said he wasn't wiring the money to some stranger but to an archbishop of the Nigerian Apostolic Church. He said he trusted Archbishop Mfune implicitly and would not wish to insult him by appearing to hesitate, and I must wire the money as soon as the bank opened today. I said okay. But when I got to the bank, something came over me, and I didn't.

TUESDAY, JUNE 14

Well, Larry got around that by wiring the money himself this morning. There goes most of our pitiful retirement savings. I hope he knows what he is doing.

WEDNESDAY, JUNE 15

Somehow I keep going over that weird kidnapping false alarm in my mind. When I was saying goodbye to the Client/Boss in the front hall and Margaret was in the kitchen, he kind of swooped at me and tried (I think) to kiss me, but I dodged and went on saying whatever I was saying. In truth, friends, I was almost thinking, "Oh, what the hell—go ahead if you want to so much." He had this tormented look on his face, all gray like he'd been rubbed with pencil dust. I felt a little sorry for him, and if I thought about it, I guess I could be attracted to him, too, if that weren't too ridiculous to think about.

In a different life, things could be different. But I'm not in a different life, I am in this one, and it's what I've got. I think that is actually the guy's problem: He doesn't have any one life, because he's so rich he thinks he can choose any life he wants. So there is no limit to his greed and torment.

THURSDAY, JUNE 16

Ninety-nine degrees with a temperature-humidity index that made it even hotter at the kids' graduation ceremonies today. Kyle's took place in the morning, when the air was slightly less hot, and fortunately none of the other kids fainted in their caps and gowns. I told Gail the weather was unseasonable, and she replied that she couldn't think of any season this weather would be seasonable *for*. Alice, whose daughter is also in a third-grade class, suggested early springtime in hell.

All the kids got diplomas and trophies, for things like being tardy fewer than ten days. When I went to school we had only one public school graduation, for the high school seniors. Now you graduate from each grade. The third-grade graduation was cheerful, with lots of Mylar balloons and shout-outs during the ceremony. But the sixth-grade graduation (Trevor's class) was more difficult, because some of the kids were even more medicated than Trevor and by that time, two thirty in the afternoon, the parking lot had grown pretty hot. Fortunately there were several doctors attending, and the kids who were unable to endure these conditions could remove their robes and rest by the construction vehicles in what little shade was to be had.

FRIDAY, JUNE 17

"Great day in the mornin' hallelujah!" (as Gramma Pat used to say when anything especially good occurred). Destiny and Antony, those precocious youngsters, managed to get Russ, their dad, released from Fresh Springs Research Hospital. They called me last night and asked if I would drive them over there this morning to pick him up, and I did. Thanks to their preparations, he was allowed to sign himself out. I then brought all three to their house and the kids seemed happy to be home. Russ now has very short hair, probably the result of a hospital trim, and it stood out all around his head sort of like the fuzz on a tennis ball. He talked quietly and calmly, until I pulled into his driveway and he was unable to get the car door open. I kept explaining—it's simple, really, there's just this little lever under the armrest—but somehow he couldn't find it and he kept pushing buttons randomly and making the window go up and down and locking and unlocking the door and so on. Destiny and Antony got out of the backseat and opened his door from the outside. Then, half out of the car, he turned to me and began to explain why all car doors should be standardized. Eventually the kids led him into the house. He and Angie were lucky with those kids, I can tell you that.

SATURDAY, JUNE 18

It's funny to get the day off, now that reconstruction of the school has been suspended for the summer. So today I will turn to the problem of removing the wreckage of the garage.

SUNDAY, JUNE 19

Apparently you need a permit to burn a heap the size of our garage. We've had plenty of rain recently, so there was no risk of sparking other fires. But I probably should not have left the job to Trevor, because the diesel fuel he soaked everything in created a plume of black smoke that alerted the county fire department and some watchers in a forest-fire observation tower fifty-eight miles away. At one point we had seven fire trucks here. I suppose I should just build a fire lane through my flower beds for the inevitable next conflagration.

By the time the trucks arrived, though, the whole heap was pretty much incinerated. Takes care of that problem!

MONDAY, JUNE 20

Today is the summer solstice, that unique day in the celestial calendar when the sun rises directly at the end of the street perpendicular to ours and the shafts of golden light stream through our front window as I face eastward for my calming daily yoga ritual and *where the fuck are my fucking sunglasses*?

TUESDAY, JUNE 21

Larry called Archbishop Mfune this morning to make sure he received the wire transfer, and the phone number we had for him is no longer in service. On my suggestion, Larry called Lagos directory assistance and found that there are five Archbishop Kwesi Adjoa Mfunes listed, all at different addresses, as well as an Archbishop Kwesi Adjoa Mfune Eyebrow-Threading Parlor. I told Larry this did not look good. He said he didn't want to call all the different numbers searching for our Archbishop Mfune because he felt that would be "an overreaction," and he was sure Archbishop Mfune would soon get in touch with him. I then told Larry that was fine, but if he has lost that IRA money he will see a fucking overreaction, all right—FROM ME!!

WEDNESDAY, JUNE 22

Ol' Larry is snoring away in bed last night, not a care in the world, as usual, and I'm sleeping fitfully, also as usual, and in my half-waking dream I hear the snoring, and all the furniture in the entire house gathers around Larry's nose when he inhales, and when he exhales it all goes back to where it was. Inhale, exhale—the furniture clusters around his nose, then settles back down again—and suddenly I'm fully awake at 3:25 a.m. And there is the horrible obnoxious ceiling looking at me. The ceiling tells me, with a knowing wink, that we are never going to see that money again. I tell the ceiling to shut up and fuck off and leave me the fuck alone. It laughs.

THURSDAY, JUNE 23

Ahhh, summer! That slow, sweet, savoring time of year, a season of ease and lushness, when you can almost hear the earth sigh with pleasure at its own fecundity! I remember as a little girl visiting Gramma Pat and Grampa Hub at the farm they had for a while, all of us sitting on the old wooden porch swing with the removable ashtrays built into the arms, and rocking back and forth while Grampa Hub's slow voice went on and on dreamily describing the Hutterite conspiracy he said was trying to take over the township, and eventually, the world. Lazy summers of yesteryear, never to return!

Well, if we cannot recapture the past, we can at least make the best of the present, by reconfiguring our own outdoor spaces to take advantage of the slow-paced, sensuous living that summer provides. By that I mean a kind of feng shui reordering of patio, garden, or yard so that it is—how shall I put it?—more "summer-friendly." Today, I want to give you:

Gracious Outdoor Living, Cursing Mommy Style: Turning Unused Patio Space into a Valued Summer Friend!

As you can see, what I've done with my own patio could not be simpler: six molded white plastic "uniblock" lawn chairs—comfortable, handsome, and inexpensive—a round glass patio table, and a pink canvas beach umbrella on a pole for shade. To this setup I have added a trumpet vine that grows over the beach umbrella and is actually a bit of an invasive nuisance if not trimmed regularly. So what is missing? Yes, you guessed it: a hammock.

Which came first, summer or the hammock? Were any two aspects of our lives ever more intertwined? For myself, I don't consider summer officially under way until I've had my first lovely hammock snooze. Today I have resurrected the old hammock that was in our garage and that I yanked from the recent blaze just in time, or almost, which accounts for these singed areas. What I will do now is attach this cord here to this screw eye in the side of the house, and the other cord to this nearby tree, and then I will sit in the hammock like so—whew! What a moldy smell! I'll have to do something about that later. Then I lie back, and the hammock is—*hey!*—spinning over, wrapping me in it—goddamn thing—but if I push like so—goddamn it! Now it spun over the other way! Temporarily I am wrapped up in it like a cocoon.

All right, this is no problem. Though my arms are now pinned at my sides and the moldy smell is almost suffocating me, I simply push with my one free foot against the ground like so and . . . *whoa!* I'm spinning like a goddamn top! GODDAMN FUCKING HAMMOCK!! Now I'm wrapped so tightly I can barely breathe and YAHHHHH!!!! NOW I'M SPINNING THE OTHER WAY!! NOW I'M GOING BACK THE *OTHER* WAY! NOW THE OTHER WAY AGAIN!! AAAAAAHHHH I'M FEELING RE-ALLY WOOZY!!! NOW THE OTHER WAY AGAIN!! I'M GO-ING TO BE SICK!!! AHHHH!!! NOW THE OTHER WAY AGAIN!!! FUCKING GODDAMN HAMMOCK LOBBYISTS WHO PUSHED THIS HAZARDOUS GODDAMN HAM-MOCK THROUGH CONGRESS WITH THE HELP OF THE BUSH ADMINISTRATION!!! GODDAMN FUCKING KOCH BROTHERS (WHETHER THEY HAD ANYTHING TO DO WITH THIS GODDAMN HAMMOCK OR NOT)!!! HELP!!! HE-L-L-L-L-L-LP!!!

[pause]

Now I am lying on the patio itself, as you can see, after the fucking moldy killer hammock finally unwound and dropped me out. I think I am going to stay here for a while, for no particular reason. Soon one of the kids will come out and see what happened. Remind me to throw this awful fucking hammock into the trash.

Oh, what a fucking horrible day this has been.

FRIDAY, JUNE 24
Still lying on the patio under the hammock. As a concession to comfort, I brought one cushion from the sofa to rest my upper body on, and another to put on top of my head to block out

thoughts. Yesterday I did get up and make dinner and so forth. But today I felt irresistibly compelled to lie here again.

In just a minute, or in several hours or days, I am going to get up.

SATURDAY, JUNE 25
Still lying under the hammock. My family is strange enough that they don't think this is strange. I roused myself yesterday, finally, after a man who came to read the water meter noticed me and asked if I was all right. I hopped to my feet to show I was. But I don't know—I like it here. There's something summery about sprawling on cement.

SUNDAY, JUNE 26
I don't see why I can't lie under the hammock as long as I feel like, but I guess I should quit soon, because now it seems to be making the kids nervous. (Larry, on the other hand, is down in the basement and does not notice.) Kyle and Trevor have their first day of day camp tomorrow, so I can resume lying under the hammock then if I still feel like it.

MONDAY, JUNE 27
As we went to get in the car this morning on the way to day camp, such a gorgeous burst of birdsong! Something was singing its little heart out from the hickory tree behind the house. I made the kids stop and listen, not that they had any great interest in doing so. Peering upward, I spotted the singer—a bloodred cardinal, with those lovely black markings around the eyes. Kyle said some of the chirps sounded like the sounds the starship troopers' ray guns make in *Star Wars*, and Trevor said that was lame, and they got into a fight. As I looked at the bird singing away in

the morning sun, I suddenly remembered I had forgotten to put sunblock on the kids. Another struggle—they hate sunblock, but they really need it because their day camp is in a field.

TUESDAY, JUNE 28

The latest from the goddamn assisted living (Sabrina calls to tell me) is that "Dad" is now able to do the splits. No one else there, even including the employees, can do the splits. The local newspaper may send a photographer to record this achievement, she says.

Isn't that super.

WEDNESDAY, JUNE 29

Thanks to the fucking sadistic ceiling needling me relentlessly at 3:00 a.m., I can't stop worrying about that money transfer. If Larry found the capacitors in a dump, why did he have to buy them? Aren't things in a dump things that have been thrown away? And, therefore, wouldn't they be free? Also, why would an archbishop be in charge of selling these items? Does the Nigerian Apostolic Church somehow "own" the dump? If so, why does a church own a dump, or the capacitor supply in this particular dump? Is this perhaps a local practice in Nigeria, or in this part of Nigeria? And how did Larry meet this archbishop, anyway? Was he just hanging around the dump? Is it common in Nigeria, or anywhere, for archbishops to hang around dumps? In Nigeria, I understand, it is even hotter than here—was this archbishop wearing his robes and bishop's miter and stole and so on while at the dump? Or was he in civilian attire? If so, how did Larry know he really was an archbishop, as he claimed? He might very well have been just a guy out at a dump—a guy to whom we have now wired the bulk of our retirement savings.

Oh, the ceiling would NOT let up, I tell you.

I know if I asked Larry even one of these questions he would become all defensive and huffy. In fact, there probably is a rational explanation for everything, and I shouldn't let the ceiling get to me. But I can't help it—the whole thing does seem odd.

THURSDAY, JUNE 30

Oh, my wonderful unseen friends, I never forget that you are out there. Whenever I get to feeling down, I remind myself that we are accompanying one another on our path of life. And this morning it just occurred to me—the journey of a year that we began together in January is halfway done! Whatever this year's destination may be, we are halfway to it already. When you think of it, isn't that amazing?

Suddenly out of nowhere a great feeling of blessedness and abundance came over me, and I almost . . . I don't know, not cried, but maybe a combination of cried and laughed and sang. Does that ever happen to you? I had a kind of full, humming feeling of the abundance and joy and sadness and kookiness of life, like I was taking a breath just for a second at the very top of a roller coaster hill with the whole crazy amusement park spread out below. I thought of poor Russ trying to reopen a resealable package of provolone slices—he called me yesterday evening to ask if we could come over and help him with that, and Larry got on the phone and talked him through it—and I thought of Angie in her tropical paradise with that awful M. Foler Tuohy, and of my fucking horrible father, and of the wonderful Gail, and of book group, God bless them, and of the kids and Larry and me and the horrible Client/Boss and Sphagnum Health that I would like to blow up—oh, I guess I can't explain it. But I remembered all of that at once, somehow, and I thought of you, too, my wonderful unseen friends.

People say time goes by quickly, and it does. But you don't really sense its passing, you only notice that it has gone. The earth is moving through space at twenty-six thousand miles an hour, but it's impossible to feel it like sticking your head out a car window. Wouldn't that be something—if you could go up in a supertower into space high above the earth and feel what the earth's speed is really like? But of course you can't. You can only see the effects of it, which, in our case, is that suddenly it's the end of June and another year is already halfway over.

Well, we proceed onward anyway, friends, knowing that our distant destination, wherever we may find it, will be glorious and grand!

JULY

Up early with the larks on this sunny summer day, bursting with energy and ready to tackle my problems one-two-three. First, I made a big decision: For now, anyway, I will stop shopping at Stuff, Etc . . . The experience has simply been too draining. Last time I was there I noticed that right by the entry doors they have big displays of an herbal pill made of gingko root and biloba powder and bee extract and I don't know what-all to increase concentration and stamina, which Margaret says everybody uses just for the purpose of shopping at Stuff, Etc . . . That seems kind of cuckoo to me. I don't want a store you need to take a special pill to shop in. Would you?

Instead this morning I went to U-Drug-It, the local megapharmacy, which also sells groceries and live bait and earthmoving equipment and so on. Its produce department is perfectly fine, though it adjoins the jewelry aisle. I also looked at their huge rack of magazines that had all these articles like "Budget This" and "Save Money That" and I wondered when I'll see one about "Having Absolutely No Money at All," because I sent off the bills this morning, and when the checks clear, assuming they do, that is approximately what we will have.

Then again, we may be due for some kind of lovely refund I know nothing about right now, so there is that to look forward to! We must keep our fingers crossed.

SATURDAY, JULY 2

Of all the nerve. I overlooked making the payment on the biggest of our credit card bills last month and a Ms. Sparks of that particular company began calling early and late to inquire about it, and for days I didn't answer, but this morning I picked up just to straighten things out, and this Ms. Sparks, acting as Ms. Prosecuting Attorney, asked me why I hadn't paid the bill when at the very same time I had enough money to go vacationing in Africa! Apparently she had seen some charges Larry made in Lagos. I explained to this well-informed total stranger that Larry had gone to Lagos on business, not for vacation. I explained it without cursing and sent the check. Wasn't that civilized?

SUNDAY, JULY 3

An assistant to an assistant to an assistant to Mr. Sandor A. Stattsman, CEO of Sphagnum Health, called and said that Mr. Stattsman had suggested my name as someone to appear in an ad for Sphagnum Health. The assistant assistant assistant said that all my family and I would have to do is pose for a photo while smiling and hugging one another. The photo would be for a Sphagnum Health roadside billboard. They are on a rush deadline and need to get it done over the weekend—and what would we receive in return for interrupting our holiday, hugging one another like idiots, and having our faces plastered along the interstate? A fee, perhaps? A reduction in our insurance rates? No, we would get, according to the ass't ass't ass't, "valuable exposure."

I did not curse in this conversation, either, although I did make some offensive gestures, which she could not see, of course, since we were on the phone. That was the best I could manage and I thought it was restrained, considering. The woman was just doing her job, but if I am quite honest I must admit to harboring a few negative feelings for her anyway, i.e., she and Sandor A. Stattsman and Sphagnum Health CAN PLEASE GO AND FUCK THEMSELVES RIGHT AWAY!!

Excuse me. Believe it or not, I was really trying not to curse there. I have been hoping to cut down.

MONDAY, JULY 4

Ahhh, the glorious Fourth! I've loved it ever since I was a little girl, lying on a blanket on the still-warm hood of Grampa Hub's Bonneville out at the racetrack and looking into the summer night sky at the wonderful, ground-shaking, phantasmagorically fabulous Fourth of July fireworks bursting up above. We used to bring a picnic made by Gramma Pat and spread our red-and-white-checkered tablecloth under the trees in the picnic grounds while she chain-smoked her Chesterfields to beat the band and Grampa Hub snored in the Bonneville's backseat; oh, and the silly sack races, the egg-coddling contests, the fish scrambles in Paint Creek, the colorful red, white, and blue Paint Creek paint spills from the paint factory, the bus-parking finals, the police action, the stun guns, and on and on into a happy summer haze of Fourth of July memories . . .

To be honest with you, I would like to skip the whole thing this year. Somehow I cannot face it. Wouldn't it be great, friends, if every once in a while we simply dropped a holiday? Said the hell with it—didn't do it, totally missed it, took a rain check— just for that one time?

Oh, well, I'm only saying this because I'm about to go to the goddamn assisted living and pick up my fucking father. Every year the staff takes off for the Fourth and the relatives of the patients or inmates or whatever they are must come and get them for the day.

However, I am determined that this will be fun!

TUESDAY, JULY 5

Well, although the determination was there, circumstances in-
tervened, as they say, which is to say, IT WAS A TOTAL FUCK-
ING NIGHTMARE!!! In the first fucking place, WHY in the
WORLD did I decide to go to the goddamn assisted living by
public transportation? I thought I would avoid Fourth of July traffic that way, was why. So, as a result, I am sitting on a bus stuck in
Fourth of July traffic while my insane senile-dementia father is
offering insane directions to the driver and chinning himself on
the bar that you hold on to when you have to stand in the aisle.
Oh dear God, that journey took hours. Then we finally got to our
house and my fucking father and Kyle and Trevor shot bottle
rockets in the front yard, bouncing one off a passing car whose
driver stormed out threatening to sue until Larry gave him thirty
dollars. Plus, the picnic at the fireworks was sheer chaos. We had
asked Russ and his kids to join us, out of misplaced pity, and Russ
kept failing to get a folding chair to work and he began to weep.
Destiny and Antony had brought an extra dose of his medications, luckily.

WEDNESDAY, JULY 6

Returned my fucking father to the goddamn assisted living (by
car this time). I never appreciate my house more than when my
father has just left it.

THURSDAY, JULY 7

Life tumbles us along, friends, and the moments when we can
stop and reflect and simply savor one another's silent presence
are too few. I am seizing the day, right now, to enjoy a moment of
spiritual serenity and communion. Won't you join me? Today we
can contemplate a saying by O. O. Mattingly, a writer, thinker,
and wealth-repatterning consultant whom I've been reading in

the hope that he will fill the void left in my life by my discarding that awful fraud M. Foler Tuohy. O. O. Mattingly writes, "We re-pattern wealth, as we repattern all of our daily life to our own advantage, primarily by the engagement of the unjudgingly re-ceptive mind."

I guess the idea is to make ourselves attractors for the good energy in the universe by letting ourselves be available to it, and the way we go about that, somehow, apparently, is by using the unjudgingly receptive mind to engage with . . . something or other. So, basically, we just sit here and try to get our minds to be un-judgingly receptive and engaged. But engaged with what, exactly? Seeing as how we're trying to keep them open and unjudging and whatnot . . . Oh, I don't know.

In fact, I would like to go back to M. Foler Tuohy. At least I understood him every once in a while. In the author photo, this O. O. Mattingly has a thick white beard, and in chapter 1 he writes several pages about his beard and what it signifies to him and how he uses his beard to repattern wealth so that big checks show up in his post office box through yadda yadda of the cosmos and so on. I tried, but I must admit that I honestly had no idea what he was talking about. I kind of regret even bringing him up in the first place.

But I cannot go back to M. Foler Tuohy! I refuse to.

FRIDAY, JULY 8

The summer heat has settled in to stay, and in fact we have had no rain for weeks, and people are talking about the possibility of a drought, and thus we find ourselves relying more and more on that good ol' trusty appliance—our friend the air conditioner! On scorching days, all praise for the merciful genius who invented air-conditioning!

In order to keep our air conditioners working smoothly and efficiently, we must provide them with regular basic maintenance, and that means giving their filters a good cleaning. This task is simple, quick, and beneficial for the environment, too. So today I'm going to hold a brief master class (if you will) in air-conditioner-filter how-tos, with my:

Clean up, Turn on, and Chill out: Air-Conditioner-Filter
Basics from the Cursing Mommy

Many of you may think, "Oh, I can't do such a complicated job of maintenance on my own—I'd better leave it for a qualified repair person." Well, that attitude went out with whalebone corsets, and let me show you why. Anybody can do it. All you need is a simple extendable ladder, such as I'm using—ouch! It's heavy!—to gain access to the outside of the air conditioners outside the house, and you're on your way. Starting with the air conditioner in our bedroom window, which has been making some strange noises as well as not cooling at all, I simply climb up to it and remove this—ouch! shit!—goddamn fucking housing. Ooops! Dropped it into the yard. Oh, well. It didn't hit anything.

Now, using the instruction manual, which I have previously brought along, I reach in here and—what is that strange humming? I reach in here and disengage the filter frame attachment from the inner cowling manifold like so and *what* in the *hell* is that goddamn humming and then I lift out the filter, easy as pie! Pretty neat, huh? And now I begin to climb down and GAAAAAAHHHHH! I AM BEING ATTACKED BY HUMMINGBIRDS!! They must've been nesting in here and YIIIIII!!! THEY'RE HUMMING AROUND MY HEAD AND POKING ME WITH THEIR GODDAMN POINTY FUCKING BEAKS!!! GO AWAY GO AWAY GO AWAY YOU GODDAMN THINGS!!! I AM WAVING MY HANDS AT THEM BUT THEY KEEP COMING!!! NOW THEIR BABIES ARE ALSO ATTACKING ME!!! THERE MUST BE A DOZEN OF THE FUCKING GODDAMN THINGS!!! Now . . . the goddamn fucking ladder . . . has . . . STARTED TO *SLIDE* AND—

WHOA!—I JUMPED OFF AT THE LAST MINUTE INTO THE HICKORY TREE!!! AHHHH!!! FUCKING GODDAMN KARL ROVE AND THE BUSH ADMINISTRATION!!! THE BIRDS ARE STILL ATTACKING ME!!! YIIIIII!!! HELP!!! H-E-E-E-E-E-E-E-LP!!!

[thrash scream hum hum chirp thrash yell]

[pause]

Actually, it's not so bad up here in the goddamn leaves. The birds finally seem to have flown away, and if they come back I'll call a bird exterminator, assuming there even is such a thing. Fucking hummingbirds in the air conditioner—Jesus. I guess nobody's home in the neighborhood today because I don't see a rush to rescue me. So what the fuck? In just a minute I'm going to climb down. Remind me never to try this again.

Oh, what a fucking horrible day this has started out to be.

SATURDAY, JULY 9

Once again, friends, I have a secret communiqué I can share with no one but you. (Or almost no one, as I'll explain.) This morning Kyle and I were in the front yard weeding the hosta beds while Trevor dozed on the lawn, and suddenly Kyle said, "Look, Mommy, that airplane just wrote your name." Bent over my weeding, I hadn't noticed, but sure enough, there in the blue sky right above, huge white capital letters spelled out my first name. The little plane was just finishing the final *E*. I knew right away this had to be the work of the creepy Client/Boss, but I didn't react. I said, "Hmm, isn't that funny?" or something like that and brushed it off and kept weeding. Kyle roused Trevor, and he said, "Wow! Awesome, Mom!" I told them it was just a coincidence. In ten minutes the name had become an unreadable white cloudy patch in the blue. I hoped the boys had forgotten about it.

Later I checked my cell phone and there it was—the Client/ Boss had sent a long, sappy text taking credit for the skywriting, like a secret creepo terrorist saying he's responsible for a car bomb. Okay, jerk, I'm impressed—now please go away. I didn't answer, per usual. How to get this man to leave me alone?

SUNDAY, JULY 10

So at dinner last night Kyle told Larry (who had been in the basement all day preparing for the Nigerian capacitors that are due to arrive any second now), "Daddy, a plane wrote Mommy's name in the sky today." That got Larry's attention, and he said, "Really? Far out!" Then we started speculating about what product has my name, or what nut was trying to surprise his girlfriend at the beach. I hate being deceptive, but I don't see how I can explain this to Larry, or even why I should, really. Let sleeping dogs . . .

But that was not an end to it, because just after dinner I got a call from Gail. She had seen the writing, too, and after the incident with the limo in front of our house, the party, and the kidnapping scare, she knows something is up. On the phone I didn't confirm or deny, but I assured her that whatever it was, it was one-sided—I hadn't encouraged or participated in anything. The only problem was, I felt kind of guilty even saying that, somehow. But Gail and I trust each other, so it's okay she knows.

MONDAY, JULY 11

It's so hot and dry that dust is blowing around and you can water your lawn only on Fridays if your address is an even number or Tuesdays if it's an odd number. Other uses of water are forbidden, like washing your car. We must all pitch in together on this because the reservoirs are rapidly going down and it's approaching an emergency. Last week the Enviro Rangers at Kyle and

Trevor's day camp were on a day trip in McKinley Springs Park and as they hiked back to the drop-off point on a residential street they saw a stream of water running from under somebody's closed garage door and down the driveway. The quick-thinking kids deduced that somebody must be washing a car in there. So their camp counselor, a very capable girl from the high school, called the county on her cell phone and reported it. I like that the kids are learning valuable lessons not only about the environment but also about being good citizens (of course the two go hand in hand).

TUESDAY, JULY 12

Next year Trevor moves up to the junior high, which is run by a private company, so all its account books are closed, and we can only assume it will be opening on schedule. Kyle will still be attending the elementary school, of course. Although it's a bit early to think about back to school already in July—and Lord knows the kids don't want to!—some of the elementary school mothers are worried that the transient workers hired at the last minute for spot repairs over the summer have not been doing all the school board expected and will not be finished by the Labor Day deadline.

These workers (who are very inexpensive) follow the teachings of a nineteenth-century "prophet" named Hulot Henderson, who believed in finding Divine Truth through the installation of home and office furnishings. We had a cultural awareness session about them at the meeting that informed us of their hiring, and these Hendersonites, as they're called, generously agreed to do a free presentation at an all-school assembly in the fall. For the time being, many Hendersonite families are living in what used to be the school cafeteria, keeping down their costs (and ours!) while they work.

WEDNESDAY, JULY 13

Well, all holy Hades has broken loose, if you will forgive my blasphemy. The house that the Enviro Rangers reported for wasting water, which was indeed breaking the law, and washing not just one car but a whole fleet of them, belongs to . . . Sandor A. Stattsman! It was the same house where Trevor and I raked gravel last spring or whenever. I don't know why he didn't recognize it—maybe because of the drugs. Anyway, when Sandor A. Stattsman was presented with the ticket and the fine, he just went absolutely over-the-top crazy, threatening legal action and getting on the phone to everybody in the county and then filing actual lawsuits left and right, with the result that the kids were charged with criminal trespass—if you're even on the street in McKinley Springs Gated Community without an invitation you're trespassing, apparently—and a judge issued an injunction shutting down the day camp pending the court's decision.

"Goodness gracious mercy me land sakes saints alive *fuck this bullshit*," as Gramma Pat sometimes used to say (minus the last part). But, seriously—FUCK that FUCKING SHITHEAD Sandor A. Stattsman, and I mean that permanently!! Now that the camp is shut down, Trevor and Kyle are home all day with nothing to fucking do. And I have to deal with that.

People sometimes suggest to me, gently, that I should drink a bit less, and after moments like this, I countersuggest, not as gently, that I should drink a lot more. Today, with the kids rattling around the house too bored even to watch TV, I am having a schnapps day. On ice. And I don't even really like schnapps.

THURSDAY, JULY 14

I am trying to keep upbeat, I really am, but the news that Trevor has to report to Fresh Springs Juvenile Center—a new youth-detention facility out by the racetrack, near Fresh Springs Research Hospital, the mental institution Russ was in—oh, friends, that discovery laid me low. The notice arrived this morning by registered mail. We have to hire a lawyer to get a stay of sentence within thirty days, and Larry is looking into that. The problem goes back to the fire Trevor set at the commuter rail station last March. He was supposed to remain out of trouble for a year, and this criminal trespass charge triggers some mandatory confinement clause—oh, it's all too much. He's only twelve.

FRIDAY, JULY 15

So what did I do? Yes, friends, I called the Client/Boss. He was surprised and thrilled to hear from me, or he sounded like he was, and when I asked him this favor he said, "It's done." He got off and ten minutes later he called back. Stattsman has dropped all charges. He'll pay the water-wasting fine and the camp will reopen on Monday.

Jeez, Louise! What does Boss/Client have over the guy?

SATURDAY, JULY 16

Larry thinks the lawyer he hired, a buddy from school, accomplished all this singlehandedly. Let him think that. Let him even pay him, I don't care. I would prefer not to discuss this stupid business anymore.

SUNDAY, JULY 17

This morning I sat Trevor down and tried to impress upon him the seriousness of what almost happened—he almost was locked up in Fresh Springs Juvenile, and no fooling. I said if he could get into such a near scrape for something that wasn't even his fault, think what the outcome might be if he really did something wrong! I told him he had to be extra, extra careful now, and I went over this point several times. Finally I asked if he understood, and he nodded solemnly and assured me that he did. I said he should tell me if he had any questions or concerns. He thought for a minute, then asked, "If you swallow your chewing gum, how long does it take to digest? Matt Z. said it takes seven years."

Why do I even bother? I am talking to myself here.

MONDAY, JULY 18

Sheltering with Larry and the kids in the basement last night during the tornado watch, I wandered among the capacitors, which are now filling up one room and spilling into another. I couldn't help myself, I brought up a touchy subject: Has Larry heard anything recently from our friend Archbishop Mfune? Oh, yes, Larry said, he and the archbishop have been in constant communication and everything is proceeding swimmingly. In fact, the full shipment of capacitors will be sent as soon as Larry makes the final payment.

At this, quite naturally, I screamed, "The final WHAT?" Well, as it turns out, the previous wire transfer, which drained most of our retirement savings, was only the *deposit*. Now Larry will send the rest, which will wipe out the savings entirely, as well as a small account where I keep the berry money I inherited from Gramma Pat.

Well, this upset me so much I couldn't even talk to him for a while. In fact, I still can't.

TUESDAY, JULY 19

Still not speaking to Larry. He says that I must believe in him, and it will all work out, and I'll see. All I can think of is those hundreds of mason jars of blackberry jam Gramma Pat put up, and the bushels and crates and buckets of berries we picked, and the clouds of Chesterfield smoke coming out of those prickly bushes as my old gramma picked away back in there, and Mr. Zook, the nice Amish man with the produce wagon who sold them for her, and Ted, Mr. Zook's nice horse . . .

Oh, *boo hoo hoo hoo sob, sob!* I am sorry, I can't . . . all that berry money, gone to Nigeria! I want to believe in Larry, and I probably would, if only he weren't such a total fucking clueless idiot.

WEDNESDAY, JULY 20

Well, Cursing Mommy, cheer up! A few good curses—FUCK STUPID GODDAMN LARRY AND HIS STUPID GOD-DAMN FUCKING CAPACITORS!!!—shouted down the basement stairs today with nobody home, and I am back on the right side of the world and ready to proceed.

Today, since I would not for the life of me DREAM of going outside in this heat, and the Ajax AC Repair guy has got all our air conditioners working properly (I will *never* mess with an air conditioner myself again, I promise!) and it's nice and cool in our bedroom, I plan to devote this time to rearranging my closet—a perfect task for a summer afternoon. I cannot wait to have my entire closet area shipshape and immaculately organized, and I'll be happy to let you peer over my shoulder as I

Banish Those Clothes-Closet Gremlins! A Few Handy
Organizing Rules from the Cursing Mommy

Before we begin, friends, I want to say a word about the Cursing Mommy's household advice columns of the past. In almost every one of them—okay, in every one of them—the Cursing Mommy encountered setbacks that caused her to become upset, lose her temper, scream curses, give people the finger, hurl objects, shout obscenities, make inferences against individuals (e.g., in the Bush administration), and more. In fact, this has happened as recently as the week before last, with the unfortunate business of the air conditioner filter.

These outbursts are regrettable and should stop. Today the Cursing Mommy has taken a couple of mood-leveling pills—very pleasant—in order to accomplish the important chore I have before me in a dignified and trouble-free manner, for a change. Calmness, and no cursing, *por favor*, Cursing Mommy!

So, to begin: Rule #1 of closet reorganization is: If you have any clothes, shoes, or accessories that you have not worn in at least a year, you are probably never going to wear them. So get rid of them! Here, I am making a pile of the rejected items on the floor. We must be brutally honest with ourselves about this. Later I will take the items to the Goodwill or some other charitable organization, where they will be very welcome, I assure you. For example, I haven't worn this boa since I don't know when, haven't worn this serape, almost never wear this pair of disco heels . . .

So after an afternoon of sorting and choosing, look at the great heap of culls I have accumulated! Wonderful to think of these no longer clogging up my space. I feel like I can breathe once more.

But now it is coming up on dinnertime, so I will continue my organizing tomorrow.

THURSDAY, JULY 21
Today, friends, we resume the work of yesterday with:

Conquering Clothes-Closet Chaos, Part II: Be Ruthless,
Because the Mess Surely Will Be!
Wire coat hangers seem to just adore one another, don't they? Was there ever a more gregarious group of objects in the world?

Look at how this bunch of hangers is all tangled and mixed up with themselves. Normally a situation like this might be enough to make me curse, but I've forestalled that possibility with my new calmness policy (plus the pills). No matter how long it takes, I am now going to disentangle these hangers from one another and get them all pointing in the same direction and put them in neat piles to take to the dry cleaner, who always is grateful to receive them.

Goodness! There are also a whole bunch of wire hangers back here on the closet floor in an even bigger tangled mess than the ones I have just pulled out. What a very large bunch of hangers. Well, that's the job for today, I guess. I'll just sit here on the bed untangling these hangers. That means I will probably not finish the overall closet reorganization until tomorrow, but, hey—no problem! Whatever it takes, letting the new calmness policy (plus the pills) be my guide.

FRIDAY, JULY 22

Until you start on a project like this you never are aware of just how many hangers are in your home. Lots more turned up in Kyle's closet and in Trevor's closet, and I have gathered those, too, as they slipped and slid around in an unhelpful way that otherwise might have made me curse, and I have sorted them and got them all facing in the same direction, and now all of the hangers are in these many neat piles by the clothes closet in our room. And the closet itself, I am happy to report, has now been completely reorganized. The shoes are in boxes in their shelves up top, the belts are hung on this hook designed for that purpose, these ties, scarves, and other accessories are all in order here on the sides and in the handy holders inside the door, and now I close the door with a good push—*ooof!!*—like so. In fact, the closet is still rather full, and a bit of effort is required to push the door shut, but that's a definite improvement on how it used to be, when the door would not even close.

Larry will take the heaps of discards down to the front stoop for pickup, and tomorrow I will put the piles of sorted and stacked hangers in the car for transport to the dry cleaner. Friends, I want to recommend the good feeling the Cursing Mommy gets from the successful completion of this task. And all without cursing, I might add—thanks to the new calmness policy (and the pills).

SATURDAY, JULY 23

This morning I went first thing to admire my closet-reorganizing job and . . .

AHHHH! HELP! THE FUCKING CLOSET DOOR SPRUNG OPEN THE MOMENT I TOUCHED THE KNOB! IT KNOCKED ME ON THE FLOOR! NOW THE FUCK- ING SHOES ARE—OW! OW! OW!—FALLING OUT AND HITTING ME ON THE HEAD, ONE BY ONE!! NOW THE ACCESSORIES ARE TUMBLING OUT, AND THE CLOTHES ROD IS BREAKING, DUMPING ALL THE CLOTHES—YIIIIIII!!—KNOCKING OVER THE FIRST PILE OF HANGERS!!! SHIT!! NO!—WHICH IS KNOCK- ING OVER THE NEXT PILE OF HANGERS!! NO, PLEASE, NO!!—KNOCKING OVER THE NEXT PILE!! WHICH IS KNOCKING OVER THE NEXT!!! JESUS FUCKING GOD- DAMN CHRIST, STOP FALLING OVER, YOU!!! GAH- HHH!!! NOW THE GODDAMN HANGERS ARE FALLING OUT OF THE BEDROOM, AND DOWN THE HALL, AND DOWN THE FUCKING STAIRS!!! FUCK THE WHAT'S THEIR NAME FUCKING REPUBLICAN SCAIFE BROTH- ERS AND THEIR FUCKING GODDAMN THINK TANK THAT PROBABLY INVENTED WIRE COAT HANGERS!!! FUCK THIS GODDAMN COAT HANGER MESS THAT I KNOW IS SOMEHOW THE FAULT OF HALLIBURTON

AND BRITISH PETROLEUM!!! FU-U-U-U-CK!!! HELP!!!
HE-E-E-E-E-E-E-E-E-LP!!!

[*pause*]

Actually, it is pretty uncomfortable lying on coat hangers. In just a minute I'm going to get up. Fucking closet reorganization—what a disaster. I'll cram all that stuff back in the closet, then dump the hangers into plastic trash bags, which they will punch holes in, but what the hell. Let the dry cleaner figure it out. Remind me never to do this again. What the fuck was I thinking, trying not to curse? I am the Cursing Mommy.

Oh, what a fucking horrible several days—make that a week—make that a life—this has been.

SUNDAY, JULY 24
Sat on the couch in my housecoat and watched the local access channel and did nothing. Somebody report me to the authorities, please.

SUNDAY, JULY 24 (CONTINUED)
Hard to believe it is still Sunday.

SUNDAY, JULY 24 (LATER)
Whew—what an unscheduled detour *that* was! Such an awful hangover those pills gave me! And the side effects! I was seeing triple for a while, and I developed a rash on my stomach that spelled out "Turn back, Dorothy." What in the world could have been IN those pills, anyway? The elderly clerk at U-Drug-It promised me they were "mellow," and I guess they were, up to a point. But the aftershocks were real lulus. That's the last time I get my medications from the remainders bin.

Oh, well—lesson learned. It's a relief to feel relatively normal again!

MONDAY, JULY 25
Recently there has been quite a bit of parental concern about the Hendersonite workers living and working in the elementary school. Lights are on in the building at all hours, and loud religious-sounding music has been heard, and many cars with license plates from all over North and South America are parked on neighboring streets. The president of the school board went to inquire, and the Hendersonites' spokesman told her that it is a part of their core beliefs to hold all gatherings in buildings that are under renovation. I am sure we will learn more about this custom and others at the group's presentation in the fall.

TUESDAY, JULY 26
Just because I asked the awful Boss/Client for a favor, and the guy immediately did it for me, and it saved Trevor from the lockup, does that obligate me to read or answer Client/Boss's text messages, or in fact pay him any more mind than I was paying him before? I gave this question a lot of serious thought today and finally decided—nahhh.

WEDNESDAY, JULY 27
Margaret is in bed with the flu and her husband is on call until the weekend, so I took their kids, Walker and Miles, to the beach. Along with Kyle and Trevor, whom I kept out of camp, I also had Destiny and Antony with me (Russ is building a model aircraft carrier). Six kids in all. So there we are by the water and I'm getting ADD trying to watch them all, and I look up, and the Boss/Client in his Guccis or Shmuccis is walking toward us across

the sand. How had he followed me there? He didn't really answer when I asked. He somehow tracked my cell phone, I believe.

He took us back to his limo and showed it to the kids and gave them ice cream bars from the freezer—it has a freezer—and they climbed around in it and had a wonderful time. I didn't get in, myself, because I felt awkward in just my bathing suit, wrapped in a towel.

Anyway, friends, here is a fact about certain kinds of unscrupulous people that is worth remembering. To get what they want, they will do absolutely anything—*even be nice*!

THURSDAY, JULY 28

When the kids told Larry about our day at the beach, he accepted Client/Boss's showing up there as a perfectly ordinary coincidence. Larry only wished he had been there himself, to talk about some work thing or other.

FRIDAY, JULY 29

Here I am alone again at my kitchen table with newspaper and coffee cup, and a chance to reconnect with you, my wonderful unseen friends out there. Through all the bumps and byways of my life I always keep you in my heart. The reason I was wrong to try to stop cursing recently was that, as the Cursing Mommy, I have a responsibility to curse with all my strength on behalf of each and every one of you. I take that responsibility very seriously.

Oh, life is a fucking goddamn nightmare, is it not? But in many ways, we choose to be who we are and to live the life we do. "Happiness is not something you *have*, it is something you *choose*," in the words of M. Foler Tuohy—

Oh, goddamn it to hell, I just quoted that crum bum, M. Foler Tuohy. Honestly, friends, I have not found another poet/philosopher to replace him, and I simply can't stand him. Such a dilemma. But do you know what? Just because I have a problem with him doesn't mean *you* have to. So let the words stand and overlook the source. The guy says we should choose happiness, and he is absolutely right. Let us choose to be happy no matter what, and share our happiness openhandedly with one another, and live willingly into the happiness we choose.

A good goal for this summer day.

SATURDAY, JULY 30
Bought a new f-Fone this morning, and this afternoon I dropped it in a toilet in the U-Drug-It ladies' room. Goddamn fuck goddamn shit fuck John Ashcroft fucking goddamn shit Halliburton Cheney Richard Perle FUCK FUCK FUCK!!

SUNDAY, JULY 31
Late last night the water heater exploded. Holy Toledo, what a mess—water two inches deep from one end of the basement floor to the other. "No capacitors were harmed in the explosion!" crowed Larry, after a quick inspection. (They are up on tables and benches, off the floor.) That made him happier than if the water heater hadn't exploded to begin with. He went off to the office, whistling, to put in some extra weekend hours. I got out the Shop-Vac and started to Hoover. All day I sucked up water and such yucky trash on the basement floor, cursing aplenty, I will admit. The plumber said you have to turn the water heater temperature down when the outdoor temps go up into the hundreds, like they've been, or else the water gets too hot and trips this safety-valve dealie, which then releases the pressure by spewing all the water out.

Life is a wonderful learning experience, friends, and I am happy to pass along this bit of water heater wisdom to you.

And now we approach August, summer's height!

AUGUST

Everybody in book group, and probably a lot of other people, received a joint e-mail today from Angie and M. Foler Tuohy. I found it hard to read, but maybe that was just me. It had a lot of eyewash about how happy they were to find each other blah-blah-blah, and about the good life on the endive ranch now that endive prices are soaring, plus a big news flash—they are writing a book together, to be called *Loving Skip, Loving Angie.* Much as I believe in people expressing themselves, this book did not sound promising to me, but then I am not an author. They included some poems they had written together and photos of themselves in the surf.

About one minute after getting the e-mail, I had a call from poor Russ. He was crying and yelling, both. In a separate e-mail just to him they had suggested that he bring the kids and live in a gardener's outbuilding on the ranch. She was missing the kids, Angie told him. Mostly Russ was incoherent, but I did understand that he thinks M. Foler Tuohy is "a little fat man," and that he, Russ, will win Angie back by working out and improving his physique. He kept talking about his "revenge body." I do not know what will become of the guy. He plans to organize an endive boycott and has stopped working on his model aircraft carrier.

TUESDAY, AUGUST 2

Nothing is more damaging to our hair than summer heat. Therefore, on the hottest days we must take special precautions to
keep our hair from suffering the ravages of heat punishment and
UV rays. The best way to do this is to go into some cool and moist
area like northern Canada or the Faroe Islands (which are off
England, I believe). Or, if we can't, a visit to our local hairdresser's
high-humidity cooling chamber will leave our hair much im-
proved. When we venture back outside, those special cooling-
humidifying helmets they have now will preserve the necessary
miniclimate in our hair's vicinity.

Well, this is all fine, I guess, if a person can afford it and
wants to carry around a miniclimate on her head. But for pity's
sake, how much are we expected to do for our hair? I mean, it's
just this stuff on top of our heads, not Follicle the Merciless rul-
ing our lives! A little sun-damaged hair never hurt anybody,
friends, and if your husband makes remarks, tell him to try carrying a miniclimate around on *his* head and see how *he* likes it.
And tell him the Cursing Mommy said so!

WEDNESDAY, AUGUST 3

Why Larry invited Russ and his kids to come with us on our vacation, I will never know. Oh, hell, I do know, of course—Larry
feels sorry for the poor guy. Every year we go to the quarry up by
Brainardsville where we rent a cabin that used to be the explo-
sives shack. (It's nicer than it sounds, although you do have to be
careful about hanging pictures and so on, because of some nitro
that leached into the walls.) Grampa Hub worked there for years,
back when forty-nine out of every fifty stone sash weights came
from Brainardsville. The quarry shut down some time ago so now
it's a resort. We'll be there for a week. Larry has rented the cabin
next to ours for Russ, Destiny, and Antony. A nice gesture, I
guess—but how about Angie contributing some of that M. Foler

Tuohy dough to her family's holiday? I insisted that at least we go in separate cars. We could never all fit in ours, anyway.

THURSDAY, AUGUST 4

Today's *Sammy* comic in the newspaper was so cute I cut it out and put it on the refrigerator. In the first panel, Sammy, the parakeet, is standing inside a metal crusher-compactor thing, and he says to the robot, Lenny, "Leonard, my good lad, I am ready for my close-up," and Lenny replies, "Right you are, sir," and pulls a lever and the compactor compresses Sammy to the thickness of a piece of paper, and he falls out and rolls like a coin, going "*W-ling W-ling w-ling-ling-ling-ling-ing-ing*" on the floor. In the last panel we see Sammy lying there, completely flattened, and he is saying to the robot, "Let me rephrase that."

Isn't that just marvelous? Don't we all feel like that sometimes?

FRIDAY, AUGUST 5

A useful item to take on your vacation is a waterproof map holder, to hold local maps and other information in an easy-to-access format when you travel on smaller roads or hiking trails. What's more, this is an item we can easily make at home, as I will demonstrate today, with my summer prevacation edition of:

The Cursing Mommy's Crafts Day, Part VII(a): Five Steps to a Nifty Map Holder You'll Thank Me For!

I first saw this map-holder design in the Boy Scout handbook, and I have modified it slightly for family vacation use. The key element in this map holder is clear plastic packing tape—the widest you can find will be about right. I happen to have here a thick roll of this tape that I have not needed since last Christmas. Whoever used this roll before me did not fold back the end as I always recommend we do, so I now have to rotate the roll back and forth in the light to see where the edge of the tape, in actual fact, is.

Okay—goddamn fucking shit. Let's get that out of the way right up front. FUCKING GODDAMN LARRY DID NOT FOLD BACK THE EDGE OF THE FUCKING TAPE AS I HAVE INSTRUCTED HIM ONE MILLION TIMES TO DO!

Okay, I am fine with that. I accept it and breathe normally. By scraping with my fingernail I should be able to locate the tape edge not apparent to the naked eye . . . and when that fucking doesn't fucking goddamn work—wait! I found it! Here at the top of the roll I have scratched up a piece of tape, and I begin to pull it, trying to pick up the whole edge—but it just keeps tearing around the ENTIRE FUCKING GODDAMN ROLL, a fucking little strip about an eighth of a fucking inch wide, fucking up the whole goddamn roll, so I take scissors and CHOP AWAY AT THE FUCKING TAPE . . . BUT IT DOES NO FUCKING GOOD!! JUST MAKES A BIGGER GODDAMN MESS!! So I begin to calmly SLICE AT THE GODDAMN TAPE ROLL WITH A BUTCHER KNIFE, aha! Now it's coming off, but the roll . . . FUCKING SLIPS FROM MY HAND, AND I GRAB FOR IT . . . NOW I HAVE TAPE ALL OVER ME!!! YIIIIII!!! I AM STUCK LIKE A FUCKING FLY IN FUCKING FLY-PAPER!!! GET ME OUTTA THIS SHIT!!! GODDAMN FUCKING CHENEY!!! GODDAMN ATTORNEY GENERAL GONZALES!!! Help! HE-E-E-E-E-E-ELP!!!

[snip slash thrash slice tangle thrash]

[pause]

Actually, it's not so bad lying here, now that I got most of that goddamn tape off of me. That shit is like some kind of alien life-form. Remind me never to touch it again. So much for the fucking map holder. The car has GPS anyway, and who the fuck wants to ever get farther than ten feet away from the car? The kids will be home soon. In just a minute I'm going to get up.

Oh, what a fucking horrible nightmare I predict this vacation is going to be.

SATURDAY, AUGUST 6

As I was packing the car this morning Larry kept asking me questions like, "Have you seen my blue bag?" He has about seventeen blue bags of various sizes and I had to figure out which goddamn one it was, and then it inevitably turned out to be the one I had packed first, way back in there under everything else, and I had to dig it out . . . A real headache! Then ten minutes later he's asking, "Have you seen my *other* blue bag?"

This is to be a "working vacation" for Larry, which means he will be driving back to the office from the quarry at least three days next week, leaving us without a car, or rather, leaving us with the necessity of borrowing Russ's car. Larry is afraid if he really takes a vacation—you know, the kind where you actually don't go in to work—he will be fired. I now am sure that no matter what Larry does or does not do, our associate and buddy the Boss/Client will never fire him. I just know this to be true. To convince Larry of it, however, I would have to say more than I want.

SUNDAY, AUGUST 7

And so here we are at the quarry, with the sun coming through the pines and spilling its golden coins of light on the forest floor, and the ripples on the clear, cold water making lovely zigzag reflections of the trees. Such quiet, such peace! A sign posted at the resort office says that a kind of spider called the brown recluse may be found in some of the outhouses, and guests are to watch for them, because their bites can cause a lot of discomfort

and even gangrene and death and so on. That is a good thing to
be aware of!

MONDAY, AUGUST 8
Also, we should have checked to see what the water level would
be in the quarry ponds, because of the recent drought. In Echo
Quarry, our favorite, the level is so low that boats have to be low-
ered by winch, and although you can dive in, there's really no
way to climb out.

Fortunately, the resort has minigolf and go-cart tracks for
the kids, and cable for the TV and computers. With Larry gone
all day today at the office I am grateful the kids are occupied
with their video games.

TUESDAY, AUGUST 9
A guest in cabin five was bitten by a brown recluse spider last
night in the outhouse and had to be taken to the hospital by helicopter. That is difficult not only for the unfortunate person who
was bitten, but also for our kids, who never were very keen on
the outhouse to begin with. Staff say they have gotten rid of most
of the remaining spiders—but try persuading Kyle and Trevor
of that! They say they will use the bathroom at the clubhouse,
which is a bit of a walk.

WEDNESDAY, AUGUST 10
Destiny and Antony have completed a very thorough survey of
the local trees and preserved samples of their leaves and needles
and so on in wax paper in anticipation of a project they might
have next year in first grade. Russ spends all day composing
angry letters to Angie and M. Foler Tuohy on his computer, and

exercising. I hate to mention this, but his "revenge body" is not really there yet. I'm afraid it's still more of a "you were right to leave me" body. Of course Larry and I say he looks great, in order to keep his spirits up. Russ does try so hard.

THURSDAY, AUGUST 11

Many paths, one journey.   —*motto of the Ecumenical Council*

Walking down a trail through the forest this morning before breakfast I found myself for some reason thinking of Winona Crandall, the ice skater, who was a hero of mine in high school and who once gave me her autograph. What a skating angel she was! I wondered what lovely figures she might be tracing on some indoor rink at that very moment, and whether our lives would ever cross again. As the birds sang around me in the shafts of morning sunshine, and the pine needles on the forest floor released their intoxicating balsam smell combined with the smell of smoke, I also thought of you, all my wonderful unseen friends. Where might each of you be on this Thursday morning? I happen to find myself on this particular path in this particular woods—what paths are you following? I imagine all our different paths, like lovely handwriting in their many windings, yet unified by common purpose and by love. We might seem to be inscribing our paths alone, but we are all in this together, you and I. The paths are many, my friends, but our journey truly is one!

FRIDAY, AUGUST 12

Sunrises and sunsets are absolutely spectacular here, owing to the smoke and atmospheric particulates caused by the adjacent wildfires, which are also driving many more brown recluse spiders into developed areas, naturalists say. There were such gorgeous peach-colored patches and swaths of fiery orange combined with purple and magenta in yesterday's sunset, and they created a really breathtaking effect, which became all the more so because the wildfire smoke made it a bit hard to breathe. Under these conditions the brown recluse spider is drawn to water, bedding, and anyplace insects gather, like outhouses, cabin windows, floors, shoes, and undergarments.

Sunrise this morning, which we all happened to be awake for because we are on the alert for brown recluse spiders, dawned even more beautifully, with a bloodred tinge overall and certain brown-and-white sections reminiscent of the markings on the male brown recluse spider (according to a cautionary leaflet distributed yesterday).

SATURDAY, AUGUST 13

Trevor did a naughty thing last night for which he will be punished severely when we get home. Poor Larry, who hardly slept a wink the night before, crawled into his sleeping bag early and asked not to be disturbed 'til morning. The rest of us went to bed soon after, determined to get some shut-eye ourselves and not worry about brown recluse spiders. Little did Larry know that Trevor, that badly misbehaving boy, had balled up a piece of fishing line in a spider shape and put it at the bottom of Larry's sleeping bag. Not only that, but Trevor also left the line connected to the "spider" so that it trailed out of the sleeping bag's top, where he could keep hold of it.

Well, no sooner had Larry drifted off to sleep than Trevor, on the cot next to Larry's, began to give some gentle tugs to the line, moving the "spider" at the bottom of Larry's bag. All at once Larry woke up and went rigid. "I think there is something near my foot," he whispered to me. (I was on the cot on the other side.) Trevor then gave another tug, and Larry, by now quite thoroughly alarmed, whispered, "What in the hell *is* that?" Trevor then pulled the line so that the "spider" was touching Larry's bare shin. Well, that did it, and Larry came up off the cot as if he had been shot from a gun and jumped straight up to the rafters, where he hung on with both arms while kicking the sleeping bag off his legs for all he was worth and shouting.

This is just the kind of unacceptable behavior on Trevor's part that we have been trying to correct. Clearly, more progress needs to be made, as Trevor himself agreed. After the neighboring cabins had been awakened by Larry's screams and a group examination of Larry's bag had uncovered the deception, Trevor fessed up and admitted he had been in the wrong. That is an essential first step—taking responsibility for his actions. Trevor and Larry and I will discuss an appropriate punishment when we are back in our own house (thank God!) tomorrow afternoon.

SUNDAY, AUGUST 14

Our vacation at the quarry did not end well, though no one was really at fault for that. After the upsets of Friday night, Larry was a bit of a wreck, and when I sent him to buy the ingredients for our final night's cookout, he did not pay attention to what he was doing. (I should have never let him shop, but I was marinating the lamb and sampling a good local cabernet.) I told him to get salad greens, so he went to the store in Brainardsville and picked up three sacks of endive, prewashed. Somehow he had absentmindedly forgotten all about the endive boycott Russ is leading. And as if that weren't bad enough, the dope then buys M. Foler Tuohy Brand All-Organic Hawaiian Endive, in the package with M. Foler Tuohy's picture on it! Larry set about making the salad when he got back and left the wrappers lying out on the counter, where of course they were the very first things to catch Russ's eye when he came by with Destiny and Antony to join us for the meal.

Well, one look at those wrappers and Russ completely fell apart. You can hardly blame him. The whole label is M. Foler

Tuohy's round face, with two stalks of endive on either side of it, a big smile, and sparkle lines coming off his eyes. Russ had to be sedated, basically. His kids dosed him with the strongest pills they had brought along and put him to bed. It was a rather downbeat end to our stay.

MONDAY, AUGUST 15

Home again, home again! So wonderful not to be in that awful cabin and not to have to worry so much about brown recluse spiders (although I am going through our luggage item by item with oven mitts on to make sure none of the spiders "hitched a ride" in our things!). Larry is happy not to have to drive so far to work. Trevor and Kyle are back in day camp for what's called the Last Stragglers Session. I think camp activities now are mainly watching videos in the picnic shelter. At least it gets the kids out of the house.

Trevor's punishment is that he can't watch videos at home for a week. Instead he has to read for half an hour every day. We needed to be so hard on him in order that he will know he mustn't pull such a stunt ever again. And I am going to talk to Trevor's therapist, when we go back to seeing him, about adding a medication with components to block out pranks.

TUESDAY, AUGUST 16

All of us book group members have sorely missed our get-togethers, which were sort of suspended over the summer because of conflicts with vacation and travel plans. We can't wait to start up again—our next meeting will be in a few weeks. Sandra made an interesting suggestion for our next book. She said that we've been concentrating on the horrible Bush administration, but the Reagan administration, way back when, was even worse in many ways, and we might enjoy books on that topic just as much. She recommended *Liars, Thieves, and Morons: A Catalog of Reagan's Henchmen*, by Audra Partridge and Kevin Schultz. It sounds perfect for us, and we are all ordering it right away.

WEDNESDAY, AUGUST 17

Russ, that bad-luck lightning rod, just cannot catch a break. This morning he came by in a terrible state because he has received notice from the company that manages the quarry informing him of a judgment against him for importing a nonnative wildlife species, namely, the prairie dogs that Destiny and Antony brought on the vacation. The kids thought it would be easier to take the prairie dogs in cages they made themselves from Popsicle sticks, rather than schlepping the whole terrarium. They really were cute little cages—I saw them—but apparently some of the animals chewed through them and escaped. Now the quarry has a prairie dog infestation that is changing the entire ecosystem, and Russ is on the hook for all related expenses. I do not think the unfortunate man will actually make it. He is very overwrought, as anyone would be.

THURSDAY, AUGUST 18

One of the tornadoes that touched down in our vicinity last month apparently moved the Stuff, Etc . . . store off its foundation and cracked some load-bearing beams, so the whole building has been shuttered by the county pending an inspection. The store has moved to a temporary site next door—the huge concrete slab with weeds growing on it where the cat food plant used to be. Now the Stuff, Etc . . . trucks park out there with their back doors open and you drive from truck to truck. You pull your shopping cart on a trailer hitch they give you (for a

returnable deposit), and you're not allowed to put anything into
your car until you go through the checkout ramps. Margaret says
it's a good system, and the prices are now even more reasonable,
but . . . I don't know. Does a bunch of trucks parked on a concrete slab really qualify as a store? I'm not switching back from
U-Drug-It. I am more of a traditionalist, I guess.

FRIDAY, AUGUST 19
It sounds like the Hendersonites have made good progress at
Kyle's school. I am told they are completely redoing all the rest-
rooms and have taken out the old fixtures and copper pipes.

SATURDAY, AUGUST 20
Some of the parents have voiced concern that the Hendersonites
are melting down the pipes in small forges they have in their
vehicles and are converting the copper into jewelry and imita-
tion coins. The Hendersonites say they do not want to do this but
are required to by state law. Unfortunately all state offices have
been shut down since June and will not reopen until after Columbus Day, so it is difficult to check.

SUNDAY, AUGUST 21
Spent a wonderful day reading *Liars, Thieves, and Morons*, which
really is like a prequel to the Bush books we've concentrated on
so far. Some of the same people appeared in the Reagan administration, such as Cheney and Rumsfeld, who were younger then, of
course, but just as big assholes. Plus, *Liars, Thieves, and Morons*
has some characters whom I remembered only vaguely but who,
as the book shows, were actually complete horrors, like James
Watt. I enjoyed learning a little bit more about him. All in all, an
excellent read!

MONDAY, AUGUST 22

More questions raised about the Hendersonites' construction methods—this time, their selling bricks from the school at booths on Main Street. When asked about this practice, they again cited state-mandated red tape and urged the school board to take their concerns to the appropriate officials in the capital. When the state offices reopen, I think we certainly should do so, in the interest of removing government interference from what is, after all, a purely local issue.

TUESDAY, AUGUST 23

Larry goes back to Nigeria on Friday. Something came up with the job he had been doing there, and his presence is required again, apparently. I do not know all the details. Even though the kidnapping scare was just a false alarm, and the result of miscommunication, still I have some lingering questions about Larry's safety. Without telling him, I stated these questions in a text to the Boss/Client this morning, and he texted back, saying the company has hired a Nigerian security firm for Larry's protection. The firm's people will do their oversight unobtrusively, however, and Larry will not even know they are there.

I was not supposed to reveal this to Larry, so as not to make him self-conscious while he works, but I told him anyway. I said I had gotten in touch with the Client/Boss—i.e., I just told the truth. Larry barely heard me, because he is so excited to be going back to the Promised Land of Capacitors.

WEDNESDAY, AUGUST 24

In no uncertain terms I let it be known that if Larry buys any more capacitors while he is on this trip, I will take the children and leave him and, for good measure, burn the house to the ground. I do not know if the message got through.

THURSDAY, AUGUST 25

Keeping what you have found means letting go of the belief that you still possess what you have already lost.   —Joachim Mesoander, 657 B.C.E.

Finding, losing, learning to let go, and finding once again are the daily measures of our lives. As we see in this meditation by Joachim Mesoander from so long ago, losing things has been the sad destiny of humanity since day one. For example, I have lost my trust in that worm M. Foler Tuohy, which is partly why I have turned to the ancients such as Joachim Mesoander. And simply on a daily basis, I lose all kinds of essential items, like for example right at this exact moment—MY FUCKING GODDAMN CELL PHONE!

Isn't it funny how upset we can become from such a minor matter? What does it mean, really, to lose one's cell phone? Especially when it is often so easily recovered, as I am about to do right now, simply by calling my cell phone from our house's landline and listening for my cell phone's distinctive ring. And so I call, and . . . I do not hear my cell phone. Maybe it is in my coat pocket . . . No, I open the closet door, no ring . . . I find my purse and look in it . . . nothing ringing there . . .

All right, it occurs to me that perhaps I left my cell phone in the car. So I go out in the driveway, I open the car door, and— AHA! Yes, I hear my cell phone's distinctive ring. Success!

However, upon examination, it appears that my cell phone has fallen between the driver's seat and the metal slide-thingy that slides the seat back and forth. Okay, I will reach under, but unfortunately . . . fucking goddamn unfortunately . . . I cannot reach the fucking goddamn cell phone, which is still fucking annoyingly goddamn ringing! I can even see the light from my cell phone display the dark under the slide rail thingy, BUT I CANNOT REACH THE GODDAMN CELL PHONE!!! I simply cannot FUCKING GODDAMN REACH THE GODDAMN THING!!! All right, you fucking thing, I'll get a fucking crowbar from Larry's tool bin on the patio and I will FUCKING PRY UP THE GODDAMN RAIL THINGY UNTIL—YES!—I REACH THE GODDAMN CELL PHONE!!

"Hello? . . . Hello?" Nobody there. Oh, I forgot—I was the one who called. Okay, never mind. Okay, I have the cell phone. It looks as if the goddamn car seat is now about three inches from the fucking steering wheel, what with the bend I put in the rail thingy, but what the hell. Let Larry worry about that when he gets home.

FRIDAY, AUGUST 26

He worried about it, all right, and pried it so much with the crowbar that now the seat is so far back that I could barely reach the pedals as I drove him to the airport this morning, but I darn sure could reach the horn as I honked at the GODDAMN FUCK-ING IDIOTS in the obligatory goddamn airport fucking traffic jam blocking the goddamn Arrivals lane, which Larry pointed out we did not want to be in, and I asked him, "Why do we not want to be in it? Aren't we ARRIVING at the goddamn airport?" and he said, for Christ's sake, no—Departures was what we wanted, because he is departing for Nigeria. As if that made any fucking goddamn sense.

So I screamed various other things at him and at an asshole taxi driver, who screamed back, and Larry jumped out at the curb, and our leavetaking was not as affectionate and mutually sup-portive as it might have been.

SATURDAY, AUGUST 27

Oh, friends, my spirit is once again "down in the dumps" on this rainy Saturday morning, with the kids bouncing off the walls, too bored to play their video games, although they can still watch TV, thank God—they rarely get to where they will not even do that.

I believe parents and caregivers all over the world should go down on their knees once a day in gratitude for television. But Gramma Pat taught me not to be a complainer, so instead today in my terrible mood I am having a pick-me-up vodka gimlet with lip-smacking tart, bright green lime juice—oh, so tasty!—and not thinking about how I am stuck with the kids now for TWO GODDAMN WEEKS while Larry is in fucking Nigeria again and I have to handle everything here by my goddamn self including all the hoo-raw involved in getting the kids back in school, not that he's ever much help when he's here, but still.

No, rather than complaining, I will enjoy the simple pleasures of the moment, as Gramma Pat would advise. This vodka gimlet with tart, sweet, tropically green lime juice was so delicious and restorative that I believe I will mix myself a whole pitcher of them!

SUNDAY, AUGUST 28

Once when I was a little girl I asked Gramma Pat what made her so wise, and she said she had a secret she would show me. Lighting up a Chesterfield and putting two packs into the pocket of her apron along with a big box of "strike anywhere" matches (the old-fashioned kind that they don't make anymore), she led me to a big old maple tree in her and Grampa Hub's backyard. "My wisdom comes from right here," she said, rubbing the bark with her old, wrinkled, nicotine-stained fingers while the Chesterfield dangled precariously from her mouth. "I call this my Wisdom (and Smoking Chesterfields) Tree." Then she showed me how to sit at the base of the tree with my back against it and let the tree's quiet strength work its way through me. A little place among the roots was perfect for stubbing out her butts and she settled in next to it while I snuggled beside her. Next to my gramma and that big old tree I never felt so protected in my life, and I went back to it often, until the lease they had on that house expired and they had to move out by the racetrack.

MONDAY, AUGUST 29

Today is my birthday. I never say how old I am, and I don't see anything wrong in that. I also don't make a big deal about celebrating the day, because as the years go by, what is there to celebrate? A nice dinner out with Larry, a couple of presents, a card the kids made themselves—that is enough. I'm happy to change the subject, honestly.

But if you want an example of true deviousness and cleverness, check out the latest from the Client/Boss. Somehow he knew today is my birthday, and at about five in the afternoon he rolls up in the limo with flowers and champagne. I almost was not surprised, and suddenly I understood why the business that required Larry's presence in Nigeria had to be taken care of now. Friends, it may not be my place to say it, but the Boss/Client is a wreck. If he weren't who he is, I would say he is almost as big a wreck as Russ. I swear his hands were shaking as he came up the walk. I did not let him in the house, but I politely accepted the flowers and champagne, then sent him on his way. He complimented the blouse I had on and said I looked "amazing." (And yes, I had gotten dressed up for purposes of basic morale on my birthday, and I did not entirely hate that he noticed that.) But what is it with this guy? Maybe I supply him with the necessary nutrient of rejection that he can get nowhere else in his life.

I went back inside, popped the champagne, and drank it all straight from the bottle like soda. Oh, gracious, did I get sick, after! I let the kids fix their own dinner. Larry didn't call, but he texted "Happy Birthday." Another birthday, in the books.

TUESDAY, AUGUST 30

Summer is so fleeting. As another summer goes by, I realize that's really the whole point of summer. Midsummer days seem so long that they give you the illusion of time suspended and unmoving, when really it's going by so fast it might as well be in the past already.

I feel mournful this morning with my coffee cup, my friends, as I see the first few yellow leaves in the hickory tree. Last night the ceiling pestered me with remarks about the Boss/Client and how I'm treating him. Oh, I truly despise the ceiling and its big mouth that sort of grows out of its white flatness when it comes to life at about 3:00 a.m. It never shuts up when I want it to shut up, that ceiling. Last night it was making unflattering observations about my character, saying I was just as ruthless as the Client/Boss, and heartless, too. I did not give the horrible obnoxious ceiling the satisfaction of arguing back, merely said, "Shut up shut up shut up shut up shut up," with a pillow over my head. But if I *had* argued back, I would have said that it's impossible to mistreat people like the Boss/Client. You can tell them all kinds of awful things right to their faces and they don't even hear you, it's like they're walking around the world in hazmat suits, and the hell with him anyway, let him find somebody as rich and powerful as himself to bother, and pay his goddamn fair share of taxes, and leave Larry and me alone.

Somehow none of my arguments made me feel much better. I may still be having a reaction from the champagne.

WEDNESDAY, AUGUST 31
Such a wonderful surprise, at the Parent-Student Welcome Back and Housewarming event this afternoon at Kyle's school! The Hendersonites have done a fabulous job! In all the years of our kids going there, the school has never looked so good. The construction problems we labored on last year have been repaired, the classrooms are all replastered, and the cracked linoleum has finally been replaced. The Multi-Purpose Room has reopened, with a colorful mural depicting scenes from Hendersonite history on the walls. Everyone was exclaiming over how bright and clean

the whole school is. The windows are so new they still have labels pasted on them, saying SHIP TO SUMMIT RURAL SCHOOL DISTRICT NO. 5 (whatever *that* may be). And the brand-new school buses! The workers say that they got them at less than cost as factory seconds because they are scratched (although I did not see any scratches, personally), and that the lettering on the buses, U.S. ARMY CORRECTIONAL FACILITY, FORT BENNING, GA, can be painted out.

After everyone had been given a tour, the Hendersonites explained that some of their families would be living in what used to be the kindergarten and first-grade classrooms to supervise the transition. They will also be buying and selling automobiles and parts, as they have been doing all along. The school board had already agreed to these conditions—as how could they not, after the fine job these folks have done? Kindergartners and first graders will have to double up in the second-grade classrooms, which may be a bit inconvenient for those pupils, but it will not affect us because Kyle is in the fourth grade.

I cannot tell you what a great joy it is, friends, finally to have this school problem taken care of. When I think of all the work we put in, and the little amount of progress we made! Just to see the Hendersonites' interesting vehicles of all description with many different license plates from North and South America parked around our school building is a geography lesson in itself. We are looking forward to their schoolwide presentation about their culture, which will be in just a few weeks. I can see that the fall is shaping up to be exciting, friends—a glorious opportunity to learn, for kids and parents both!

SEPTEMBER

THURSDAY, SEPTEMBER 1

> *The September fields lay green and lovely*
> *Just as faithless summer left them.*
> —M. Foler Tuohy *(deceased)*

I have decided that I can stand to quote occasional lines by M. Foler Tuohy if I regard him as a poet who lived and died a long time ago. The addition of a simple "(deceased)" or "(dec'd)" after his name improves it a whole lot, I've found, and the poems and other writings are even more affecting in light of the fatal accident I imagine having befallen him.

Tuohy is very perceptive, we must admit, about these tag-end days of summer. They are like a pitiful, mortally wounded animal walking on in ignorance that, for all practical purposes, it has already died. I had been meaning to spend these tag-end days drying berries for winter storage by placing them on cookie sheets on top of our car out in the driveway in the blazing sun. Berries dried this way keep well, retain their fresh, wild flavor, and make welcome high-vitamin snacks in kids' or spouses' lunches. I planned to take you through the whole drying process, with reminders not to use old cookie sheets impregnated with years of cooking oil, because the oil will give the berries a disagreeable taste; however, after I had put out sixteen quarts of berries on new cookie sheets all over the car roof and luggage rack, and as I was waiting for the sun to do its work, I temporarily suffered a minor brain malfunction and forgot that they were up there, and drove off in the car to do an errand. As I accelerated quickly out of the driveway, the cookie sheets, quite naturally, went flying off the roof with a clatter, and they and all the berries were run over by many cars. I cursed quite a bit, and I almost got run over myself in a stupid attempt to salvage just a few elements of this goddamn fucking stupid totally unnecessary catastrophe.

The reason, in fact, that I am not cursing bloody murder right now about this mishap is that I have taken a few of the pills I saved from that remainder-bin batch that got me through the closet reorganization in July. I vaguely remember that these pills had bad consequences, but I don't care. They are indeed "mellow," as the elderly clerk at U-Drug-It assured me.

FRIDAY, SEPTEMBER 2

Awoke this morning and drank several cups of 38-percent-more-caffeine coffee, that old standby, hoping it would counter the continuing effect of the pills. It did, sort of—with the result that half of me was going about ninety miles an hour while the other half remained cement. I found this to be sort of an interesting combination—not that I would really recommend it, because the two mental states didn't exactly add up to normal. My right eye would barely open while my left was rather prominent and bugging out, with an enlarged pupil. Kyle asked if I was doing that on purpose, as I was driving him and Trevor to the mall to shop for school clothes. I said it was part of a yoga exercise. Both kids accepted that. They remember the time they had to get me unstuck from the lotus position, and I suppose compared to that a strange facial expression is no big deal.

SATURDAY, SEPTEMBER 3

It's been a while since we've heard from Larry. I'm not really worried that he's in danger, but if he's on a hunt for more capacitors I hate to think what might be the outcome. I am not going to contact Boss/Client about him again. I intend to keep all communication with that person to a minimum, thank you.

SUNDAY, SEPTEMBER 4

Took the kids, and Destiny and Antony, to the county fair. It really was lots of fun, with all the rides and the exhibits and booths. In the evening I sat on a bench by the kiddie rides and read *Liars, Thieves, and Morons* and let the kids wander wherever they wanted, saying only that the four of them had to stick together and check back with me every hour. As an extra precaution I told Destiny and Antony to watch Trevor and report to me if they felt he needed to be restrained. That might seem a lot to ask of five-year-olds, but they are very responsible, and in fact had already won Best of Show in the eight-years-old-and-under category for their series of tempera paintings, *Medicating the Chronic Depressive*, part of the fair's youth science competition sponsored by Medium Pharma. Their portrait of Russ was a remarkable likeness, I thought.

I was sitting not far from the water-gun booth, where contestants squirt water from little machine guns into target balloons that fill up and then explode, and then a bell rings and people cheer and the winner gets a saltwater-taffy horseshoe. I put the book down and listened to the pops of the balloons in the background, and the calliope sounds of the rides, and the crazy laugh from the Laugh in the Dark Haunted House. And the smells—the taffy, and the corn-dog fryer, and the catfish fryer, and the deep-fried cookie fryer, and the deep-fried cookie refryer.

But I missed the smell of cigarette smoke—because there wasn't any! That still seems strange to me. The county fair became a no-smoking zone some years ago. I remember how mad Gramma Pat was when they did that—"Who ever heard of a county fair you can't smoke at?" she said. When they made the parking lot no-smoking, too, that was it for her. For a while she used to sit in the parking lot on the tailgate of the station wagon with her Chesterfields when we went on the rides, and now she couldn't even do that. She vowed she would never go back and she never did.

The sun went down and all the fair's lights came on, and it got chilly, and my thoughts were almost *too* gloomy. I was glad when the kids came back and we could finally go home.

MONDAY, SEPTEMBER 5

Labor Day is a wonderful opportunity for us to regroup and clear the decks for another year. Some philosophers say that the real New Year's Day should be in the early fall, the way the Chinese do it, I believe. There's a lot of smart thinking in that approach. On Labor Day, a fall crispness in the air (if by chance it's not incredibly hot, as often is the case) promises a fruitful season both physically and spiritually. With the coming of the new season it's the perfect time to hit Restart.

Are you ready for what is up ahead? That is what I ask myself, and my answer is—God, no! Spare me! I do, however, enjoy a lovely autumn cocktail made with fresh apple cider, dark rum, a dash of grenadine, and a festive stick of real cinnamon for a stirrer. Too early yet for cider, you say? Not possible to go to the store and hunt up a stick of cinnamon? Out of grenadine? We still have rum, thank the good Lord. Let's pour a great big snifterful and make a Labor Day toast to labor, especially the unpaid domestic kind— i.e., you, my wonderful sustaining friends out there, and me.

TUESDAY, SEPTEMBER 6

Larry finally called last night, and right away I asked him if he had been buying any more capacitors. He knows what will happen if he does. He ducked the question, said he had inspected some of the shipment we are supposed to be receiving soon (according to Archbishop Mfune), and raved a lot about how fabulous these Nigerian 000-series capacitors are. I asked him again if he had bought any more and he said, "No, no, no, not exactly." It turns out he has taken another huge batch of them on consignment. I guess he has not put down any money for them, just signed promissory agreements to remit funds only for what he can sell and return the unsold ones. He was in that ecstatic frame of mind again. Then the phone became staticky and the connection broke off.

Am I wrong to worry? I must try to keep a positive attitude about this potential goddamn fucking disaster I am sure Larry is leading us into.

WEDNESDAY, SEPTEMBER 7

Kyle swooned so much this morning I did not know what I would do. He was all pale, the poor little guy. I felt sorry for him and I hated to send him off to his first day of school in that condition, and without any breakfast. I did point out to him that the last time he fainted and broke out in hives was back in June, on the second-to-last day of school. He has been absolutely fine all summer. I tried to be reasonable—if he faints only when he has to go to school, and I keep him home whenever he faints, how will he ever go to school? He seemed to see the logic, and he manfully hefted his forty-five-pound backpack and started out the door. Oh, it pained me to see his unhappiness, it truly did. I told him to try not to faint today, especially in gym, and he promised he would do his best. Also, I reminded him not to be afraid of the Hendersonite hall monitors because they are really helpful and nice and cost-effective for the school district, and are there to help him learn. (He had said they scared him when we went to the opening last week.)

Trevor is off to middle school, an unknown territory. The for-profit company that runs our middle school does not publish any statistics or reveal proprietary information. I am assuming that they have a seventh grade and Trevor will be in it.

THURSDAY, SEPTEMBER 8

Kyle made it through day one, glory be! He is a brave little guy. And after some preliminary swoons this morning he went back for day two. Keeping my fingers crossed that I would not have to go and pick him up, I made a lunch date with Gail to celebrate our kids' being back at school.

Well, Gail and I went to Oso's and we had such a good time. We talked about all kinds of subjects, and oh, friends, I finally told her everything about the Client/Boss. I omitted no detail, confident I can trust her not to tell anybody.

Gail listened carefully and then came out with a remark that surprised me. She said, "It sounds as if this guy is in love." Somehow the idea had never occurred to me—I mean, that the Client/Boss might have human-type feelings like anybody. You could've knocked me over with a feather. Gail went on to explain that certain people go through life all the way into their forties or fifties (the Boss/Client is fifty-five or so) never having been in love, and then suddenly they find themselves experiencing it, and they have no idea what to do. It overwhelms them and causes them to behave crazily. It's as if they've caught some illness like measles that most people develop an immunity to in childhood. They are rendered helpless.

That's an interesting possibility, I guess, but it doesn't give me much of a notion about what I should do (if anything). It was a real relief to talk to Gail, however. She is so smart, and such a sweetie pie!

FRIDAY, SEPTEMBER 9

So, speak of the devil, the Client/Boss pulled up in the ol' white limousine this morning. He should just put some velvet ropes or something out there in front of the house and reserve himself a space. He gets out, walks up the sidewalk like the world's most proper undertaker, and knocks on the door. Again he says he has something to tell me and asks to come in. I let him in, he sits down, I sit down. Then he tells me that he has some terrible news—Larry fell in the sauna at his hotel in Nigeria and hit his head and died. Normally such a shocker would have upset me, but I did not take it too seriously, because I was at that very moment talking to Larry on the phone. Boss/Client had not noticed I was holding our cordless telephone in my hand. I simply passed it to him and let Larry clear up the misunderstanding.

As I've observed Client/Boss's face and how it reacts to unexpected news, I've noticed that it can go from white to red like one of those megabillboards in the city that flash different messages and change the light on the entire street for a block. This time it continued from red to fiery crimson, most likely from deep relief combined with embarrassment. How can he keep getting such unreliable information? He and Larry had a short conversation straightening things out. Then he hurried back to his limo almost without saying goodbye. File under: Strange!

SATURDAY, SEPTEMBER 10

Larry got in late last night. I didn't go pick him up but let him take a taxi home. He is very happy about his growing capacitors "empire," which he says will make us wealthy. For business purposes, he allowed Archbishop Mfune to baptize him in the Nigerian Apostolic Church—a very moving ceremony, he said—and he also accepted a position as Deacon Pro-tem of a church in Lagos that some of the best capacitor experts attend. I believe he

is even developing a bit of a Nigerian accent. He says he has
found himself a second country that feels like home.

SUNDAY, SEPTEMBER 11

Trevor's therapist was late for the seven o'clock appointment this
morning. He drove into the lot just as we were getting out of our
car, and I could read his lips through his windshield as he spotted us and said, "Oh, no!" Really, if he cannot be more positive
about the patients who pay his fees, he should find another line
of work.

Again I sat in the car and waited while Trevor had his appointment. The pieces of tree are still stuck in the chain-link
fence as they will be for eternity, I expect. As I looked at them, I
tried to think about nothing. Do you ever do that? It's hard, because you end up thinking about something no matter how hard
you try. I tried to imagine a huge white mattress stretching as far
as one could see in any direction. That's not nothing, but it's
close to nothing. But then I imagined the mattress cover—I
could not help myself—and then I started thinking about how it
always pops off the corners of the mattress. And then I started
quietly cursing about mattress covers in general and how much
I fucking hate when that happens. There's nothing you can do
about it but lift up the corner of the goddamn heavy mattress
and put the mattress cover back in place, but then it comes off
again! Goddamn it, it is annoying. So in the end, my attempt to
think about nothing was not a success.

When the hour was over I went in to get Trevor and I had a
few words in private with the therapist. I informed him of Trevor's
part in the brown recluse spider incident and asked what kind of
adjustment to Trevor's medication would take care of that type
of problem. The therapist just looked at me for a long time. Then
he said he would get back to me about it next week.

I'm thinking it may be time to start shopping for another therapist. But it was such a long process to find this one!

MONDAY, SEPTEMBER 12

Kyle brought home a packet from school today that explains the school's new Hendersonite-based curriculum. According to certain educational theories, children learn better in an environment that stresses practical skills like comparing paint samples through prayer. These real-life-oriented teaching methods are said to promote development of the knowledge acquisition areas of the brain in children ages five through twelve. The packet also contained a lot of interesting facts for parents' or caregivers' information. I had not known, for example, that President James A. Garfield was a practicing Hendersonite. That may have been why he was assassinated.

TUESDAY, SEPTEMBER 13

Today, friends, we are going to put on some old clothes, roll up our sleeves, and clean out the refrigerator! Yes, it's an often disagreeable task, but it has to be done sometime, and we can whistle while we work and try to make it interesting. So, please join me this morning for:

Getting Down and Dirty with the Vegetable Drawers: A Cursing Mommy Trek into the Wilds of the Refrigerator!
To do a really first-class job on the refrigerator you must build up a good head of steam before you start. And how to do that? First, find the right energy drink. I have noticed that athletes and other active people drink a lot of beer, so that's what I will try today. Normally I don't enjoy beer—it's too fattening and causes bloat— but today I'm making an exception because this twelve-pack of

Grain Land Lager has been in the basement since who knows when. It is warm, which is not ideal, but of course inside the refrigerator the temperature will be cool, so that will balance out.

Excuse me—isn't that a nuisance? Before I even open my first can, I must answer the telephone. Let's hold that thought, and I'll be back in a moment.

WEDNESDAY, SEPTEMBER 14

The moment stretched into many hours as I had to go to the goddamn assisted living and replace "Dad's" supply of toiletries. I've been sending bottles of Jade East goddamn cologne supposedly at his request, and he really has been going through it at an amazing rate. When I arrived there yesterday after Sabrina's call, I noticed that all the attendants smelled of Jade East, too. That is probably just a coincidence—it's a popular scent, after all—but I still don't quite understand how my fucking father is using two twelve-ounce atomizers of Jade East per week. Well, the old wretch always did love his cologne.

THURSDAY, SEPTEMBER 15

One very important key to maintaining our daily sanity is a simple scheduling tactic I call Putting Things the Hell Off. Today I am Putting the Hell Off Cleaning the Fucking Refrigerator, and the reason is simple: I just don't fucking feel like it. Looking at my calendar I see a whole raft of blank days during the rest of my life that I can devote to this stupid task, when perhaps I will be in more of a refrigerator-cleaning frame of mind.

FRIDAY, SEPTEMBER 16

I feel even less like cleaning the refrigerator today, but the problem is that it is starting to develop a rather overpowering aroma.

In fact, every time the refrigerator door is opened, the inner compartments release a breath of God knows what. However, I have the perfect solution: Jade East cologne! Instead of sending these latest atomizers to my fucking father, I'll just give the inside of the refrigerator a good Jade East spray-over!

I am kidding, of course. I would never do such a thing. But I do have a suggestion for myself that perhaps you, my friends out there, can also benefit from. We all know that a simple box of baking soda, opened and left to sit on a back shelf in the middle of the refrigerator, will absorb odors. Well, if one box will do that, how much more effective will a dozen boxes be! I have gone to U-Drug-It and purchased a whole case of baking soda and opened all the contents into this very large mixing bowl. Now I put the mixing bowl in the refrigerator with a simple readjustment—GODDAMN FUCKING MAYONNAISE—of the racks and some of the goddamn items in here, and . . . presto! Maybe all the unpleasant refrigerator odor will be gone.

As a reward for this great idea, I am putting my feet up on a stray box of capacitors in the living room and opening one of these Grain Land Lagers and—*ptuie! Yuck! How do people drink this stuff??!!* Please hold on, friends, while I pour this disgusting swill down the sink and throw the other eleven cans in the trash!! I guess beer is not like wine with that whole improving-with-age thing. I believe these particular beers are from a neighborhood association meeting five or seven years ago. Remind me never to drink seven-year-old beer again. I'd brush my teeth but I don't think that would help. *Gahhh!* I want to scrub my tongue.

SATURDAY, SEPTEMBER 17

Sphagnum Health has a new system of premium adjustment where the company sends small armored vans into local neighborhoods to collect subscribers' extra valuables they might not need anymore. The vans are convenient, because they will actually go house-to-house. If you have any jewelry, let's say, or gold-plate dinnerware, or sterling silver serving dishes you no longer think you need, you just give them to the Sphagnum Health van and their onboard computerized valuables appraiser tells you how much each item is worth and what will be deducted from your next premium. It's simple and money saving, all in one.

Russ, for example, has basically stripped their whole house of all nonessential household objects. Due to his recent hospital- ization, he has very high premiums, which he wants to reduce as much as possible. I believe that Destiny and Antony now keep the basic pots and pans and flatware locked in a chest in their room. So, following his example, and looking to add some extra dollars to the family budget, I gathered up the collection of ster- ling silver berry spoons left to me by Gramma Pat—she always told me they were owned by Betsy Ross, a distant relative—when I heard the van's bell coming down the street.

But as I stepped out the front door, I suddenly thought, "ARE YOU OUT OF YOUR FUCKING MIND?" and simply gave the Sphagnum Health van the finger and went back in the house. What goddamn difference does it make? Our rates will probably go up 27 percent in October anyway.

SUNDAY, SEPTEMBER 18

Do you sometimes have what I call "Of course!" moments? Mo- ments when some previously hidden or forgotten truth reveals itself all of a sudden in a flash out of the blue, and you say to your- self, "Of course!"? These moments can be the blessed illumina- tions and inspirations of our lives—or, sometimes, not. Sometimes the truths we see at those moments can be rather painful experi- ences that teach us about life.

Take this morning, for example. I got back from driving Trevor to and from the therapist, and then I set to work making a vinai- grette sauce for the salad I will bring to our book group meeting tonight. It's a big salad—there are now seventeen or nineteen people in book group!—so I mixed a really huge amount of vinaigrette. It has some real mayonnaise in it, so I thought I'd better keep the vinaigrette in the refrigerator 'til this evening, when I would add it to the salad. As I put the container of vinaigrette on the top shelf of the refrigerator, it bumped against a little jar of maraschino cherries we keep there for no known reason, and somehow the container tipped over, and all the vinaigrette spilled out into the bowl of baking soda on the lower shelf below it.

So what was my "Of course!" moment? Simply, this: If you combine vinegar (the main ingredient in vinaigrette) with baking soda, it sort of . . . explodes! "Of course!" I had forgotten about that. In school, my brother used to make baking-soda-and-vinegar volcanoes every year for earth science. He would mix the two ingredients together, along with some red food coloring, and create a lifelike eruption that always got an A. So, "Of course!" in my refrigerator, the fucking goddamn spilled vinegar and the goddamn fucking baking soda went *Fooof!* and foamed and bubbled and surged up all over the FUCKING GODDAMN inside of the stupid FUCKING GODDAMN RUMSFELD-LIKE GODDAMN REFRIGERATOR!!!

. . . Creating a HUGE GODDAMN FUCKING MESS!!! GODDAMN FUCKING ARI FLEISCHER AND THE BUSH ADMINISTRATION, AND FUCKING MARGARET THATCHER, TOO!!! GOD, HOW I DESPISE THEM, AND THIS FUCKING GODDAMN STUPID HORRIBLE GODDAMN HALLIBURTON REFRIGERATOR MESS!!!

"Of course!"

MONDAY, SEPTEMBER 19

I won't even describe the awful cleanup I had to wade into and the big garbage bags of ruined food and scrubbing everything down and taking out the racks and the vegetable drawers and so on. It was simply awful and I cursed until Larry said he was going to install a Swear Jar where I would have to pay a quarter for every curse word I said. Ha! What a joke! (He was not being serious, because the idea is impractical.)

No, what I want to tell about instead was last night's book group. Oh, it was a riot! First we watched a video Angie and M. Foler Tuohy had sent. They were on this Hawaiian cliff with the ocean in the background and describing their new life. Angie is very tan and looks relaxed, which made some of us envious, though I kept my thoughts about that to myself. M. Foler Tuohy (deceased) read from his new poetry collection, which either is "boldly erotic" or is titled *Boldly Erotic*, I forget which. The video included a commercial for M. Foler Tuohy brand endive. We are divided about whether we will ever purchase that brand of endive again.

Then we had dinner and talked about *Liars, Thieves, and Morons*, which everybody had really gotten into because of how perfectly horrible the Reagan administration turned out to have been. We were interrupting one another and laughing, and one or two people (besides me) were cursing, and Susan pointed out an interesting footnote in the book's "Minor Functionaries" section, which listed bagmen, petty thugs, and so on. There was the name of Sandor A. Stattsman (currently of Sphagnum Health)! Who would've guessed? It even had a little photo. He looked the same, except with hair.

TUESDAY, SEPTEMBER 20

And after all that my salad was a big hit! Almost all of it was eaten. We discussed how Sandor A. Stattsman got into the book, and what exactly he had been up to in Central America, and whether he was as much of a toad back then (we decided not, just barely). As the evening was ending, the tail of the typhoon that's been in the area hit with such a huge volume of water that it washed out parts of the long driveway to Sandra's house (where we were meeting), and each one of us's car had to be winched back to the highway by the AAA guy from prison whom we called. I did not get home until 1:30 a.m., rather wet and bedraggled, but very pleased with the meeting overall and looking forward to our next.

WEDNESDAY, SEPTEMBER 21

I still do not have any idea what is going on in Trevor's school. All the students there must sign nondisclosure contracts. After much cajoling, I got him to concede that there is a seventh grade and he is in it. Other than that, anybody's guess is as good as mine.

THURSDAY, SEPTEMBER 22

It is always Thursday.   —*Paul Tillich*

Friends, by any chance, have you noticed this fact, too? I don't know how or why it should be true, but somehow or other, it *always* seems to be Thursday (as it is today). You wake up, you remember it is Thursday, and you wonder, "Wasn't it Thursday just a few minutes ago? And now it is Thursday AGAIN already? How can that be?"

Some philosophers, like the eminent theologian and auto insurance executive Paul Tillich, explain that we live in a permanent present, and everything that was before, is now, and shall be exists simultaneously in it—and it all happens to be Thursday! There are actual math proofs of this, I am told.

FRIDAY, SEPTEMBER 23

Today the local papers are full of the prairie dog invasion that has taken over the state park up by the quarry, with Russ always mentioned prominently as the one at fault. The unlucky guy certainly could do without the notoriety! He is quoted with a long spiel about how M. Foler Tuohy is really to blame, although the connection is rather tenuous, as the newspaper editorial points out. Many prairie dogs drowned in the recent typhoon, which won Russ the ire of animal-rights groups, but some prairie dogs also floated into new areas and established colonies there, so several homeowners' organizations are demanding redress as well. Russ called us up early this morning really beside himself.

SATURDAY, SEPTEMBER 24

Larry is feeling more confident about his job because of a lateral promotion he just received, which involves no raise in pay (natch) or any other benefit but does come with a new title. The only real upside is that Larry now thinks he can take an occasional Saturday off. So today he and Kyle and Trevor have gone to the air show.

So, friends, on this September Saturday I am "home alone," as the saying goes. How to spend this time? Well, I'll tell you what I did. Just for fun I did some looking into the ol' Client/Boss's background online. And do you know what I found? Before thirteen years ago, when he founded the company that owns Larry's firm and made him his billions and so on—NOTHING! Isn't that strange?

I could not help myself, and I sent Boss/Client a text message asking, "What were you doing in 1998?" So far I have heard nothing back. That is very unlike the Client/Boss.

SUNDAY, SEPTEMBER 25

As I was driving Trevor to his therapist this morning, I thought I would catch him off guard, and I asked, "So, do you like your new algebra teacher as much as Miss Bellardi?" (She was the teacher last year who had a soft spot for Trevor and persuaded the school not to file charges. Once or twice he said he didn't hate her.) But, no luck. If I thought I would get him to reveal anything about his school this year, I was wrong, because he quickly put me in my place with a recitation of the confidentiality clause in his nondisclosure contract. And all from memory! Pretty impressive.

MONDAY, SEPTEMBER 26

Early fall is the time to plant those springtime bulbs—your crocuses and tulips and daffodils and so on. We can make this a rewarding task as we daydream about the super show of floral colors we are laying up in our lawns and gardens, ready to unfurl next spring. If you live in a place with squirrels, as I do, you know that the little dickenses will chow down on the delectable bulbs as soon as they are planted, so we must remember to protect them before putting them in the ground.

One effective way to do this is by wrapping each bulb individually in fine-mesh chicken wire. That is what I am doing today. I have this great big rather unwieldy roll of wire and I am using these metal shears to cut out sections in which to wrap the bulbs. It's time-consuming work, but it pays off, as we will see. (The wire will not hinder the bulbs from sprouting, if we were wondering about that.)

Chicken wire certainly is not the easiest material to work with. It sort of bends around in directions you might not want it to go—ouch!—but you must be firm with it—doggone it!—it just slipped out of my hands, but luckily I'm wearing gloves, but that isn't completely a help because it makes me more awkward, and now the wire has *hooked a loop of my goddamn sweater,* and as I try to unhook it—hey, wait!—the goddamn sweater starts to . . . UNRAVEL, goddamn it, goddamn it, stop that, ouch, and as I pull more on the goddamn fucking stupid Cheney-like fucking goddamn chicken wire it pulls more yarn out of the fucking sweater, goddamn THE WHOLE SWEATER IS FUCKING UNRAVELING, so I take this aluminum softball bat that's here on the goddamn patio where the kids left it and SMASH THIS GODDAMN CHICKEN WIRE FLAT, GODDAMN FUCK-ING USELESS GROVER NORQUIST GODDAMN FUCKING CHICKEN WIRE DISAPPEARING SWEATER GODDAMN FUCK ALL!!!

[smash crash hammer bash yell smash crash smash]

[pause]

Well, I guess that pretty much does it for the chicken wire. Looks like the sweater has had the schnitzel, too. Oh, well, I sup-pose I can find another gardening sweater among our assorted rags. Actually, it's not so bad lying here amid the chicken wire and the bulbs and the softball bat on the goddamn driveway by the patio. The asphalt has a smell that I find sort of soothing. In just a minute I'm going to get up.

[pause]

Oh, what a fucking horrible autumn I am sure this is going to be.

TUESDAY, SEPTEMBER 27
"This is the day which the Lord hath made. Let us rejoice and be glad in it."

I woke up this morning with this lovely Bible verse in my head, combined with a powerful desire to smash Sphagnum Health and steamroller my other enemies—but in a way that would be positive and life-affirming, as well.

WEDNESDAY, SEPTEMBER 28

Janeen, a new member of book group, has volunteered to make a whole survey of books about how awful Reagan was and report back to us with a recommendation. I can't wait to be reading about this topic again!

THURSDAY, SEPTEMBER 29

See what I mean about Thursdays?

FRIDAY, SEPTEMBER 30

Last night was the Hendersonites' presentation at the school: "Hulot Henderson: Teacher to the World." It was a big deal, with videos, old-time hymn-type songs, and a speech by a Hulot Henderson impersonator (the original having passed away in 1831). You could also get your fortune told in a special séance—lots of fun, and interesting, too. Larry learned he is soon to become very rich! (Capacitors, no doubt!) Apparently, the Hendersonites have been involved in the American educational system from the beginning. There were pictures of frontier Hendersonite learning clinics like the one Abraham Lincoln attended as a boy in Kentucky. After the presentation, we broke up into small groups for classroom visits. Kyle whispered that he still finds the Hendersonites scary and he does not want to memorize their carpet-sample charts. I told him that he has to, and that's that! He is lucky to be going to such an innovative school. When we got home, Larry had somehow misplaced his wallet.

OCTOBER

SATURDAY, OCTOBER 1

Friends, do you ever get those notices from your insurance company that say "This Is Not a Bill"? I got one of them today, and what it should have said is, "This Is Not a Bill—It's Worse!" Sphagnum Health, the official most horrible company in the entire world, sent us notice today that our monthly payments are going up 36 PERCENT!

How do you like that? Is that a kick in the pants, or what?

SUNDAY, OCTOBER 2

This morning as I was sitting in the parking lot at Trevor's therapist's office, I heard my old companion, the radio preacher from the crypt, talking about the Last Days. He said they had already occurred about twenty-eight to thirty-six weeks ago, but the present time has not yet caught up with them. This delay is unavoidable and actually prophesied in the Bible, according to the preacher, because Scripture (Numbers 1:37–38) reminds us that we should allow "from sixty to ninety days" for the Last Days to take effect. That waiting period has now passed, obviously. A lot of details still need to be worked out, or something, but as soon as the world registers that they have already happened, the Last Days will be upon us, and that will be the actual end. As I sat there, the car windows were icing over in this morning's temperature inversion and I could see nothing out the window. I was not looking forward to talking to the therapist at the end of Trevor's session, and in my mood of the moment I thought when the Last Days finally do arrive, and everything is finally over with, it might be a big relief, frankly.

But then I decided such a view is too negative. Don't you agree? Last Days—"Oh, fiddlesticks and fuck it all," as Gramma Pat used to say (except for that last part). I don't believe in any Last Days, just in the Current Ongoing Awful Goddamn Days We're Living in Right Now. They are challenging enough.

MONDAY, OCTOBER 3

Russ did not receive his "This Is Not a Bill" notice from Sphagnum Health until this morning, and it completely unhinged him, the poor guy. He called me up the minute he opened the envelope—why does he always call Larry or me?—and he was making a sort of *yip-yip-yip* sound, and weeping, and I imagined I could actually hear the little bubbles popping as he foamed from the mouth. Then there were these *thud* sounds as he ran around crashing himself into walls. I don't know what room of his house he was in, but it must have been one where he has already sold off the pictures and sconces and other wall hangings.

When he calmed down and was only wailing, he began to look at the problem rationally. He does have several options, after all. He could write a tell-all book dragging M. Foler Tuohy's name through the mud for a big amount of advance money, or perhaps simply threaten to do so. (I did not encourage him in this.) He could sell his car, although it is not a valuable one. Or, he suggested, he could simply present himself to Sphagnum Health, inform them that he gives up, and ask to live in the basement of their offices in return for letting them harvest his organs and vital fluids. To me that seemed the likeliest choice. But then what would he do with Antony and Destiny?

I talk about Russ—but what about Larry and me? We have the exact same problem and don't know what we will do, either.

TUESDAY, OCTOBER 4

Another "This Is Not a Bill" lulu—our car insurance also is going up! This one came with a personal note from our car insurance guy. He said that the increase was because word had gotten out among people in the industry that Trevor will be old enough to drive in three years. They are upping the premiums in advance sort of as an escrow contribution.

Great God in heaven, what next?

WEDNESDAY, OCTOBER 5

Long ago I learned never to ask "What next?" because life will surely bring you what *is* next, and it might be something you don't want even more than you didn't want what made you ask "What next?" in the first place. Exhibit A in this category is, of course, MY FUCKING FATHER! Sabrina called and he needs fifteen hundred dollars. No reason given—he just has to have it, and if it is not in his hands today he will shut off the building's electricity. She sounded quite desperate and put the director of the whole goddamn assisted living on the line, who was even more frantic than she. Apparently my fucking father has some sort of an in with the power company back from when he was a real estate tycoon. I did not know this, but my fucking father turned off the power once before. He was bought off with several cases of Rust-Oleum, which he resold. Now the price has gone up to fifteen hundred dollars. I suppose he splits it with the power company guys, or some damn thing.

Now I must go over to the goddamn assisted living to sort this mess out, wondering the entire time, quite reasonably, "Why doesn't my fucking goddamn father just fucking DIE?"

(Is that so terrible of me?)

THURSDAY, OCTOBER 6

So I get to the goddamn assisted living and my fucking father has completely forgotten about the whole business. People were tiptoeing around him but they didn't need to. The entire episode had fled his Swiss cheese mind. Instead he wanted to tell me, who he still thinks is Marjorie, that same old stupid not-true story about himself and the actress Dyan Cannon. His purpose was to make me, "Marjorie," jealous. Oh, won't he please, please, please just die?

FRIDAY, OCTOBER 7

Larry's wallet still has not turned up. It's been missing since the presentation at the school a week ago. We have searched high and low and I absolutely cannot imagine what could have become of it. Now he is going to have to cancel his credit cards and get his driver's license replaced, and all that hoo-ha. What a pain in the gluteus maximus!

SATURDAY, OCTOBER 8

Do the little things with great love, always, or I will give you such a smack!
—Mother Teresa (the younger)

On this Saturday morning amid the racket of family life, I retreat to a little nook under the basement stairs with my cup of coffee where Larry and the kids can't find me. It is time to look inside and take inventory, and friends, I hope I like what I see. The words of Mother Teresa (the younger) are a guidepost which, I must confess, I do not follow to the letter every day—as, for example, two days ago at the goddamn assisted living, which I would rather not think about, as usual.

And yes, I do little things all the time, like rewashing the cat food cans Larry throws into the recycling bins without washing adequately, so that horrid red ants get in them and swarm on my arms when I go to put the bins by the curb, and why in hell can't goddamn Larry just *rinse the goddamn cans*, for Christ's sake . . . In any case, that is just one of the many little things I do every day.

And I ask myself, do I rinse the cat food cans with great love? After much self-examination, and soul-searching, and quiet time with just myself alone contemplating the question, I decided, JUST GIVE ME A FUCKING BREAK, ALL RIGHT??!!

So, yes—I guess I do rinse the cans with moderate to great love, plus rage.

SUNDAY, OCTOBER 9

This morning at the therapist's, I had Trevor wait in the car after the session while the therapist and I discussed fine-tuning his medication. Right now he's on Dystopial, Simulose, Ridiculin, and Benzo-dystupophane, which acts as a booster for the Ridiculin and prevents the mumps caused by the Dystopial. I thought this combination was working fine, until Trevor's disappointing relapse during our vacation, which I have described. The therapist informed me that no medication he knows of is specifically targeted to the center of the brain associated with pranks, though I am welcome to research this for myself online. As an alternative, he recommended deep-immersion hypnosis. We would have to go to Europe for this, and even if we did, he said, the treatment works in only about a third of the cases, and most patients will revert to pulling smart-alecky stunts and pranks again over time.

Not a very satisfactory answer, so I don't know what we will do now.

MONDAY, OCTOBER 10

The kids had today off for Columbus Day so I took them to the doctor for their annual checkups. In the waiting room I ran into

Margaret, whom I haven't seen (except at book group) for a while. She asked about the Boss/Client, and I described how he had come by the house again with even more terrible news about Larry in Nigeria that again turned out to be wrong. Margaret said she had seen his white limo recently out by Stuff, Etc . . . She now spends much of her time (and lots of gas) driving around that "store" as she shops, and she says the white limo is parked near there sometimes. Stuff, Etc . . . does not really have a parking lot because it *is* a parking lot, but you can park in the weeds next to it. She said she saw Sandor A. Stattsman's Sphagnum Health Co. Humvee out in the weeds last week, too. I wonder why in the world they would be hanging out there.

Margaret's older boy, Walker, is an eighth grader at the same middle school Trevor goes to. Walker is completely faithful to his contract, Margaret says, and has never told her anything at all about the school. Apparently they do not even send home the kids' grades! (This is the first I've heard of that.) She says she has never been given one single piece of information about what Walker does or doesn't do in school, and it's the most wonderful, relaxing experience she and her husband have ever had with their children's education. She wishes all schools were like the middle school. I guess she is looking on the bright side. Personally, not knowing makes me uneasy. With Trevor, you can be sure that something *must* be going on.

TUESDAY, OCTOBER 11

This is National Casserole Week, friends, so today I thought we'd make a special extra-large deep-dish Cursing Mommy casserole that will feed your family all week if you (and they!) so choose.

Watch now as I put together my:

Trouble-Free, Three-Step, Oven-Ready Cursing Mommy
Souper-Duper Oh-So-Tasty Casserole!

I don't know if it's really that tasty, to tell the truth. The reason it's called "Souper-Duper" is that a main ingredient in it is soup. As you know, the Cursing Mommy does not endorse any product or brand name, but what the hell, I make it with Tressel's Cream of Mushroom Extra Creamy. I mean, Jeez Louise, everybody knows that's the main kind of soup in 90 percent of all casseroles on the planet, so why not just say so? The best wine to go with this casserole is a sprightly chilled Riesling. (I don't mean to go with eating it, of course, but with making it.)

Now, Gramma Pat used to call this dish "Tuna Fish Mish-mash," and it was my favorite comfort food except for the time I found a Chesterfield butt in it, but that happened only once. Other than that, Gramma Pat's Tuna Fish Mishmash soothed my spirits every time. The main item you need to start this recipe is a can opener. You line up the seven cans of soup and three cans of tuna next to the can opener—I prefer an automatic can opener, myself, although you can use the old-fashioned manual kind, which of course just means more cranking for the cook to open the cans. The Riesling to accompany this part of the casserole making is best served in a great big glass—a goldfish bowl, really—because opening the many cans is a tedious chore.

To operate this automatic can opener, I simply hold the first of the soup cans next to this gear thing and press down the handle, which turns on the machine's little motor and . . . goddamn it to hell, it did not "catch" on the lip of the can. Take a great big swallow of Riesling—mmm, so fruity!—and try again. And once again, goddamn this can opener, it does the same goddamn thing and fails to engage the lip of the soup can some-fucking-how. God, how I despise this can opener. And, even worse, the goddamn FUCKING CATS think the sound of the opener means that Larry, who actually knows how to make the goddamn can opener work, is opening their cans of cat food for their supper.

Get out of here, you cats. They are rubbing themselves back and forth along my shins while I am trying to solve the mystery of making this goddamn can opener function, and I really don't think I can deal with this right now, and GODDAMN FUCK-ING CAN OPENER! WHY WON'T YOU FUCKING WORK? So far I have crimped the edges of this first can a little BUT I HAVE NOT OPENED SO MUCH AS ONE GODDAMN CAN!!! Now the cuff of my fucking blouse is caught in the god-damn gears, FUCKING GODDAMN REAGAN AND THE AMERICAN ENTERPRISE INSTITUTE, THAT'S WHO'S PROBABLY RESPONSIBLE FOR MAKING GODDAMN CAN OPENERS SO NOBODY BUT BILLIONAIRES' PRI-VATE FUCKING CATERERS CAN OPERATE THEM!!! And—GAHHH!!—Now . . . I'VE TRIPPED OVER THE GODDAMN CATS!!! WHOA!! I'M FLAT ON MY BACK ON THE KITCHEN FLOOR!!! AND NOW THE CAN OPENER WON'T TURN OFF!!! IT'S GRINDING AROUND ON THE FUCKING FLOOR, SCARRING THE TILE, AND SOUP THAT IT SOMEHOW FUCKING OPENED IS SPILLING ALL OVER, AND, OH, GODDAMN IT ALL TO HELL!!! FUCKING CATS!!! GODDAMN CASSEROLE!!! GODDAMN FUCKING REAGAN!!! FUCKING GODDAMN SCALIA CAN OPENER!!! HELP! H-E-E-E-E-E-E-E-E-E-E-E-L-L-L-L-L-P!!!

[*pause*]

Lying here on the kitchen floor is not so bad, really, except for the goddamn cats. No, cats—it is not your suppertime. For-tunately, this also happens to be National Take-Out Thai Food Week, at least in our house, so it looks like that's what we're going to be having. I think there's still some of that Riesling left, thank God. Remind me to throw that goddamn can opener in the goddamn trash *tout de suite*. In just a minute I'm going to get up.

Oh, what a fucking horrible goddamn day this is going to be, and, in fact, has been already.

WEDNESDAY, OCTOBER 12

Larry got home last night, and he opened the goddamn cans, and I threw the casserole together, and it turned out okay—believe it or not. Friends, it just goes to show the benefits of persistence and a positive attitude. It wasn't finished until late, so we had to order Thai anyway. But now I won't have to cook tonight. Nothing is impossible if you set your mind to it and some good luck comes your way. At some future point, if I'm up to it, I will show you how that damn casserole is made.

THURSDAY, OCTOBER 13

Goddamn fucking horrible extortionist rip-off do-nothing thieving goddamn fucking SPHAGNUM HEALTH to eternal fucking goddamn hell, and its asshole reptilian criminal CEO, Sandor A. Stattsman, too, fuck them all, because they are an extortionist bunch of criminal fucks.

I just thought I would say that.

FRIDAY, OCTOBER 14

This year Gail made the noble gesture of volunteering to serve as secretary-treasurer of the school board, and a few days ago she took it upon herself to check up with the state about the Hendersonites' claims that state law had mandated the various things they were doing last summer at the school, such as turning the copper pipes into jewelry. Now that the state offices are open again, finally, Gail sent some inquiries to the proper authorities. She says she hates to bring this up, in light of all the Hendersonites have accomplished, but apparently there is no state law or regulation requiring that the pipes be melted down and jewelry be made of them. Also, she could find no state regulatory basis for the selling off of some of the bricks in sidewalk booths, as was also done. She is continuing to look into this, though I advised her to just let it go. Why bring up old news when the school is running so smoothly?

SATURDAY, OCTOBER 15

After much searching, the book Janeen suggested we read next for book group is *Mr. Reagan Goes to Washington: A Study of a Horrible Administration and the Destructive and Possibly Sociopathic Individuals It Employed,* by Grady Aberthwaite, Joyce LeBeau, Rachel Pearlstein-Stein, and Andrew Bishop, D.Econ. (1988). Janeen says this book has it all, including lots of previously unknown horrifying facts about Reagan and some very obscure horrible assholes he promoted to positions of power, as well as information about what a con job the late William F. Buckley, Jr., was. All the book group members have ordered it and we can't wait to get started on it. Thanks to Janeen for unearthing this jewel.

SUNDAY, OCTOBER 16

I tried to do my yoga in the car today, without screaming, as I waited in Trevor's therapist's parking lot. I brought along my yoga slippers (which are made from pieces of real yoga mats!) and changed into them to get myself in the proper mood, and I concentrated on the cut-off tree branches in the chain-link fence, and tried to inhale their elusive scent of eternity, as the fall colors in the surrounding leaves filtered the sunrise like those pieces of colored gel on spotlights in the theater.

Anyway, friends, I regulated my breathing and calmed my

mind and thought of you. We feel a sadness when the leaves turn colors and fall, but it's a sweet sadness. Do your cars have those illuminated reminders on the dashboard that say, "Service Engine Soon"? Not only does my car have one of those, but also the stupid light is on ALL THE GODDAMN TIME! (Sorry to disturb our meditative mood with inappropriate cursing, but it drives me fucking nuts.) Even after the car has just been serviced, the stupid "Service Engine Soon" light is still on! And, in a way, that is what our internal "dashboards" are like, is it not?

We go through the glorious world unmindful and distracted, because somewhere on our inner control panels some warning light or another is blinking, telling us of something we forgot, or must watch out for, or worry about. So right now, friends, as an exercise, let's let those little red warning lights go out one by one. Off goes the light that scares me about what will happen with Larry's goddamn capacitors, and the one blinking so red about our health insurance, and the one that reminds me about Trevor's penchant for pranks, and the Kyle-may-be-fainting-at-this-very-moment light, and the one about the awful Client/Boss. All go out and go dark. Dark, dark, dark. My control panel is now blessedly blank—how about yours? I inhale great deep columns of air to the very base of my diaphragm. Isn't this just wonderful?

Then of course—*sigh!*—Trevor's session is over, and he raps on the car window with his scout ring to get me to unlock the door and climbs in, and I start up the car, and naturally the goddamn fucking—excuse me—"Service Engine Soon" light is still fucking ON. That is life. But we had a few calm moments there, didn't we, friends? And for that we should be glad.

MONDAY, OCTOBER 17

A tragedy has befallen the Hendersonite community—one of its members has died in a terrible accident. The unlucky man, whose name was Stefan, was shopping out at Stuff, Etc . . . when a huge stack of cartons full of canned goods fell over on his car and crushed him inside it. This stack had recently come off a container ship and had shifted dangerously in the voyage, according to reports. The dead man had just gone through the gate and presented his Stuff, Etc . . . membership card. It was a brand-new one because he had just become a member. As a newcomer to our community, he did not have much experience shopping at Stuff, Etc . . . , and now we see the sad result of that.

TUESDAY, OCTOBER 18

Today Kyle's school canceled classes so that the funeral of the poor departed Stefan could take place. Hendersonite funerals are very austere, with much weeping and collection of money for the loved one's family. Larry and I gave generously, and after the service was over and the hearse had left for wherever they are going to bury him, an elder took us aside and returned Larry's wallet! He said Stefan had found the wallet in a window well and had been meaning to return it when he died. The cash was missing but the IDs and credit cards were there. That made us feel even sorrier for the man. He had no wife or children or other family besides his twelve brothers, who are distraught.

WEDNESDAY, OCTOBER 19

I love to look through the bright and cheery pages of the new holiday gift catalogs as much as anyone, but don't you think some of these retailers are overdoing it a little? Already the season's catalogs are piling up in the place where I throw away the mail. The goddamn catalogs weigh a ton, and slide around when you try to carry them, and fall open on the floor, and then the whole bunch of them slides, and I begin to curse and scream. Christmas is such a lovely time of year, but not on fucking October 19—excuse me—when it's eighty degrees outside with heat lightning. The truth is, friends, I actually secretly despise fucking Christmas, because all it is is more work for me, and a lot of junk to throw away—like these goddamn fucking catalogs. And I'd rather not think about all that, if I can help it, until *actual fucking goddamn Christmastime*!

Or is that not very "Christmassy" of me?

THURSDAY, OCTOBER 20

Aunt Dot, Gramma Pat's only surviving sister, sent me a sweet but nutty letter of condolence and included a clipping from her local paper that had a list of recently deceased individuals in the county. The list had Larry's name on it! Aunt Dot had circled the name, in case I didn't notice. The people at the paper, when I called them, said they had relied on a photostat of Larry's driver's license, which somehow must've been used in error when Stefan died, because the man was carrying Larry's wallet. They said they would print a correction. What a ridiculous mix-up! I called Aunt Dot and had one heckuva time persuading her that Larry was still with us. Finally I think I got through to her. I really must go up and see her soon. She is still living by herself but I'm sure she will have to go into a home. I warned her off the goddamn assisted living where my fucking father is, but I need not have bothered. She said she would never go anywhere he is because of her loathing for him.

FRIDAY, OCTOBER 21

Got a weird text from the Client/Boss: "I'm here if you feel like talking." What is that about? Talk about what? The guy really is losing his marbles. I texted back, "Glad to know you're here. Where were you in 1998?" To that I received no reply.

SATURDAY, OCTOBER 22

Poor Russ has been having one problem after the other. He's trying to save on gas so he came over today on his bicycle, weaving and wobbling among the potholes. Then he jumped off and started pacing back and forth on our front walk, searching his pockets for a note he had written to himself. I saw him there and went out. He started explaining that he was having trouble getting the metal drain filter in his kitchen sink to work. It won't let the water out when he wants it to, and then it lets it out when he doesn't want it to. I tried to tell him that you just adjust the little plunger thing in the middle of the drain filter to block the holes in it so the water doesn't drain, or to open the holes so it does drain. It's not that complicated. I even brought him into the kitchen and showed him on my own sink. But he said the water drained differently at his house because of the altitude above sea level and Coriolis effect. Then he ran out and climbed on his bicycle and rode away.

SUNDAY, OCTOBER 23

Today at Trevor's therapist's only two other cars were there, and I got out and walked around the parking lot. The day was dark and gloomy, and the rain of the night before had turned the asphalt a dark, dark black, while the recently painted lines were very white. On top of that, the rain had pasted down hundreds of bright yellow maple leaves fallen from the nearby trees. Anyplace can be our private zone of respite, friends, and the gorgeous black, white, and yellow color scheme of the parking lot, with the charming random scattering of leaves, really spoke to me this morning. It was as if someone had taken the colors of a school bus and shuffled them and fanned them out like cards. Does that make sense? Looking at the yellow leaves and the black asphalt and the white lines gave me a shiver of joy. I think I bring

Trevor to the therapist every Sunday morning at this early hour as much for the parking lot as for anything else. Isn't that crazy?

MONDAY, OCTOBER 24

Larry is all excited because the first shipment of Nigerian capacitors was loaded aboard a cargo plane over the weekend, according to Archbishop Mfune, and it should arrive at our door this week. I don't know how many capacitors there will be, or what Larry proposes to do with them when (and if) they actually do show up. If and when that happens, he is going to have to think of something fast. According to him he has already received many inquiries about them from buffs all over the country. The 000-series capacitors were the Cadillacs of capacitors, he says (back when Cadillacs were good), and now he has the largest 000-series capacitor trove outside Nigeria. A reporter from the capacitor buffs' newsletter has been calling him. Larry believes this is going to be big, big, big. He is kind of cute when he gets like this.

TUESDAY, OCTOBER 25

My doctor says I have not been getting enough alcohol. I am suffering from an alcohol deficiency, which can have serious consequences.

Oh, I am kidding, of course. My doctor did not make any such diagnosis, and in fact I rarely even go to the doctor, and neither do Larry and the kids, because we have to save our money to pay the premiums to GODDAMN FUCKING SPHAGNUM HEALTH!!! In this case I am making the diagnosis on my own by means of an educated guess. I do have a surefire remedy, however, and that is scotch. Of all the beverages in the world, alcoholic or non, I think I like scotch the best, so this morning I am going to put my feet up, pour a scotch, and watch the soap operas.

As you may know, there are almost no soap operas on TV anymore. This is completely mystifying and terrible. Gramma Pat used to love them—her "stories," she called them. With her "stories," and a little light ironing, and four or five packs of Chesterfields, she could have a whole afternoon. How is it that soap operas can no longer find a place in the world? Are we not allowed to waste a minute of time anymore? There are few remaining certainties in this life, but one of them, thank God, is scotch. With only one cube of ice and a splash of cold water.

WEDNESDAY, OCTOBER 26

Just an ordinary day, when there are no major holidays, or anniversaries, or big events on the schedule—what a simple godsend a day like today can be! The fall leaves have turned their lovely shades, and the sky is a hazy blue, and the sun streams down, and the day is so ordinary it gives us a standard that we can compare the not-so-ordinary days to. And now that I think of it, the not-so-ordinary days seem to be a lot more common nowadays than the ordinary ones, as a matter of fact.

Anyway—a perfectly ordinary day. Let's enjoy it together!

THURSDAY, OCTOBER 27

Thank God I appreciated an ordinary day while I had the fleeting chance, because, oh, friends, what a busy time followed it! At nine fifteen this morning the UPS trucks started rolling up. I was doing my yoga, the doorbell rang, and . . .

The goddamn capacitors were here! Ten trucks—not the usual vans, but trucks—were lined up in front of the house. Leave it to Larry not to be home when the goddamn things arrived. I didn't want to go outside in my yoga slippers and possibly mess them up (they are made from pieces of real yoga mats!) so I asked the UPS folks to bring the boxes in, and my God! The first truck-load alone filled the entire downstairs. We had boxes of capaci-tors piled up in the halls, in our bedroom, on the stairs, and filling the basement up into the kitchen and still the goddamn things kept coming. Holy moly you have never seen such an avalanche since Mount St. Helens blew! And then they had to just stack the rest up in the yard, and the pile out there is also huge! And this is just the first shipment!

Right now I am in shock, friends—capacitor shock. The boxes all have writing on them in Nigerian, and the shield, cross, and spear of the Nigerian Apostolic Church. They even smell like Africa. (It's kind of a nice smell, like tarred rope and cardamom.) But okay, okay—enough already!

FRIDAY, OCTOBER 28

When I woke up this morning I had to remove boxes of capaci-tors from the shower stall before I took my shower, and I dropped a box on my foot, and oh, did I let out a holler! I told Larry he must do something with the capacitors today or I was going to call the police. I didn't know exactly what I would say to the po-lice, but I would call them anyway. Larry got very hurt and said I should be patient, he couldn't do anything today, because he would be fired if he didn't go in to work. I did not buy this malar-key for one second. Larry will never be fired. I insisted he stay home and deal with this problem this very day, and after some whining and grumbling and phone calls to the office, he did.

SATURDAY, OCTOBER 29

Larry's solution to the capacitor problem is temporary at best, but I guess I will have to live with it. He rented an inflatable dome that usually holds displays for industrial fairs, and he floored it with plastic and stacked most of the capacitors inside it in our backyard. He hired some moving men to help him. The boxes are stacked on steel racks that go up to ten and fifteen feet high. What a monstrosity to have in the yard! A gasoline-powered air pump that burns I don't know how many gallons an hour keeps the whole thing inflated, and oh my God I wish we had never gotten into this. I can't wait to hear what the neighbors will think, not to mention the municipal zoning board. Plus we still have the odd pile of capacitors lying around the house, and the basement, of course, is still full to the top. What, *what* in the world was I thinking of ever to have agreed to such a crazy scheme?

Larry has unpacked two of the prized 000-series capacitors and shined them up and put them on the mantelpiece for display. I don't get what is so special about them, quite frankly. They just look like regular capacitors. But I have never seen Larry so happy. He is like a man on fire.

SUNDAY, OCTOBER 30

Last night a blizzard of snirt—snow combined with dirt, from the recent dust storms—hit our area, depositing ten inches of the awful stuff everywhere. It was followed in the wee hours by what they call a "hail-locust"—hail combined with a plague of locusts, all of them dead and frozen solid, fortunately, though on top of the snirt they made driving difficult. As a result we were almost fifteen minutes late to Trevor's therapist appointment this morning, and then, wouldn't you know, the therapist himself had not yet even arrived. Trevor passed the time by singing that old top-forty hit, "Stop! In the Name of Love," substituting new letters at the beginning of each word, for example, "Bop! Bin ba Bame bof Bove," "Cop! Cin ca Came cof Cove," "Dop! Din da Dame dof Dove," "Fop! Fin fa Fame fof Fove," and so on. Trevor has such an imagination and I hated to interrupt his creative processes, knowing how important this kind of play is to a child's development, but really he was driving me out of my fucking mind, and I finally did have to say something.

When the therapist showed up at last he looked very unhappy—the man does not enjoy his work, that is clear—and he walked through the snow, dirt, and thawing locusts with a disgusted expression. He had not remembered his boots. Then Trevor (who *did* have boots, thanks to my foresight) went in to his appointment, leaving me blessedly by myself in the car in my ashram / parking lot.

Sometimes, friends, we must re-remind ourselves that we are all in this together, and that you are out there invisibly sustaining me as (I hope) I do my own small part in sustaining you. Where are you right now—all of you? Where do you find yourselves this Sunday morning? Some of you are at places of worship, some are getting a welcome chance to sleep in, some are already up and doing chores that will only need to be done again. Here in the parking lot I close my eyes and concentrate and try to get a better sense of you, and I do get it—hallelujah!—and I imagine all of us linking hands, invisibly, one to another, until the vibrating energy of all our beings runs through us in a warm, strong current unanimously. And in that wonderful moment, I am restored.

MONDAY, OCTOBER 31

The Halloween Parade around town for the elementary school kids had to be suspended today because of the weekend's weather events, so the kids just paraded in their costumes in the school's newly renovated gymnasium and then were bused out to the mall so they could trick-or-treat there. Not all the businesses at the mall were expecting them, so instead of candy or similar treats they gave out other little items, like paper clips or staples or business cards. Kyle was disappointed in the slimness of the pickings, and when he got home he wanted me to run right out and buy big bags of candy just for him. When I refused he threw quite a fit, unusual for Kyle. I hope he is not on the way to becoming a second Trevor, who, on the other hand, is not that interested in candy. Trevor generally spends Halloween holed up in his room, as he did this year, giving all of us a break.

NOVEMBER

TUESDAY, NOVEMBER 1

This morning brings disturbing news. Two more shoppers have died out at Stuff, Etc . . . Although police have not yet released their names, both, it appears, were brothers of the late Stefan. One was killed while sorting through a produce display when a large vegetable truck backed over him. The other somehow fell into a seafood tank and drowned. To have such a series of awful accidents occur at our local grocery store in such a brief span has cast a pall over our community.

WEDNESDAY, NOVEMBER 2

You would expect Stuff, Etc . . . to shut down, given its recent great dangerousness to its customers, but it has not done so. Nor does it have to, Larry says, because of the clause in the agreement all Stuff, Etc . . . customers must sign, which indemnifies the company from accidental death, or even, in some cases, willful manslaughter on the store's part. Stuff, Etc . . . shoppers know full well what they are getting into, Larry says, and looking to their own well-being is up to them. I guess that's the trade-off, considering the amazing bargains you get there. All the same, it seems rather cold to me, and I am even less inclined to switch from U-Drug-It, my current store.

THURSDAY, NOVEMBER 3

The Hendersonite victims' names were Prospect and Lott. They were both younger than Stefan and had looked up to him, it is said. In a really peculiar turn, both were carrying state driver's licenses in Larry's name! Apparently Stefan had made exact copies of the ID, for what purpose I cannot imagine, and had given them to his brothers to hang on to until the licenses could be returned. (?) It is all too confusing for me. Anyway, the medical examiner informed Larry of this and he went down to the municipal building before work this morning and picked up the IDs. Now Larry has three copies of his own driver's license. What a crazy deal! Again today Kyle does not have school because of a Hendersonite funeral—a sad lesson for the children, but perhaps a good one.

FRIDAY, NOVEMBER 4

> *Even in life, we are in death, which is really a down.*
> *—Ecclesiastes (W. Gravy, translator)*

Our wobbly earth turns on its axis, the days darken into this often-gloomy month, and an indefinable sadness fills the soul. As the ancient poets told us, our lives are short, and the end of life, i.e., death, is never far away. Thinking about those young men and their sudden, sad ends gives us all a solemn reminder to stop and consider the meaning of our own lives.

This morning I put on Larry's knee-high rubber boots and got a garden rake and stood by the storm drain in front of the house as the rain and meltwater coursed down our street. The awful mix of fallen leaves and thawed-out dead locusts was clogging the grates, causing the water to back up and flood. This terrible leaf-and-locust stew would be in our basement soon enough if I did not keep the outflow moving, and I raked and raked, putting tons of locust muck up on the lawn, only to have the grate clog up again. What a nightmare. I was at it all day with just a brief break for lunch and several glasses of sambuca (which warmed me nicely, I must say).

Raking dead locusts from a storm drain: Today, friends, that was my life.

SATURDAY, NOVEMBER 5

As a reward, I did not get out of bed today—just stayed in and buried myself in our book group book, *Mr. Reagan Goes to Washington: A Study of a Horrible Administration and the Destructive and Possibly Sociopathic Individuals It Employed.* I got comfortable and curled up with it and had a cozy time. It is written in a very lively and readable style, and although it is almost eight hundred pages long it is lavishly illustrated with old photographs from that period. I have not yet looked at all of them thoroughly, but there is a cornucopia of information just in the photos. This is so great. I am not budging out of bed today. Whatever needs to be dealt with, I'll let Larry deal with it.

SUNDAY, NOVEMBER 6

Goddamn it to fucking hell and fucking Halliburton FUCK! I forgot the fucking time change! Last night we were supposed to turn the clocks back one hour for daylight savings, and we forgot, and then at four in the morning Larry remembered—only the dope remembered it backward! Instead of "Spring forward, fall back," which it actually is, he remembered "Spring back, fall forward," which, I have to admit, makes about as much sense. (I mean, if a lion comes at you, you spring back, and if you pass out from drinking, you generally fall forward—right?)

Anyway, Larry set the clocks forward, erroneously, which meant the goddamn alarm soon went off, and I dragged Trevor out of bed and drove to the goddamn therapist appointment, and we got there in pitch darkness *two fucking hours early*! When I figured out by listening to the radio what time it actually was, I saw no point in driving all the way home and coming back again. So we just sat there and talked. Or, rather, Trevor described to me the various strategies he was using on his video game, such as, "When his Jiggly Puff is coming to get my Wiggly Puff I morph into a star and go through a galaxy portal until my energy pack is back at ten . . ." and so on. Not very interesting. But I think it was the best talk Trevor and I have had in a long time.

MONDAY, NOVEMBER 7

Another wonderful book group last night. We carried on a very illuminating discussion of this month's book, although not everyone has had a chance to read it all. (It is quite long.) Many of the other book group members had been as fascinated with the photos as I was. Julie had even gone over some of them with a magnifying glass because she said you entered the scene when you did that and noticed details you might otherwise miss, and it gave you much more of the flavor of that era. Remarkable—I would never have thought of doing that.

Even more fascinating, in the book's "Where Are They Now?" section at the end, there were a few paragraphs about our old friend Sandor A. Stattsman (current head of Sphagnum Health)! It said he had once worked as a lightning-rod salesman and had been tarred and feathered by citizens of the Canal Zone for financial irregularities. There were mug shot photos of him that did not flatter him at all. An interesting find!

I felt lazy yesterday and did not make any special dish to bring to our evening. Instead I got some stuffed peppers from the Italian deli—a mistake. People hardly touched them, they were not tasty at all, and I was quite embarrassed. Next time I will do my cream-cheese-and-crabmeat appetizer. It has been a while since I made that.

TUESDAY, NOVEMBER 8

Following Julie's example, I got out my own magnifying glass this morning and started looking at the photos in the book. It really is fun because the picture becomes this place you enter in 3-D, you almost feel like you're exploring a different dimension. I was going person by person through a group shot of a bunch of minor Reagan donors when I made a discovery that gave me a start. In the far back, his face just visible at the end of a row, next to the young Sandor A. Stattsman, was a young dark-haired man who was an absolute dead ringer for . . . the Client/Boss! He had a surly expression and could have used a shave.

Is that wild, or what? I must remember to ask the Boss/Client about that.

WEDNESDAY, NOVEMBER 9

Fruitcake season will soon be upon us. Since everybody decided some years ago that fruitcake is a complete joke and always horrible and something you hated to be given as a present, this might not seem an important topic anymore. But fruitcake used to be such a special thing! I remember right about this time every year Gramma Pat would begin her fruitcake planning. She had a whole fruitcake regimen that had been passed down to her by her mother, Great-gramma Sallie, who in turn had got it from her mother, Great-great-gramma Lil, and so on back to cavewomen fruitcake makers, probably.

Traditionally, all the best fruitcakes were steeped in brandy, and now that we generally don't make fruitcake anymore it would be a shame to let the brandy be forgotten, too. This morning I am having a nice big glass of it in order to remember how integral it is to a holiday spirit, in memory of fruitcake. The truth is, you'll never catch me making goddamn fruitcake—what a slog it is! And then everybody hates it, and mocks you for making it, and you end up throwing it away. I say forget all that noise—I learned my lesson. For me, brandy alone is what remains of fruit-cake, which is fortunate, because I believe it is a very meaning-ful and essential part.

THURSDAY, NOVEMBER 10
I got the strangest phone call this morning. The person did not identify himself but I recognized the voice, because it was my old tormentor, Assistant Principal Molkowski—the guy who used to call up and lecture me for sending poor Kyle to school when he was fainting and covered with hives. Of course I know what Molkowski sounds like over the phone because I talked to him dozens of times, and his horrible voice is practically corkscrewed into my ear. I never hear from him anymore because he was laid off in the Hendersonite takeover of the school—good riddance—and I'd been told he'd got a job at Stuff, Etc . . . as a stock boy at minimum wage (serves him right).

Anyway, Molkowski's voice said he could only talk for a minute but I must listen. Larry must never, ever shop at Stuff, Etc . . . or go out there for any reason, or his life will be in danger, the voice said. What in the world goofy goddamn nonsense is that? I started to ask, but the voice then stopped and the line went dead. I guess the guy needed something else to bug me about for old times' sake. I will put this creepy weirdness from my mind.

FRIDAY, NOVEMBER 11
Just for laughs I photocopied the photo in the Reagan book that has the Client/Boss look-alike in it, and I blew it up and circled the guy and wrote "Funny coincidence?" in the margin, and then I mailed it off to him this morning. I know I resolved not to be in touch with the Client/Boss at all, but I just couldn't resist this, it was so nuts. I wonder what he'll say.

SATURDAY, NOVEMBER 12

Well, give me fifty lashes with a wet noodle for doubting my dear husband! The orders for the capacitors have begun rolling in! Some by e-mail, some by ordinary mail—dozens and dozens of them! And, some, glory be, with honest-to-God checks enclosed! I don't know whether to laugh or cry. The 000-series capacitors turned out to be just as big a hit among collectors as Larry had predicted. He is in a happy frenzy, packing up capacitors in the special containers he ordered and shipping them out by UPS. Chris, the UPS lady, stopped by here several times today to pick up another load. I even pitched in and helped, buying bags of packing peanuts and sweeping the goddamn things up all day as they scattered around the house and the backyard—but hey, even the goddamn packing peanuts did not bother me. I simply cannot believe this is working out.

SUNDAY, NOVEMBER 13

Sitting in Trevor's therapist's parking lot this morning, I was thinking that with the recent increase in Sphagnum Health's rates we would have lost our coverage, or at the very least cut it back to the point where it covered us only if we didn't need it. And now we are depositing actual checks from actual capacitor sales in the actual bank. Pinch me, I must be dreaming. It seems we will not have to cut back on our insurance after all! We may even be able to splurge on dental.

MONDAY, NOVEMBER 14

With Thanksgiving only ten days away it is time to begin to plan for that most community-oriented of holidays, when we give thanks for what we have and share our blessings openhandedly with family, neighbors, friends, and strangers. Oh, how I despise it sometimes. But that is wrong and unhelpful thinking, which I will set aside this morning as I turn to a fun, important task: making a centerpiece to decorate the Thanksgiving table.

Because I have been so busy with all this capacitor business I have decided today to revive an old column some of you may remember, called "How to Make a Decorative Holiday Centerpiece out of Used Coffee Filters and Throw It at Your Fucking Husband's Head."

Now, I do not literally mean you should throw this centerpiece at your husband's head—not unless you really feel like it, that is. If you do throw it, I can promise it will probably not break the skin because it is fairly light. Its main elements, as we see, are old coffee filters and pinecones, which will be the body of the turkey. Simply take this bottle of Ferdinand's Glue-All and pour it all over one end of this cone, which will be the turkey's head, and glue it to this larger cone, which will be the turkey's body. Then stick on the coffee filters like this. Now the glue has to dry. So let's forget about this project for the time being and fix ourselves a nice big drink.

TUESDAY, NOVEMBER 15

Checks keep arriving in the mail and I am giddy with glee as I open each new envelope. Checks from all over the country, and some from Canada, and one from England, and one from Switzerland! I simply cannot believe Larry guessed so right about these 000-series capacitors. I remember last Thanksgiving, when I actually *did* throw the centerpiece at his head, we were so low on money and my fucking father was coming and Trevor had been suspended and everything was awful and Larry came up from the basement with a capacitor he was tinkering with and he asked me some dumb question and—*wham-o!*—I let fly with the centerpiece. It missed him and hit the refrigerator and broke. This year I must remember to reinforce it with small bungee cords, although, in truth, I am feeling so charitable toward Larry these days that I think it's unlikely I will throw anything at him.

WEDNESDAY, NOVEMBER 16

The guest list for our Thanksgiving dinner this year will be: Margaret and her two kids, Walker and Miles; Russ and his kids, Destiny and Antony; my fucking father; and the four of us. Margaret's husband is invited, too, of course, but he will no doubt be on his rounds at the hospital that day and unable to attend. In fact, I have never actually met the good doctor, nor do Margaret and the kids see much of him, I believe. So that will be eleven people, just enough to fit at our dining room table with both leaves in it.

THURSDAY, NOVEMBER 17

No word from the Boss/Client about the photocopy of that picture I sent him last week. This is really uncharacteristic of him. Usually he is faster on the uptake.

FRIDAY, NOVEMBER 18

The glue attaching one pinecone to the other and to the coffee filters has dried completely and the bond is quite strong, so this morning we can proceed with the continuation of my classic column on how to make that decorative holiday centerpiece. This year I am following the basic instructions but changing them a little bit in a way I think will be interesting. At the gourmet butcher in the next town, where I always order my turkey, I made a special request that the butcher set aside for me the turkey's actual bill and feet, and I have them wrapped in this white (if slightly bloodstained) butcher paper here. So instead of a cardboard bill and pipe-cleaner feet on my centerpiece, this year I will try the real things and see what that looks like!

This is sure to be more realistic, anyway. As I open the butcher paper—Whew! It sure smells realistic, anyway—I see that the bill is . . . well, it is a turkey bill, with bits of feathers and flesh hanging from it, so I take it to the sink and clean it—uh, it's a little gross—and then I pat it dry with paper towels. Never attempt to glue anything that's at all damp. We know that rule. Now I take the bill and, using this extrastrong miracle cement that can glue anything to anything, I attach the turkey bill to the pinecone head. Okay, seems like we have a pretty good fit, thank God the pinecone is a big one, because this is quite a good-sized turkey bill and it does look a bit weird connected to a pinecone and used coffee filters. But it will be perfect once I do the feet.

Going back to the butcher paper, I take out the feet and—they're kind of . . . scaly and creepy, like dinosaur feet. I hadn't counted on that. Well, forging onward, I take the turkey-dinosaur feet and glue them by their topmost bones to the pinecone representing the turkey's body and . . . yes, I am gluing them and the glue is holding, really quite a lot of glue is required, it is running down the feet onto the newspaper I put under them, and . . .

Time for a short recess while I savor several shots of sloe gin I happen to have close at hand. Mmmm, very nice. And very warming! That reenergizes me.

So now I return to the centerpiece and . . . wow, it does look kind of . . . horrifying, really. Maybe centerpieces are not supposed to use real animal body parts. I'll make a note about that for next time. Well, live and learn. Now, wishing to see what the centerpiece will look like on the dining room table, I pick it up off the kitchen counter where I have been assembling it . . . I say, I pick it UP OFF THE KITCHEN COUNTER—

I cannot believe it.

I have just miracle-glued this goddamn monstrosity TO MY

OWN GODDAMN KITCHEN COUNTER!!! JESUS CHRIST!! WHAT THE FUCK WAS I FUCKING THINKING???!!! The glue ran down the feet and permeated the paper and while I was enjoying my sloe gin it DRIED LIKE FUCKING CONCRETE AND ANNEALED ITSELF TO THE GODDAMN FUCK-ING COUNTER, GODDAMN FUCKING MIRACLE GLUE!! Now I'm taking a spatula and scraping at it, IT FUCKING BROKE THE SPATULA! and I'm prying at it with a claw hammer, *turkey feet glued to my goddamn counter* WHAT A FUCK-ING GODDAMN MESS!!! Now I've tripped over the spatula handle on the floor and fallen among the smashed pinecone pieces GODDAMN FUCKING HALLIBURTON CHENEY PAUL WOLFOWITZ GODDAMN!!! Help! FUCKING REAGAN AD-MINISTRATION!!! GODDAMN GEORGE W. BUSH AND HIS STUPID RANCH, TOO!! HELP!!! H-E-E-E-E-E-E-E-E-E-E-E-E-E-E-E-E-E-E-E-E-E-E-L-L-L-L-L-P!!!!

[*pause*]

In just a minute I'm going to get up. Fucking realistic damn centerpiece—what a mistake. Cursing Mommy, where was your brain? Remind me never, *ever* to try such a terrible idea again. Soon the kids will be home from school. I'd better start cleaning this nightmare up.

Oh, what a fucking horrible Thanksgiving I predict this is going to be.

SATURDAY, NOVEMBER 19

Another long, sleepless night last night. As Larry snored, the god-damn ceiling started in on me again. I really can't stand the ceiling's attitude, its know-it-all smugness, when it needles me. The ceiling's huge features, its big mouth and nose and eyes, emerged on its deceptively bland surface at about 3:45 a.m. and then it was whispering all kinds of snide, nerve-racking remarks. It said it was watching me, and watching Larry, too, and we were fools headed for disaster. I answered back and said, "Oh, yeah? And how about the disaster you predicted with the goddamn capacitors? How about that?" The ceiling murmured that we hadn't seen how that will turn out, either—just wait. Oh, it nearly drove me mad, and I turned on the light to make it go away. But I found it even harder to sleep with the light on, and when I turned it out again the mocking ceiling was still there. Finally I ended up going downstairs to the couch and not being able to get to sleep there, either. An ordeal!

SUNDAY, NOVEMBER 20

Sat in Trevor's therapist's parking lot and wondered about the awful Client/Boss and why I haven't heard from him. This silence certainly is a new thing. I looked at the cut-off branches in the chain-link fence and they seemed full of a mystery I could not grasp. Oh, I wish I could just levitate through the roof of the car like people do in those crazy pictures of the Rapture and look down at my life and all that's around it and see it exactly for what it is. But instead I am here at pavement level experiencing everything so close I can't distinguish anything at all. Oh, for a true vision of my life!

MONDAY, NOVEMBER 21

I know I shouldn't have, but something that had me jumping out of my skin inspired me to take those other two Reagan books we read for book group and photocopy the footnote about Sandor A. Stattsman and his mug shots and draw circles around them with my Sharpie and write in the margins, "Look familiar?" and "Anybody we know?" Then I sent the copies to the Client/Boss. Just to see what he says? I'm not sure.

TUESDAY, NOVEMBER 22

Faithful old Aunt Dot sent me an update from her local paper consisting of two clippings—the first was a correction saying that Larry had not died, after all. The second was the latest list of deaths in the county, with Larry's name appearing on it twice. I guess that means they used the photostats of the driver's licenses of each of the recent Hendersonite victims, Stefan's brothers Prospect and Lott. Sometimes things are just too complicated. I called Aunt Dot and explained away the first Larry on the list of deaths, but I'm not sure I explained away the other. Dot is willing to accept that our Larry is still alive, but she is not at all clear about the other Larry. I think I will just leave that one alone.

After I enjoy a nice big shot of slivovitz—pear brandy, it's delish—I will call the goddamn newspaper and get them to print yet another correction, or perhaps two.

WEDNESDAY, NOVEMBER 23

Running around like a chicken with my head cut off today, or should I say like a turkey with its head cut off? I wonder if turkeys do that, too? That's another of those questions I wish I'd asked Gramma Pat while I still had the chance. I absolutely *insisted* Larry stay home from work this morning and move these wonderful and marvelous capacitors out of our goddamn downstairs, at least, so we can get ready for Thanksgiving. He fretted a lot about losing his job, but as soon as he started in with the capacitors he forgot everything else, as I knew he would. I helped him pack the latest bunch of them for shipping. We made a lot of progress. And how delightful to see the stack of checks accumulating on the sideboard, ready for deposit in the bank! My hat is off to Larry. It really is.

THURSDAY, NOVEMBER 24

No time to write. I was up half the night cooking and preparing for Thanksgiving, and now I'm about to drive to the assisted god-damn living and pick up my fucking father. Maybe when I get there they will tell me he has died.

If only!

FRIDAY, NOVEMBER 25

Last night as we all sat around the dinner table before tucking into the Thanksgiving feast, each of us said what he or she was thankful for, and my fucking horrible father who has been noth-ing but a blight on my goddamn life bowed toward me and said, "I am thankful for my wonderful daughter, who takes such won-derful care of me."

I almost cried. He has never said anything like that before. In fact, he hasn't even said anything that coherent since 2003. I felt all kinds of crazy feelings I could not explain or control, just deep, deep things in me rising up, and I did not know what to say. Of course my first thought was that the old manipulative bastard was just trying to drive his hooks in even deeper so he could take advantage of me more. But then I was not so sure.

SATURDAY, NOVEMBER 26

Still recovering from Thanksgiving. It really is a brutal holiday, is it not, friends? The aluminum foil industry is actually behind it, along with the makers of clear plastic wrap. My refrigerator is just yards and acres of aluminum foil crinkling all over the place as it covers the leftovers, with an assist from vast sheets of plastic wrap.

It all went okay. That's saying a lot. Russ did not dissolve in tears. Destiny and Antony became fascinated with Larry's ca-pacitors and offered to put him on a new accounting system. This is not something they learned in first grade—though with the

Hendersonites teaching them, I suppose you never know. Margaret and I had a good talk in the backyard while smoking and drinking and ignoring everybody. Her kids got along well with Kyle and Trevor, incredibly (I'm speaking of Trevor here). And the food was yummy, although, as is always the case, I did not really taste it until I tried some all by myself the next day.

SUNDAY, NOVEMBER 27

Holiday weekend or no, Trevor's therapist showed up at seven this morning, and Trevor and I were in the parking lot waiting for him. The sun was just coming up—a strange salmon-pink sun that sent lines of pinkness among the clouds, while the trees tossed in the wind. I thought the trees must be the turbulent indigestion dreams of the people still sleeping off their holiday feasts in the houses and apartment buildings all around. The low sun slid across the parking lot and it made everything, even the littlest stone or twig, stand out so clearly. I was disgusted by a pile of beer cans and soiled Styrofoam plates and other party refuse somebody had just dumped there. It actually offended me that someone had done that in my own private ashram, so I went to a nearby convenience store and bought some big garbage bags and picked all the junk up. (To handle some of the grosser stuff I used paper towels, which I always carry with me in the car.) The parking lot looked so much better after I was done—I imagined it breathed a sigh and even thanked me.

MONDAY, NOVEMBER 28

Oh, good God—calamity! Last night at about four in the morning we were awakened by what sounded like hundreds of sirens. We looked out the window and saw a bright orange glow behind the trees and houses to the north. Larry and I threw on clothes and ran outside and asked neighbors and passersby what was going on. Nobody knew, and then a police car slowed and a cop stuck his head out the window and told us to stay in our yards— the elementary school was on fire!

Well, Larry and I and everybody else ran over there anyway, and the school was a huge torch, flames and sparks shooting to the sky, and walls falling in and exposing fiery classrooms that were quickly swallowed by flames. We did not know if any Hendersonites were inside. Firemen said the building was empty, and in fact no people could be seen anywhere on the premises, and all the Hendersonites' vehicles were gone.

I must go now. That's Gail on the phone with more news. I'll know more later and pass it along.

TUESDAY, NOVEMBER 29

The elementary school is a smoking ruin. No one was inside it and no one got hurt in the blaze, though several firemen suffered smoke inhalation. The building appears to have been stripped before it was burned. None of the new fixtures were still in it— even the windows had been taken out. The new school buses are AWOL. No sign of the Hendersonites can be found, and an all-points bulletin for them on the roads has turned up nothing. They have vanished completely.

News media have been all over the place, interviewing everybody. Police theorize that the Hendersonites took this action in revenge for the three who died out at Stuff, Etc . . . (although those deaths were accidental). Who can explain what these followers of Hulot Henderson do, or why? They are a proud folk.

However, this turn of events put our school renovation project back at square one, or worse than square one, really, because for the time being we will have to hold classes in trailers. And somehow I think that the municipality will have no choice but to pass a bond levy now. And there will go the property taxes—*voom!*— up to the sky!

WEDNESDAY, NOVEMBER 30

What cannot be changed must be endured, unless you can get out of it
somehow, if possible.   —Flemish proverb

The loss of our elementary school has thrown our entire community into confusion. Getting the trailers set up to provide classrooms for more than five hundred students at short notice is a major undertaking and has caused us to reexamine our whole concept of education. We have decided to take the children's input on this, as well. Kyle, for example, is delighted not to have school, and Trevor says he is jealous and wishes his own school would burn down. I told him not to get any ideas about that, and just to be sure, increased the dosage on his Dystopial by five hundred milligrams.

The majority of the elementary school kids seem to be of the opinion that we should forget the whole idea of school, as such, and instead let them learn on their own. While we wait for the trailers, cyberclasses are available online, and that system works pretty well for other communities, we are told. The kids say they are eager to try it. So maybe we have been making too big a deal about having an actual physical school for them and a bricks-and-mortar building and teachers and so on.

The only problem is that with Kyle home all day, I go mad. I am sure I speak for many caregivers when I say this. And he has been home for only three days now! (Of course, there was the long Thanksgiving weekend before that.) I do not care, really, whether or not there is a school per se (oh, hell, I guess I do), but I and other mothers in particular *want these kids out of the house*! I have been talking to Gail and Margaret about this and we are in complete agreement. Maybe there is some warehousing-type situation we can come up with as a temporary measure, but I can promise you that having the elementary kids home with nothing to do for the indefinite future will drive several hundred mothers and other caregivers in this community right around the bend.

WEDNESDAY, NOVEMBER 30 (CONTINUED)

How anybody homeschools their kids is beyond me. Just now I tried to take Kyle through his lessons on the Internet and I got nowhere at all. Both cats jumped on the table and Kyle started playing with them, and I told him to cut it out, and he lost his place and searched for it, stopping along the way at the Home Shopping Network somehow, and we both got interested in that, and then the doorbell rang and it was Russ asking if he could drop off Destiny and Antony because they were causing him to have anxiety attacks. So then I had the three kids here, and Destiny and Antony soon got everything under control and were helping Kyle with his lessons although they are three grades behind him (they are in first, he is in fourth). I told them I was grateful for their help and then went upstairs and got in bed and called Margaret, and we commiserated. She had taken her kids to the library and simply left them there. It was packed with kids and the librarians were frantic, she said.

Margaret and I agreed that it is somewhat harder to relax with a drink when the kids are home or when you know you might have to hop in the car without warning and chauffeur them somewhere. I feel this is an invasion of my personal space, and although I know I should not resent it under these difficult circumstances, I do resent it, somewhat. I search for solutions, such as reviving the concept of "naptime." Maybe if the kids could all take a two-hour nap in early afternoon . . . No, there is no chance of that catching on. And two hours would not be enough "cocktail time," anyway—certainly not enough to get us caregivers through the day. Such inconvenience, out of nowhere!

DECEMBER

Mmmmm, December! What a lovely, cozy, warm, bespangled, delicious month this is! Didn't you just love it when you were little? And isn't it a fucking nightmare today? No—I take that back. It is only a fucking nightmare if we let its natural tendency to be a fucking nightmare get the upper hand. We must clear our minds of December's potential fucking-nightmare-ness, and, like the faithful magi of old, keep our eyes upon the star.

When I was a little girl, Gramma Pat always got us an Advent calendar with those doors you opened for each day in the month—every door slightly bigger than the one before it, until the biggest door on December 25. My brother and sister and I took turns opening the doors, and we all three delighted in the little pictures we found behind each one—maybe a little mouse in a red-and-white nightcap with a candle, or a raccoon mother in spectacles knitting a pair of socks, or two angels eating cake. Gramma Pat's calendar sometimes came with her special Christmas gift cartons of Chesterfields with big red ribbons and a picture of Santa enjoying a Chesterfield printed on the box. Some of the angels on those Advent calendars were also smoking, I recall.

As we look ahead to the rest of this month, my wonderful friends out there, let us regard each December day as another exciting calendar door for us to open. Yes, I predict we will discover something unimaginably delightful behind each one!

FRIDAY, DECEMBER 2

I, personally, would find it easier to get into a Christmas shopping spirit if it weren't so god almighty *hot*. Snow was forecast for this weekend, and we were all ready to be bundled up indoors packing capacitors and ordering gifts online and so on, and then they changed the forecast to an unseasonable heat wave. Now it's overcast, gloomy, eighty-four degrees, and dark at four thirty in the afternoon. The weather person says this is the hottest December 2 in three years. Since the previous unseasonable December heat wave we have never had to use the air conditioners so late in the year. But they are on full blast and cranking away now!

SATURDAY, DECEMBER 3

Gail told me a very interesting and useful fact today, which I bet will be as much news to my friends out there as it was to me. We all know what persistent arguers kids can be. Well, relief is at hand! Now when you get into a long and pointless argument with your children, there is a service you can call that will handle the argument for you. You simply call the number, describe the argument to the person who answers, and hand the phone over to the main arguer among your children. Then you let the service take it from there! Meanwhile, you go off and do whatever you wish until the child finally tires. Most of the service's arguers are in phone centers in Guyana. The arguers are trained, patient, resourceful, and able to endure the most boring back-and-forth. You can reach this service anytime of day at YES-NO-YES-NO-555-4444. The very next argument the kids and I get into, I plan to give this service a call!

SUNDAY, DECEMBER 4

Something so upsetting happened to me today that I cannot describe it. I am going to drink moderately heavily and go to bed.

MONDAY, DECEMBER 5

All right, I am somewhat calmer (if a bit hungover) this morning, and I can attempt to tell you, friends, about the shock I received yesterday.

It was a Sunday like any other. Up early, roused Trevor, drove to the therapist's, parked in the parking lot. The therapist arrived, Trevor went in for his appointment. I took some deep breaths, put on my yoga slippers (which are made from pieces of real yoga mats!), and absorbed the calming aura of the parking lot, focusing on the sawed-off branches in the chain-link fence as a way to get myself centered, as I always do. Closing my eyes, I began to meditate.

The car was idling, windows rolled up, and the air conditioner running in this heat. Maybe that was why I didn't hear anything. All of a sudden, in the middle of my meditating, I got a sense of something looming very near me. I opened my eyes, looked to the right—and there, about a foot away from the window, was the white limousine! It had pulled into the space right next to me and was just sitting there!

My God, it was like I was in one of those shark cages and I turned to see the face of a twenty-foot great white. My heartbeat went from yoga calm to really fast. How had he found me there? One of the dark-tinted windows in the limo went down. The heavy metal music was throbbing, but quietly, like a heart. In the window, the Client/Boss's face appeared. I looked away. He got out of the limo and walked over to my car, to the window next to me. I rolled it down and asked him what he thought he was doing, following me here? He asked me to sit with him in his limo so we could talk. I refused, said I'm fine where I am. He asked me please to just get out of my car and talk to him. He was in his scary-nice mode. I got out of the car. I looked over at his limo and—another surprise—there's former assistant principal Molkowski standing by the door! He winced slightly as if pleading with me not to betray him.

The Client/Boss took me by the elbow—*shudder!*—and led me to a corner of the parking lot. In his fake-nice earnest manner, he told me that the photos I sent him had troubled him very much, because the man in one of them, the man who resembled him, has been his nemesis for many years. This man was created by his enemies using plastic surgery in order to undermine him, the Boss/Client said. That is why there is no information about him before 1998—all records were erased because of things this look-alike did.

You might be wondering, what does the Client/Boss look like, anyway? Making a double of him would not be hard because at first glance he could be anybody. He is the same height as I am (when I'm not wearing heels), which is five seven. He has average features, brown hair, an average build. At closer inspection, though, his face is kind of thin and streamlined, like it was made in a wind tunnel, and his hair, which he mousses and combs to a ridge along the top of his head, stands up like saw teeth. His eyes are the weirdest part—they're the same dusty gray-blue as a video screen and they can seem flat or sky deep, depending. He has tiny whisker patches here and there around his mouth and probably shaves in the shower.

He was being so intense, and I felt almost dizzy with the weirdness of it. I forget all he told me. He said never to mention that photo again, or the other photos I'd sent, the ones of Sandor A. Stattsman (which are even worse, somehow), and to destroy the books they're in. I said our whole book group had copies of them, along with the entire rest of the world. He shook his head and looked at the ground, saying, please, never mention any of this again and let the subject be forgotten. Then he walked back to his limo, Molkowski opened the door for him, and they got in and drove away.

When Trevor came out of his session, I was still so stunned that even he noticed. While we were sitting at McDonald's he asked me what was wrong.

TUESDAY, DECEMBER 6

What I hated most about Sunday was that the guy came to my private, special place that I thought no one but me knew about. I mean, other people know about it, of course, but no one knows its meaning to me. And now the guy knows—he must have seen me there, in my yoga posture, meditating—and I hate that. The only reason I can't spend the day brooding about this and screaming curses is the elementary school kids, who have nothing to do and are becoming feral. Kyle wants to run with them and whines when I won't let him out. So here is Kyle, moping and whining around the house, and packs of elementary kids whooping through the yard yelling his name, and me thinking that if it's not one goddamn thing it's ten dozen.

WEDNESDAY, DECEMBER 7

Friends, you are my strength. What would you do, in my situation? We hardly have time to deal with one mess when another comes at us, like Lani in that *Loving Lani* episode where the puppies keep coming at her on the conveyor belt. So we sit back, let the puppies go by and pile up on the floor, and accept what we cannot change. If only I could stop feeling like I'm jumping out of my skin.

THURSDAY, DECEMBER 8

While doing some Christmas shopping out at the mall this morning, I was in Flood's and I happened to turn down an aisle in the sleepwear section and who do you think I ran into?

Angie! Yes, the very same! She and M. Foler Tuohy (the late) are back in town for the holidays, she said, staying at a bed-and-breakfast on Route 7 where they have rented the whole house, including the part where the owners are living. She looks fabulous, thin and tan and beautiful. One reason they are here, she said, is that they intend to get custody of Destiny and Antony, because Russ is not raising them properly. (What a laugh!) Angie said that under the stress of living with Russ the kids are not eating enough endive.

Russ does not know yet that Angie and "Skip" (ugh!) are here. God help the poor man when he finds out.

FRIDAY, DECEMBER 9

I had to bite my tongue not to tell Russ about Angie when he called this morning. But really, if I'd said anything, it would have given the guy a heart attack, in the state he was in. Apparently he had been trying to throw something away and it kept bouncing out of the wastebasket. He said he was at the end of his strength. I suggested the wastebasket might be overfull, and he said he'd check. I also told him he could bring whatever it was he was trying to throw away and throw it away here at our house— but he didn't want to do that. He said he was going to try again, and he hung up. He must've succeeded, finally, because he didn't call again. I really do not know what will become of him.

SATURDAY, DECEMBER 10

Friends, let us begin this hot, overcast almost-winter day with a list of affirmations:

We are great.
We are resourceful.
We are compassionate.
(Time for a quick cocktail.)
We are all right.
We are perfect in every way.
We are astonishing.
We are enraptured with life.
We are courageous.

We are fully licensed and bonded.
We are thoughtful.
We are ambidextrous.
(Better make that a double.)
We are splendiferous.
We are really, really, *really* great.

Whenever I recite these affirmations, I feel about the same as I did before reciting them, only more affirmed. And please note that for an affirmation to be effective it does not have to be true, only affirmative. The truth we are talking about is not "truth" truth (whatever that is), but INDIVIDUAL truth. We must claim the right to our own truth.

SUNDAY, DECEMBER 11

Feeling jumpy in the therapist's parking lot this morning, waiting for the great white to loom up alongside. But today I was left in peace, thank God. Instead I thought of all that I have before me this fucking holiday season and I almost collapsed as if a gravel truck had unloaded on me. First I have the Christmas shopping, and wrapping and mailing the presents, plus Kyle will be knocking around the house every day for the foreseeable future; also, book group is meeting at my house on the twenty-second, so I have to get the place in shape for that. Then there's Christmas itself, and then Larry's birthday and Kyle's birthday (both on the twenty-sixth, a terrible coincidence for both of them, not to mention for me). Then it's off to goddamn Encino for fucking New Year's again—I wonder what THAT will be like—and then who knows what after that. I can't face it. I am screaming silently inside.

Well, Cursing Mommy, buck up. You live a fortunate life, you are enormously blessed in your friends and some of your family, and Larry's 000-series capacitors are flying out the door. Be grateful (however goddamn grudgingly) for all you have.

MONDAY, DECEMBER 12

Did I say I will have Kyle knocking around the house? Make that Kyle AND Trevor! I went to drop Trevor off at school this morning, and there was a big commotion in the street and parking lot with parents and kids milling about. The school had handed out an announcement saying it was closed today due to an eraser shortage. I never heard of such a thing before. So Trevor got back in the car, cheering, and I brought him home again. I will get nothing done today, I can see that.

TUESDAY, DECEMBER 13

Trevor's school is still closed. Early this morning he and Kyle teamed up on me, wheedling for me to let them go out and run with their friends. Sounds of the feral kids hollering through the neighborhood backed up their pleas, and I would have given in, just to get them out of the house, except I wanted them to do their online studies. I said they could go on playdates to their friends' houses afterward. They said that all their friends were out right now running around. The other moms and caregivers must have already thrown in the towel, I guess.

After a while I got sick of arguing. Then I remembered Gail's suggestion! Right away I picked up the phone and called the arguing service. A very nice, no-nonsense Guyanese lady came on the line, I briefed her on the argument, and I put her on speakerphone. Then I brought Kyle and Trevor and let the Guyanese lady take over.

Whew! What a break! I went upstairs and lay down and enjoyed the quiet. But it did not last long. In about fifteen minutes, Trevor and Kyle came bounding up the stairs to tell me that the lady on the phone wanted to talk to me. I came down and asked the Guyanese lady how the argument was going, and she said not well at all. In fact, she had lost. She said this was the first time in seven years that she had ever conceded an argument. The irrelevant statements were what defeated her, she said, such as, "Do you know that in a lifetime the average person eats six spiders in his sleep?" She had not known that about the spiders and it upset her and interfered with her concentration. She was very apologetic and offered to bill me at half price. I thanked her for trying and rang off.

So, what the hell, I let the kids go. I said they had to be home by dark and they ran out. And somehow, even with them gone and the house empty, now I cannot relax.

WEDNESDAY, DECEMBER 14

First thing this morning Trevor received a severance packet from his school informing him that his enrollment had been terminated and the school was relocating overseas. I did not even know schools could do that. Later we got a notice from the school board announcing an emergency parents' meeting tomorrow night at eight o'clock.

THURSDAY, DECEMBER 15

This afternoon I am relaxing with an old-fashioned or four while I sign and address our cheery holiday greeting cards and mail them to the 150 friends and family on our list. I was going to include a write-up describing the notable events of the year in the Cursing Mommy's family, but then I took a second look at it and decided, as I sometimes do, fuck that. Yes, people may want to know about Larry's reduced earnings at his job and the garage catastrophe and the school fire and what medications Trevor is on, but I think just a simple card, without all the information, is more expressive. Because, honestly, why go into it? When I get one of those letters myself I sometimes think, "Oh, help!"

Is that too negative? Yes—it's the holidays, for heaven's sake! I will radiate warm holiday thoughts as I sign and try not to curse inwardly about the taste of this fucking goddamn envelope stickum combined with the alcohol.

FRIDAY, DECEMBER 16

At the communitywide meeting of parents and school officials last night they hit on a solution to our sudden shortage of functioning schools: As of Monday, all elementary and middle school students will be promoted to the ninth grade and will begin attending "classes" in the high school. Aside from Destiny and Antony, I don't know any first-grade students capable of doing ninth-grade work, so I put "classes" in quotation marks. The school board explained that the promotion will be mostly a formality, and the new ninth graders will actually spend much of the school day sitting military-style on the gym floor under the supervision of temp workers and the police. I think this is a far from ideal plan. But thank God they are at least *doing* something.

SATURDAY, DECEMBER 17

In the weekend Arts section of our local paper there is a big feature about our book group. It's a very well-done article with descriptions of the books we've read and incisive comments from many of the members (not including me, because the reporter didn't call me). One of the photo spreads includes the mug shots Julie found of Sandor A. Stattsman next to a publicity still from Sphagnum Health showing what he looks like today. The photos are to give an example of the interesting things our book group has come across. (After the upset they caused the Client/Boss, I wonder if running these photos was entirely a good idea . . . ?) The only mention of me is when it says the next meeting will be at my house, and has my address, and the day and time the meeting will be. Did they need to put in all that?

SUNDAY, DECEMBER 18

I am half dead with tiredness, dozing off in the car in the therapist's parking lot. Russ found out Angie and M. Foler Tuohy (dec'd) are in town, and he called us at two o'clock last night saying he was about to firebomb the bed-and-breakfast where they're staying. It took Larry and me three hours, talking to him in shifts, to persuade him not to. Then when we finally got him halfway quieted down and hung up the phone, it rang again. This time it was Angie, in even worse shape than Russ had been! She was calling in tears to tell us that M. Foler Tuohy is out somewhere with the wife in the couple that runs the bed-and-breakfast.

Through her weeping Angie kept saying to me, "I am turning into my mother! I am turning into my mother!" I told her that was silly. But apparently, as it turns out, her mother *also* had an affair with M. Foler Tuohy. This was twenty-some years ago, when Tuohy was going by the name of Arnold Mapes. Angie said that this Mapes (Tuohy) also left her mother for the wife in a couple who ran a bed-and-breakfast, so I guess Angie does have reason to be concerned. We never did get her off the phone. Larry was still trying to calm her down when I left this morning.

MONDAY, DECEMBER 19

Will someone tell me, please, when it became the custom for us moms to do ABSOLUTELY ALL the Christmas shopping for our families? Used to be, the dads and the kids bought a present once in a while. Not anymore! I buy all the presents Larry gives to his parents and his brothers and sisters. When they call on Christmas day to thank him, I have to hand him a list so he knows what he gave them. I also buy Larry's gifts to the kids, and their gifts to him, and I almost always pick out and buy the presents the kids and Larry get for me. It can be somewhat rewarding to shop for others, but to be honest, I am thoroughly goddamn fed up with the whole fucking deal. Where I draw the line is at wrapping my own presents. That is just too ridiculous—wrapping presents to myself so I can unwrap them on Christmas morning? I insist that Larry and the kids wrap those particular damn things themselves.

Well, Christmas crabbiness—enough out of you! This morning I am going to wrap all the presents (except my own), and I'll do it in a good Christmas frame of mind, with the help of this mug of holiday eggnog that I have generously spiked. Because we are out of both rum and brandy, the traditional eggnog spikers, I have used the only liquor we seem to have left, which is vermouth. Later I must make a preholiday run to the liquor store!

TUESDAY, DECEMBER 20

Gahhhhh! I got distracted yesterday by that *horrific* eggnog-and-vermouth concoction. My God, how perfectly AWFUL that was! Today I am proceeding with the more traditional eggnog and brandy, using some good Three Monks Special Reserve that Larry brought home last night. Yes—much better! So now, let us continue with:

You, Too, Can Be a "Wrap" Artist: Effortless Gift Wrapping
Tips from the Cursing Mommy

First, pick some pretty Christmas paper. This first sheet is pretty, but it is covered with glitter! Oh my good Christ, how I detest glitter. Excuse me, but I am throwing this entire roll of wrapping paper *the hell away*! Never, ever, allow even a single *speck* of glitter in your home! It gets everywhere, especially on the side of your nose when you are about to go to an important lunch or other appointment. No, the pretty paper I choose will not have glitter on it, but it will have little elves with hammers and chandeliers, for some reason. However . . . as I examine this paper . . . I SEE THAT SQUARES HAVE BEEN CUT OUT OF THE GODDAMN CORNERS, MAKING THIS FUCKING IRREGULARLY SHAPED REMNANT COMPLETELY FUCKING UNUSABLE!!! Thank you, LARRY! Or else it was one of the kids who did this ridiculous job of cutting.

You know, that is so goddamn discouraging I just want to give up on the whole thing. I think I will just retire to bed with my eggnog and try again tomorrow.

WEDNESDAY, DECEMBER 21

Today I am in a much sunnier mood for this goddamn present wrapping, and I will note just in passing that it is one of those tasks that if I don't do it, IT DOESN'T FUCKING GET DONE!! In good cheer, or some goddamn approximation of it, I will continue:

So, first pick some wrapping paper that doesn't have fucking glitter on it and doesn't already have a fucking piece cut out of it. Fine, this will do. I don't care that it says "Congratulations, Graduate!" That is the only goddamn paper we have. Place the box the gift is in upside down on the paper like so. Measure the paper so there's enough overlapping. Cut along here. Now make the cut edge smooth by folding it over and taping it—oh, the hell with that. Let it stay ragged, it's not a big deal.

Now, when you position the seam, you want to do it exactly at the edge of the box, so it will be less visible . . . but if it keeps slipping, as this goddamn thing is doing . . . Oh, hell, just slap some tape on there. Clear plastic tape is good, but we're out of that, too, so this black electrical tape from Larry's tool drawer will have to do. Also remember, if you cut the paper too short, it's impossible to cut it longer . . . fold the top flap down and tape it . . . and, yes, IT IS TOO FUCKING GODDAMN SHORT!!! Oh, goddamn, Cheney, Halliburton, Blackwater, FUCKING *FUCK!!! Just stick some goddamn newspaper in there to cover the rest of the goddamn present!!!* Now I will just take this stapler and [*wham wham wham wham wham*] I will staple the goddamn paper on there!! And now I have stumbled over the goddamn wrapping paper roll and fallen on the goddamn FUCKING WOLFOWITZ RUMSFELD GODDAMN FUCKING FLOOR, GODDAMN FUCKING STUPID CHRISTMAS!!! Help! HE-E-E-E-E-E-E-E-E-E-E-E-L-L-L-L-L-L-L-P-P-PPPP!

[*pause*]

Oh, what a fucking goddamn awful holiday season I have known all year this was going to be.

THURSDAY, DECEMBER 22

Tonight is book group, so I am getting the house ready. Another shipment of capacitors went out this morning, another lovely heap of checks and money orders went into the bank, and I am in a cozy mood. Tonight we will be discussing the high points of all the books we've read this year, including the ones by the long-dead M. Foler Tuohy, and picking out the important themes. Tonight's meeting will be more of a holiday party, really. I am putting up ropes of balsam branches with their heavenly smell, and red ribbons, and ornaments hung strategically from the ceiling. (We have not yet got our Christmas tree because we always do that the day of Christmas Eve.) As I decorate I am listening to the Christmas carols of the peerless Nat King Cole. Such a wonderful, happy feeling, and I know the true holiday spirit is suddenly in the air and I JUST BROKE ANOTHER GODDAMN ORNAMENT, oh goddamn it all to hell.

FRIDAY, DECEMBER 23
[Cursing Mommy unavailable due to ninja attack.]

SATURDAY, DECEMBER 24
[Police action in progress.]

SUNDAY, DECEMBER 25
The holidays are so fucking awful and I'm right in the middle of them and we had that nightmarish ninja attack three days ago that I'll tell you about soon and the cats are no longer using their cat box and I am frankly just too out of my mind to write the traditional Cursing Mommy Christmas column—so, more soon. Merry Christmas and Happy Holidays to all my dear friends.

MONDAY, DECEMBER 26
[blank]

TUESDAY, DECEMBER 27
[blank]

WEDNESDAY, DECEMBER 28
We have just started to recover from the ninja attack and Larry's and Kyle's birthday parties, which I will tell you about, and now we have to get ready for the yearly torture trip to the Client/ Boss's house in Encino (wish me luck), so I don't have time to do my Cursing Mommy's Christmas-Leftover Ten-Minute God-damn Recipe Roundup, as planned. Just throw a bunch of stuff together and use the microwave. And from our holiday house to yours, best holiday wishes—talk later!

THURSDAY, DECEMBER 29
[Redacted by order of Sphagnum Health Corp.]

FRIDAY, DECEMBER 30
[Redacted.]

SATURDAY, DECEMBER 31
[blank]

JANUARY

And so, my wonderful sustaining friends out there—each of you with your own story, and each of those stories no different, really, from my own—the year we set out upon together has now reached an end. It was delightful to have you with me, dear fellow spiritual beings, as we pursued our human journey through the days.

Now here I am again at the kitchen table with my coffee cup warming my palms as I think of you. Larry is at the capacitor warehouse he is renting near the racetrack and Kyle and Trevor are out with a new group of children they have met since Kyle's school burned down and Trevor's moved overseas. Some of these new children are not even from our area, but I hope it will be all right. At last I am by myself once again. Isn't it funny, even when you're in a family, how much time you spend alone? Well, it's a lovely, lonesome resource, being by oneself, and the loveliest part is sharing it with you.

Today is a holiday, I know, and tomorrow will be, also, but honestly, from my point of view the holidays are already gone—and not a bit too soon. They really were quite trying. You might have read in the papers about the ninja attack on our book group. Oh, it was awful! Afterward I was digging throwing stars out of the living room walls for days. These professional ninjas were sent by Sandor A. Stattsman to frighten our book group into not making any more statements about him, but of course that very night we did the exact opposite and complained to the authorities, who arrested the ninjas responsible (and, don't misunderstand me, I know there are also good and principled ninjas who would not have stooped to such a thing) as well as Mr. Sandor A. Stattsman himself. I am told his bail has been set very high. He will not be getting out for a long time, is my hope.

Of course, a few days later we received a "This Is Not a Bill" notice from Sphagnum Health saying that our rates will be going up as a result of CEO Stattsman's arrest! You can't win.

My father, whom I think it's actually okay to call "my fucking father" again, announced to one and all that he could not face the start of another year. He took to his bed, decided he was breathing his last, and summoned my brother and sister, who flew in to say goodbye, and of course I went to the bedside, too. We had a not very tearful vigil, and the next morning he woke up feeling fine and hopped out of bed and is now doing calisthenics again, the jerk. My brother and sister had their holidays ruined and wasted their frequent-flyer miles and the old fraud revives. Better luck next time.

On top of that, Larry's arrest was another major disruption. The police who took him in said he was wanted for crimes in eleven states and three Central American countries. That is impossible. How could he have committed "theft of sacred objects" in San Cristobal? He doesn't even know where that is. And "disassembling a pipe organ without a license"? Nonsense! Larry is the least musical person I know. It took many hours to get him released, and I'm sure it will be a very long time before we get to the bottom of what is going on here.

M. Foler Tuohy is who knows where with the wife of the couple that owns the bed-and-breakfast. While everything else was happening, Angie was calling me in hysterics or driving over here to cry and complain. I still feel guilty for introducing her to M. Foler Tuohy, so I had to listen. One afternoon while I was waiting for the jail to call back about Larry, she burst in. Just at that moment Russ called to ask what to do about the yellowish water that comes out before the mustard in the French's squeeze dispenser. He was very upset about it, and I just put Angie on the line and they talked the mustard-water problem through and—well, now they're back together. That's probably a horrible outcome, but at least it's one I can't feel guilty about.

As usual, Larry and I flew out to the Boss/Client's New Year's party in Encino. I don't have to tell you I was dreading seeing him again. Quite honestly, I also wanted to kick his shins extrahard, in case he had been involved in that business with the ninjas. A plush minibus picked us up at the airport and the arrangements were all red-carpet as we have come to expect, with iced tables of truffle dishes and shellfish by the pool and a heavy metal fusion revival band. People from the office were making a fuss over Larry and hanging on his words. They know about his smashing success with the capacitors and there are office rumors that he will be moved up to whatever position is above the one he has now. The weather was balmy, the fan palms were rustling in the breeze, New Year's was approaching, but—

Where was the Client/Boss? He didn't show. And he didn't show. Nobody knew what could have happened to him. Usually he would appear long before this and perform his famous strip on the diving board.

Just before dinner, some of the guests said the Boss/Client was on the evening news, and everybody crowded around the huge screen in the banquet room to watch. There he was, in a grainy photo taken earlier the same day in the tiny town of Sequel, New Mexico, where he was last seen getting on his plane. Next to him in the photo stood former assistant principal Molkowski. The report said they had flown into the desert and disappeared, and were presumed to have crashed.

I, however, knew better, because I had been getting text messages from him all day, including a text just seven minutes before the news report came on. Naturally, I had looked at none of them, not wanting to encourage him, per my usual policy. Now I opened them, one by one. They said:

Dear Cursing Mommy—

I address you by your official name, and by no other, as a sign of the respect I have for you. You will soon hear (if you haven't already) that I am missing and probably have died. In fact, while the first is true, and will remain so, the second is emphatically not. Information that has come out about my past life makes it important that I not be found for a long while. As I am disappearing, I want to tell you a few things that may put your mind at ease. I do this because of the great love I have for you.

You may wonder why I, a billionaire, have been pursuing you relentlessly now for a full calendar year. Well, I'll tell you why. First, because you are incredibly hot. We are neither of us young, but you have a beauty that is all the more fabulous because you take it so unseriously. A person has to look twice to see how beautiful you are, but that second look is a revelation! Also, you're not afraid to get mussed by the ups and downs of life. In that, you remind me of Carole Lombard, my mother's favorite movie star.

But the attraction goes even deeper, and I expect (but can't prove) that it has something to do with my childhood. You see, my own mother cursed constantly. She used blasphemies, obscenities, inferences of parentage, vulgarisms, scatological terms, invective, and general bad language of every kind, both at home and out in public. Oh, Mom could really turn the air blue! Nowadays this is common, but it wasn't back then. Mom was one of the first "nice" women to curse like that. You remind me a lot of her.

And yes, as you probably suspected, I did try to have

your husband, Larry, killed several times. There are the attempts you know about; others you probably didn't hear of (the falling payroll safe, for one—a disaster). I feel some remorse about the guys from the nutty religious sect who were killed by mistake at Stuff, Etc . . . , but that was Stattsman's fault, not mine. I tell you all this only because I want you to have the truth, and because my wealth gives me protection. For the record, I won't do it again. Do you remember the Bible story of David and Bathsheba? Look what happened to David in that one. Ouch! Point taken!

Before I go, I want to tell you again how much

But here he started getting really ridiculous, so I not only turned off my phone, but I also took out the battery.

Soon the plush minibus arrived and began to ferry guests back to the airport. Not everybody wanted to leave, but Larry and I did, so we could get home early and save a day of paying the sitter. When the New Year came in we were homeward bound at thirty-three thousand feet, ol' Larry snoring away and me reading an interesting article on molds for fruit-flavored gelatin. We arrived at our house in the morning and paid the sitter for the full weekend anyway, after we saw the capacitors everywhere and remembered we have some money now.

The poet whom I now don't have to identify as alive or dead—since he's not with Angie anymore and she's back with Russ and that whole episode can thankfully be forgotten—once wrote:

> *Let the feeling build below you and behind you,*
> *And then, at just the right moment,*
> *Jump!*
> *Spring from your toes,*

Let it send you flying!
To jump like that's the only way
Of never dying.

That is how I'm going to approach the oncoming year—I'll jump into it with a somersault, not caring where I land. May we all take such hopeful, trusting leaps! And to prepare, I plan to sit down on my living room floor right now with a big scotch and collect my thoughts. Thank you, friends, for being with me this year, and know that I will remain with you in spirit from now on, wherever you are. Never stop expecting that life will be better than it often, unfortunately, turns out to be, and know that you can count on me to curse the horrible parts of it with all my strength, on behalf of each and every one of us, because I am the Cursing Mommy.